W9-AFF-268

firefly

THE MAGNIFICENT NINE

ALSO AVAILABLE FROM TITAN BOOKS

firefly

Big Damn Hero by James Lovegrove (original concept by Nancy Holder)

Generations by Tim Lebbon (October 2019)

THE MAGNIFICENT NINE

firefly

BY JAMES LOVEGROVE

TITAN BOOKS

Firefly: The Magnificent Nine
Hardback edition ISBN: 9781785658297
E-book edition ISBN: 9781785658303

Published by Titan Books
A division of Titan Publishing Group Ltd
144 Southwark Street, London SE1 0UP

First edition: March 2019
1 3 5 7 9 10 8 6 4 2

Did you enjoy this book?
We love to hear from our readers. Please email us at readerfeedback@titanemail.com or write to us at Reader Feedback at the above address.

To receive advance information, news, competitions, and exclusive offers online, please sign up for the Titan newsletter on our website
TITANBOOKS.COM

AUTHOR'S NOTE

The events in this novel take place between the *Firefly*
TV series and the movie *Serenity*.

That is most precious which lasts least long.
—*Old Earth-That-Was saying*

The Matter of a Hat

A small ship sailed through the vastness of the 'verse.

Propelled by the twin drive pods of her trace compression block engine, the Series 03 Firefly-class midbulk transport vessel glided at quarter burn against a backdrop of steady-shining stars and the endless Black. She moved, it seemed, with barely any effort. Her forward structure of bridge and foredeck, which resembled the head and neck of a swan in flight, cleaved cleanly through hard vacuum. Her bulbous aft end gave off a gentle pulsing glow.

She was the very picture of serenity.

From the outside, at least.

Inside, it was a different story.

"That girl," growled Jayne Cobb, "is seriously damagin' my calm! She shouldn't have it. Make her give it back."

The "girl" in question was River Tam and the "it" in question was a knitted hat with pompom and earflaps. The hat was made from yarn in a trio of unappetizing colors: cheap-diner-mustard yellow, leprous apricot and moldy pumpkin, with the pompom on top mixing all three.

It was not much of a hat, but it was Jayne's and he treasured it. He was irked to his very soul to see it set upon someone else's head. Particularly the head of a young woman whom he considered as mad as a gorramn loon.

"Make her give it back, Mal," Jayne demanded, "or so help me, I'll go over there and rip it off her head. Maybe rip off her head, too, while I'm about it."

Jayne's blustering growl was loud enough to carry all the way across the cargo bay. It was loud enough to carry throughout the entire ship. But up on the catwalk at the far end of the cargo bay, River appeared not to hear.

River was dancing. Lost in music only she could hear, she pirouetted and gavotted. Her every movement was a symphony of grace and precision, her legs strong, her arms flowing. Her elegance made the hat seem all the more incongruous. Where she was lithe and supple, it was lumpy and ugly. Yet somehow the hat worked. It was part of the ensemble, offsetting by contrast the uncanny beauty of River's dance. She *owned* it.

The hat's true owner, if he appreciated this weird symbiotic meshing of headgear and choreography, would never have admitted it.

"Mal," Jayne said, pleading. "One last time. She don't stop that prancin' tomfoolery and give me back my hat…"

Mal Reynolds heaved a sigh. He had once been a warrior. He found the role of peacemaker difficult. More often than not, though, he was required to be just that aboard *Serenity*. The eight-strong band of outcasts and misfits he called a crew were nothing if not argumentative. As their leader, his job seemed to involve less dishing out orders and more putting out fires. Without really trying to or meaning to, Mal had become the head of a family, and it was a family that took the *fun* out of *dysfunctional*.

"It's just a hat," he said to Jayne, "and a sorry-lookin' one at that. Ain't as though anything she can do to it'll make its condition worse."

Jayne huffed. "Girl snuck into my bunk. Stole my ruttin' property! There's rules about such things, or if there ain't, there should be. Now, you gonna act like a captain, or am I gonna have to lay down the law my own way?"

Mal heaved a deeper sigh. He liked Jayne. Even admired him for his craftiness and the way he spoke his mind and took crap from nobody. But the fella sure could be a *bèn tiān sheng de yī duī ròu* at times.

Just as Mal was about to go over and confront River, Zoë Alleyne Washburne walked into the cargo bay, drawn by all the commotion.

Jayne spun towards her eagerly. "Zoë. You're a female."

"You say that like it's a bad thing," she replied.

"No, it ain't a bad thing. It's a good thing. You go speak to the girl." Jayne gestured at the still-cavorting River. "Talk some sense into her. Woman to woman, as it were."

Zoë cocked an eyebrow at him. "Why, Jayne? You scared of her or something? Great big hulking ex-merc like you? Bitty little creature like that?"

"I ain't scared a' no one," said Jayne, puffing up his chest, but the fact was, there was something about River Tam he didn't cotton to. It wasn't just that the girl wasn't right in the brainpan. There was more to it. She had hidden depths. Dark depths. Dangerous depths. The kind of depths it didn't do a man good to go meddling in, not unless he wished himself harm.

Didn't even have to meddle, either. River could go off at you unprovoked, as Jayne knew only too well. Like that time she'd stabbed him with a carving knife for no good reason.

They had a ticking time bomb on board *Serenity*, and its name was River Tam.

* * *

"Quite a rumpus we have going on here," said Shepherd Book, entering the cargo bay. With him were Kaylee Frye and River's brother, Simon. Moments earlier these three had been in the dining area playing Tall Card, and Simon had been losing badly. For a holy man, Derrial Book was a remarkably good bluffer, while Kaylee's winsome, heart-shaped face masked a deviousness which she wouldn't have dreamed of using to her advantage except when it came to something harmless like a card game. It didn't help Simon— but helped Kaylee a lot—that he was besotted with her. He had been losing hands to her pretty much on purpose, just so she'd like him that bit more.

"What seems to be the problem?" Book continued. His warm baritone voice was so mellow and reasonable, you could easily imagine yourself sitting up and paying attention as he delivered a sermon in church, and not just that but *enjoying* it.

"Her," said Jayne. "Hat." He had gotten himself so fired up, he was having trouble getting his words out.

"Jayne's got a burr under his saddle 'bout River wearing his chapeau," said Mal.

"You're her gorramn brother," Jayne sputtered to Simon. "You know better'n any of us how she works. Can't you just, I dunno, switch her off or somethin'?"

"She's not some machine, Jayne," Zoë chastised.

"She was, we'd have dumped her out the airlock a long time ago," Jayne muttered.

"River? River?" Simon Tam approached his sister, hands held out pacifyingly. Much as he loved River, he was also wary of her. The sinister medical experimentation that had been carried out on her at the Academy—the Alliance's bogus school for gifted students, from which Simon had rescued her—had left River very different from the girl he had grown up with. At times he scarcely recognized her. At times she even frightened him.

River paused briefly in her dance to fix Simon with a penetrating gaze. Those large brown eyes of hers didn't just look at him. They seemed to look *into* him, as though she knew his every secret. Then she whirled away from him, resuming the sequence of sinuous, athletic moves which, in another life, could have earned her a place in any ballet corps on the central planets.

"River!" Simon called out, vainly. His sister was sunk in some strange fugue state, beyond the reach of his influence.

He turned to Jayne with a hapless expression on his face. Jayne's fingers were twitching. He looked of a mind to come up onto the catwalk and settle things with his fists. Simon gulped, thinking that in the event of him and Jayne engaging in fisticuffs, one of them would end up bruised, battered, bloodied and quite probably unconscious, and it would not be Jayne.

To Simon's relief, Inara Serra now arrived on the scene. It seemed that even all the way over in her shuttle, which was docked snugly on *Serenity*'s starboard flank, she had been able to hear the furor in the cargo bay.

Simon felt that Inara, as a Companion, pretty much the epitome of tact and poise, would surely be able to soothe tensions in the cargo bay. Not for nothing was she nicknamed "the Ambassador" by the crew. She was as subtle in the ways of understanding people's characters as she was skilled in the arts of bringing physical pleasure.

Inara took in the situation at a glance.

"River," she said, and immediately River halted. "My love, that hat does not go with that dress."

"I could have told her that," said Kaylee.

Book looked at her.

"What?" Kaylee protested. "Just because I wear overalls all

day, doesn't mean I don't know fashion."

"Why not take it off?" Inara continued. "I'm sure, if you came to my shuttle, we could find you something more suitable."

River gave a quirky smile. "They can't even look at each other sometimes. It gets so it's what they don't say is more important than what they do. They're two suns in a binary system, orbiting each other. Both bright, both brilliant. But they're going to burn out on each other if they don't ever get together, and it may be too late anyway."

River was prone to making oblique announcements like this. Inara frowned, as though she did not understand what River was saying. A quick reflex glance in Mal's direction, however, suggested that she did.

"The hat, River," she said. "Jayne's upset that you've got it. Give it back to him, and then you can carry on dancing to your heart's content."

River weighed up the proposition. Then she grasped the catwalk railing and hurdled over, landing on the cargo bay floor below as lightly as a cat. She strode across to Jayne, plucking the woolen hat from her head. She held it out to him.

Jayne hesitated, looking at River askance, suspecting a trick. He snatched the hat off her, clutching it close to his chest.

"'Thank you,'" said River, like a schoolteacher reminding her class to mind their manners.

"Thank you," Jayne intoned grudgingly, wondering why he should be the one to have to show gratitude.

"This is what happens when we spend too long off-planet with too little to do," Inara said to Book.

"Captain Reynolds says we're 'between jobs,'" Book replied.

"What most other people would call 'unemployed.'"

Book nodded. "Let's stick with 'between jobs.' We should give the man a fig leaf of dignity."

River was still standing in front of Jayne, staring up at him. Then, seemingly apropos of nothing, she said, "She wasn't ever yours."

"Who wasn't ever mine?" said Jayne, taken aback.

River's voice was soft and toneless, akin to that of someone half-asleep. "She never belonged to you."

"Mal," said Jayne out of the side of his mouth. "Girl's talking crazy. Again. I don't like it."

River reached up and tenderly stroked Jayne's cheek. "But you should treat her like she does."

Then she pivoted away, disappearing off to the passenger quarters as swiftly and fluidly as her namesake.

The silence that followed was broken by a voice over the ship's comm.

"Good day to you all, my merry band of shipmates. This is Hoban Washburne, your dashingly handsome yet surprisingly modest pilot. We're receiving a wave. Originating from a private sourcebox on Thetis. Recorded message. It's been pinging back and forth across the Cortex for some while, node to node, to judge by the delivery path record. Named recipient is one Jayne Cobb."

"Jayne?" said Mal. "You been expecting a wave?"

"Not as I know of."

"Named sender," Wash continued, "is one Temperance McCloud."

"Temperance who now? I don't know no…" Then Jayne's face paled. "Nah. Nah, it couldn't be."

"You look like you've just seen a ghost," Zoë observed.

Jayne nodded noncommittally, as though he had not really heard what she said.

"Presume you'd like it patched through to your bunk," said Wash. "Doing that now. *Beep!* Thank you for choosing Washburne Telecommunications Incorporated. We appreciate your custom."

Jayne, still clutching his hat, hurried off.

"Sir, any idea who this Temperance McCloud is?" a bemused Zoë asked Mal.

15

Serenity's captain shook his head. "Not a notion. But seeing how spooked Jayne is right now just from hearin' that name, I got me a powerful hankering to find out."

Taking Unkindly to Threats

Huckleberry U. Gillis was sweating.

Hard.

Which, being as he lived on what was perhaps the driest planet in the entire 'verse, a world where water was as precious as gold, may not have been wise.

But it was forgivable.

Because there was a knife with a wickedly sharp blade right next to his throat.

And the hideously scarred man holding the knife not only looked like he knew how to use it, he looked like he wanted to use it.

Being mayor of Coogan's Bluff was not an easy job, but Huckleberry Gillis reckoned he did it well enough.

Coogan's Bluff was a tiny town, one of a couple hundred such settlements scattered across the arid surface of Thetis, a world which sat somewhere between the Border and the Rim but closer to the latter than the former.

Thetis was an ironic name. The original Thetis was a Nereid, a sea nymph in the Ancient Greek mythology of Earth-That-Was.

Only someone with a strange sense of humor—or a great deal of optimism—would have borrowed her name for a planet whose landmasses were more or less desert and whose oceans were small and so densely salty they could not support marine life.

Terraforming sometimes took, sometimes didn't, depending on environmental factors and the temperamental nature of the technology itself. In the case of Thetis it had failed to make much of the place, and only the hardiest of colonists chose to live there. They were people who wanted little to do with the Alliance and the Core. Not exactly troublemakers, but the type not to accept readily the yoke of authority, the type who reckoned folks could muddle along without being told by some bureaucrat how they should muddle along and without paying much in the way of taxes on the proceeds of their muddling along.

As mayor, Gillis interfered as little as possible with the lives of the townsfolk. He confined his duties to settling disputes, smoothing ruffled feathers, and hanging out at Billy's Bar on the corner of the town square where Main Street met Two-Mile Road. Billy's was kinda his office-away-from-office, and a damn sight nicer place to spend time at than the glorified cowshed that was his actual office. Regulars at Billy's would come up to Gillis, maybe buy him a drink, and either shoot the breeze or get something off their chest, or both.

Whenever anyone aired a grievance, Gillis would make sympathetic noises and promise to get to the bottom of the problem. Sometimes he even made good on the promise, which was rare in an elected official. He was generally well liked, which was rarer still in an elected official.

So it wasn't a bad life, and Gillis had reason to be satisfied with his lot.

Until, that was, Elias Vandal came along.

The same Elias Vandal who was currently holding a knife on him.

For Gillis, and for the rest of the inhabitants of Coogan's Bluff, Vandal and his Scourers had pretty much ruined everything.

* * *

Elias Vandal had a face like an unfinished meal. The right side of it was blemish-free; you might even say ruggedly good-looking. Unfortunately, the left side was such a mess, you hardly noticed the intact side.

Something had chewed, or burned, or clawed, or in some other manner ravaged the left side of Vandal's face extensively. Now it was covered from temple to jawline in a mass of waxy tissue, like a flow of molten lava that had solidified. A twisted hammock of skin half hid his left eye, and the white of the eye itself was so bloodshot, it seemed inaccurate to refer to it as "the white" at all; it should have been "the red." The left corner of Vandal's mouth was drawn up in a perpetual sneer. The nostril above was broader than its counterpart on the right and puckered around the rim like a dog's butthole.

Oddly, Vandal's left ear had not been damaged during whatever heinous mishap had befallen him. Its flawlessness was marred only by the earring that dangled from its lobe. An earring that, unless fake, appeared to be fashioned from a genuine human knucklebone.

This was the face that now loomed before Gillis, while the knife pressed harder against the little dewlap of flab that hung below the mayor's chin. A bead of blood welled at the knife's tip, but Gillis barely felt the pinprick of pain. He was too mesmerized, and frightened, by Vandal's face—and by the thought that it might be the last thing he ever saw.

"So let me get this straight," Vandal snarled. "We came here, what was it? A month back? Somethin' like that. And we had us a discussion, did we not? *Did we not?*"

Gillis, realizing that some form of response was being sought, nodded. Given the position of the knife blade, it was the tiniest of nods.

"We did," said Vandal. "And what was the upshot of said

discussion? Refresh my memory, Mr. Mayor."

"I said…" Gillis's mouth felt parched, his tongue like a dry sponge. Meanwhile the sweat continued to ooze from every pore, dampening his shirt collar and armpits. "I said I needed time. Weren't a decision to be made lightly. I said I'd canvass opinion throughout town. Get some feedback. Let you know."

"Let. Me. Know." Vandal spun out the words slowly. "And here I am, ready to be let known. I've given you plenty of time, ain't I? Given you all the time in the world to talk to these here good people."

Vandal swept his free arm around, indicating the patrons of Billy's Bar, who numbered perhaps twenty. All were staring at him and Gillis. None had taken so much as a sip of their drinks since Vandal and a half-dozen of his gang, the Scourers, had swaggered into the establishment a few minutes earlier. Each was watching their mayor squirm in Vandal's grasp and quietly thanking the Lord that he or she wasn't in Gillis's shoes.

"Them and their kith and kin," Vandal said. "Seems to me like you oughta got this all squared away by now. What's there to quibble over? You have wells. Aquifers runnin' hither and yon beneath the soil. Decent water supply. Enough to keep your crops irrigated and your whistles whetted. The kind thing to do—the right and proper thing to do—would be to share some a' that bounty with folks less fortunate than yourselves. In that category I most surely do include my boys'n me."

The Scourers jeered in agreement. One of them was behind the bar, having usurped the position of the bartender and owner, Billy Kurosawa. While Billy looked on helplessly, the Scourer was tucking into some of his best bourbon, necking the liquor straight from the bottle. Another of the Scourers was sat between an elderly married couple, Jake and Sally Buchholz, with an arm draped around the shoulder of each like he was their long-lost son or something. Mr. and Mrs. Buchholz sat stock still, with identical looks of frank terror on their faces.

"Now," said Vandal to Gillis, "I made you what I would term a fine offer for full and exclusive ownership rights for the wells at Coogan's Bluff. What offer did I make?"

"You told us we could sell them to you for zero credits," said Gillis.

"Correct. The princely sum of zero credits. And in return, you'd start buying your water off me, every single drop of it. But that's not all you'd get in return, is it now?"

"No." Gillis shook his head, using the action as cover to put a sliver of distance between its blade edge and his skin. "No, you told us we'd get to keep our lives, too."

Vandal grinned. Not all his teeth were present in his mouth, and those that remained were jagged, yellowed, fangsome things, dangling from his gums like stalactites. His breath would have made a sewer worker gag.

"Ask me, that's a veritable bargain," he said. "What's there to dicker about?"

"Nothing. It's just... Some things you can't rush, Mr. Vandal. Big decisions like this, they take careful broaching. Finessing. I've not been able to speak to everyone yet. Some homesteaders around here, they live far out in the barrens or up in the hills. Not easy to reach. I need a little more time. A few days, is all."

Vandal's grin broadened, before abruptly vanishing.

Gillis knew then, without a shadow of a doubt, that he was about to die. He prayed it would be quick. Vandal claimed to have been a Reaver once, however, and if there was one thing Reavers were renowned for, it was the agonizing slowness and disgusting humiliation of the deaths they inflicted.

"Hear that, boys?" Vandal said, addressing his Scourers. "Mr. Mayor here needs a few days. After all the many days we've already allowed him. Sound to you guys like a delaying tactic? Sure sounds to me like one."

"N-No," Gillis stammered. "I swear. Just got to do this right, you know what I mean? Spread the word. Let democracy take its course."

Vandal reared back. Gillis winced in anticipation of the killing blow.

Suddenly the knife was no longer at his throat. Vandal was holding it up beside his own head. The weapon had a distinctively unusual shape. The blade was curved like a sickle. The polished-wood haft, not much thicker than the blade, completed the semicircle.

"Know what?" Vandal said. "Three days. That's it. Three more days. That's when we'll be back next, at sunup, and by then you'd better have had formal papers drawn up, handing over the water rights. Else you'll be seeing plenty of liquid, Mr. Mayor, but none of it the aqueous persuasion, if you get what I'm saying."

"Blood," said one of the Scourers, a huge, apelike ogre of a man. "He means blood."

Vandal rolled his eyes. "He gorramn knows that, Shem, you backbirth. Don't need it explaining to him."

"Oh. Yeah." Shem, it must be said, did not look like being the sparkliest firework in the display. His eyes were too close together, his ears too far apart. "I see. Gotcha, boss."

Vandal helicoptered his arm in the air, and the Scourers made for the exit.

Just as Vandal was leaving, one of the townsfolk got to his feet, shoving back his chair with a scrape.

He was a frail old man, seventy if he was a day, thin as a twig. His skin looked as desiccated as the landscape surrounding Coogan's Bluff.

"Now you listen here, you bastard," said the old man, one Cecil Hanratty by name. He was the seniormost resident of the town, considered cantankerous by some, forthright by others. He had lived in Coogan's Bluff practically since the place was founded. His age-faded eyes glittered. "You can't take what ain't rightfully your'n. Our water is ours. It belongs to us. It's a gift given us by God, and we ain't sharing it with no one, no how.

'Specially not some half-assed bullyboy like you."

Vandal had halted in his tracks to listen, head canted to one side. He looked curious, almost resigned.

"You done, old-timer?" he said.

"No, I ain't," said Hanratty. "Alliance hears what you're up to, Vandal, comin' into half the settlements on Thetis and intimidatin' your way into ownin' their water, they're going to send in Enforcement and they're going to crush you and your band of halfwits like bugs."

Vandal turned. "That a threat?"

"No, it's a fact."

"Seemed more like a threat, I'd say. And I don't take kindly to threats. I'll show you in a moment how *un*kindly I take to threats, but first let me address your point about the Alliance. Alliance don't give two turds 'bout a boondocks planet like this. Alliance ain't going to dispatch no cruiser, no shuttle, no gunship, no nothin' to Thetis. Don't matter how loudly you holler, it ain't gonna happen. Your mayor here is well aware of that, 'cause otherwise he'd have sent 'em a wave already, and he hasn't. May as well ask for divine intervention. It's about as likely. Now..."

He tossed his knife in the air, making it somersault, catching it.

"As for them as threaten me..."

The knife somersaulted again.

Hanratty glared defiance at him.

Vandal swung his arm to the side, the knife leaving his grasp. It spiraled across the room in a perfect arc, whirling like a boomerang. And like a boomerang, it described a full circle and returned to its thrower's hand, Vandal catching it dexterously by the haft.

Hanratty was still standing. The knife's looping flight had taken it directly in front of him. It had seemed to pass him by, missing by a whisker.

Only it hadn't missed.

Hanratty raised a trembling hand to his neck. A ribbon of blood sprouted across his throat at an acute angle. His expression was one of shock and incomprehension. He knew something had been done to him; he just couldn't fathom what.

Then his head slid sideways, shearing away from his neck. It fell to the sawdust-strewn floor with a heavy *thunk*. His legs crumpled a split second after, his decapitated body collapsing backwards, blood spurting from severed arteries. There were shocked cries and gasps of horror from the locals.

Vandal flicked the knife so that the blood on its blade flew off. Three townspeople close by were spattered. They flinched and grimaced.

"I bid you all farewell," Vandal said, with a courteous bow. "Three days. You better have what I want ready for me by then, or… well, I guess *some* of us don't need to make threats, do we?"

He nodded over at Hanratty's two-part corpse and sauntered outside.

Nobody said anything. Nobody needed to say anything. Everybody turned to Mayor Gillis.

"Miz McCloud's gonna come through for us," Huckleberry Gillis murmured, mostly to himself. "She's got to."

A Boy Named Jayne

"Jayne Cobb," said Temperance McCloud, a woman whom Jayne had not seen in fourteen years and who, back then, had gone by the name Temperance Jones.

He paused the recorded message so that he could study her face. An added wrinkle here and there, hair a little coarser and flecked with gray, but otherwise she was exactly as he remembered. Her eyes were still lively, green as jade and twice as lustrous. They were the eyes of a smart, wily woman. The mouth looked hard, but that was a mark of inner determination. Temperance—the Temperance he had known—was somebody who got what she wanted, more often than not through polite persuasion, but when polite persuasion failed, by force. Sometimes force of will, other times sheer brute force.

Jayne's heart was beating with an odd rapidity. He felt a mite dizzy.

He unpaused the message.

"Kind of a blast from the past, huh?" Temperance McCloud-formerly-Jones went on. "I'm maybe the last person you expected to hear from again."

"Damn straight," Jayne said under his breath.

"I know it's been a long time, Jayne. Heck of a long time.

25

And I know things between us didn't end exactly how either of us mighta preferred."

Jayne did not comment on that, just pursed his lips tightly.

"It's not like I cut and ran," Temperance said. "May have seemed as I did, but that weren't my intent. We were good together, you an' me. So good. It's just it was gettin' too much for me. I was gettin' a-scared. Of what I might be with you. Of how bein' with you was makin' me think of my future in new ways."

She shook her head as though trying to shake loose the thoughts that were crowding into it.

"Look, I ain't callin' for to rake over old coals. God knows there ain't no benefit for me in dragging up ancient history, and none for you neither. All I'll say is when I think of us, I think of that ancient Earth-That-Was saying: 'That is most precious which lasts least long.' Heard that one? It's kinda become the code I live by these days."

"Maybe you do, Temp," Jayne muttered. "Maybe the rest of us not so much. The rest of us, you have something precious, you hang on to it for as long as you can."

"Jayne, the reason I'm reachin' out to you now is… I need your help."

Jayne looked hard at the videoscreen. He couldn't tell whether he was angered or unsurprised.

"Now, I ain't a woman who asks for help just any old how," Temperance said. "If you recall anything 'bout me at all, you'll recall that. I wouldn't even be askin' if it was just me involved. It ain't. It's others. Coupla hundred of us, all told. We're in deep trouble, the kinda trouble the Feds'll be no use settlin'. The kinda trouble that calls for a man of your talents, Jayne."

"You mean my talent for bein' your stooge, Temp?"

As though Temperance had anticipated him asking this question or one much like it, she said, "I ain't talkin' 'bout that first job you pulled for me, nor any of the others we did together, where you

26

were the muscle and I was the brains. That was that. The Jayne Cobb I need now is the Jayne Cobb who was tricky and underhand and could think his way out of a bad situation when he knew he couldn't fight his way out."

Jayne was not sure if he recognized himself in that description. There might be some truth in it, but then Temperance wasn't above massaging the facts and ladling on the flattery.

"I'm on Thetis these days, and we have ourselves a predicament here now. There's a guy, name of Elias Vandal, who's musclin' in on our town, fixin' to steal our water. Water's all-important on Thetis. It's the line between life and death. Vandal's got a gang backin' him up, call themselves the Scourers. He's got ordnance and numbers. Most of all he's got a reputation. A bad one. It's his reputation as does most of the heavy lifting for him. Everybody round these parts is just about piss-your-pants terrified of him, and with justification. Vandal says jump, folks chuck themselves off a cliff. *That* bad of a reputation."

Temperance hesitated. Her eyes widened. She gnawed her lip, seeming reluctant yet resigned.

"I need my boy named Jayne," she said. "I need you to get together some people, some hired guns. I know you can. You have contacts. Leastways you used to, and I doubt as you've changed much in all this time. I need you to come to our rescue. No one in this town— Coogan's Bluff, it's called—has the testicular circumference to resist Vandal. We got a lily-livered mayor and a bunch of farmers who can handle a pitchfork but not a weapon in anger. I've tried mobilizing an opposition and ain't had no joy. Vandal and his mob're going to overrun us and take our water and our livelihoods and maybe our lives. I'm askin' you—I'm beggin' you—in the name of what you and I had, come and save us, Jayne. Please. We don't have long. You're our last, best hope."

The message ended. The screen image froze on Temperance gazing imploringly out.

Jayne sat back. His mind was awhirl.

One phrase Temperance had said stood out above all the rest.

My boy named Jayne.

It had been a running joke between them. Temperance had teased Jayne constantly about his name. He had started out growling at her to stop going on about it. After a while, as she carried on, he only acted as if it annoyed him. Secretly he liked it.

Jayne met Temperance Jones at a dive bar on Persephone. He was just a kid back then, wet behind the ears but already garnering a name for himself in certain shady circles. It was said about Jayne Cobb that you could hire him to do anything you required, and you'd get what you paid for. As long as you paid, that is. If you didn't cough up the credits, woe betide you. Jayne had a code of honor: you honored your side of a bargain, he'd honor his. You welched on a deal, though, and you'd better run, because no power in the 'verse would save you from his wrath.

His meeting with Temperance at the bar was no happy accident. She was looking for a man. Not in *that* way. She was looking for a man who would teach her soon-to-be-ex-husband Kelvin a lesson in how to treat a woman. The lesson was similar to the one Kelvin had been giving her during the six ugly months of their marriage, delivered with fist and foot, sometimes his belt.

Jayne was glad to take on the assignment. He didn't tell Temperance why he needed credits so badly. He never told anyone. People did not need to know about his sick brother Matty and the medical bills that were crippling their mother. That kind of information a fella kept to himself, lest it be exploited as a weakness.

Besides, men who hit women were pretty high on Jayne's scumbag list. It was the sort of job he might have done for free, if money weren't such an issue for him.

And he could not deny that Temperance herself was a beguiling proposition. She was perhaps four or five years older than him and sophisticated, but with a ruthless streak. That and the black eye she was sporting made Jayne feel appreciative of her and protective. She was enough of a *femme fatale* and enough of a damsel in distress to make a young man's head spin, although he would realize this only in hindsight.

He duly went to the address she gave him, broke in, pulled her louse of a spouse from his bed, and dished out the kind of drubbing nobody would forget in a hurry. He stopped short of breaking any bones, and when he was finished he told Kelvin that if he ever laid a finger on his wife again, or any other woman, he'd get the same, only twice over.

At that point Kelvin spat out three words, along with a lot of blood.

Three words that rocked Jayne down to his boots.

"I ain't married."

Jayne knew he wasn't lying. What reason would a man have to lie after he had just had seven shades of *gǒu shǐ* beaten out of him? Before, maybe. After? No.

Jayne went straight back to the bar to demand his fee from Temperance and an explanation.

She laughed. "Would you have done as I asked if I'd told you that Kelvin screwed me out of my cut on a deal?"

"Yes. Maybe. But what about that shiner? Who gave you that?"

Temperance Jones touched a forefinger gently to her bruised eye. "Me. Or rather, the door edge I slammed hard into my face to make it look like someone hit me. One or other. Depends how you look at it. Made my sob story credible, didn't it? Thing is, Kelvin and me, we had a consignment of protein bars which just kinda happened to fall into our laps. No government molecular stamp. Weren't a mighty huge payday but weren't nothing to be sniffed at neither. The gorramn *hún dàn* offloads them onto some bowler-hat Limey kid from Dyton—Weasel or Badger or somethin'—then tells me the Feds caught up with him and confiscated the loot afore he could sell it. Like I wouldn't find out! You don't pull that crap with me and not expect repercussions."

"Well, that there is a sentiment I can get behind," Jayne said. "What I don't condone is lying."

"Honey, I am all about the lying," said Temperance. Sliding closer to him in the booth they were sharing, she added, "Speakin' of lying, there's another kind I'm partial to. Handsome buck like you I reckon's well built not just in height and breadth. I reckon he's well built in *every* department."

Her hand went where a lady's hand should not go without permission, but Jayne, if a tad startled, did not ask her to remove it. Least of all because the stroking, caressing motion Temperance started using left him more or less incapable of speech.

He never did get paid for the Kelvin job.

But in the weeks that followed, there were other jobs, ones he and Temperance carried out together. Money came in. He sent most of it back home. The rest he spent freely.

It was the time of his young life. Scrapes with the law, heists, scams, and all of it anchored by his association with Temperance Jones, which was business partnership and torrid affair in equal measure.

There was the bank hold-up on Beylix.

There was the bounty they earned from hauling a people-trafficker off Parth and taking her back to face the music with the crooks on Santo whom she had unwisely stiffed.

There was the theft of military skiff parts from a Blue Sun manufacturing plant on Verbena, which netted the couple the price of a luxury vacation on Pelorum. There they earned a little extra pocket money fleecing wealthy, horny male tourists with a classic "not as single as she looks" con.

There was the Silverhold caper, about which the less said the better, although Jayne had a bullet-wound scar on his triceps as a permanent memento.

And, finally, there was Temperance's desertion of him, a wound that left a deeper, albeit invisible scar.

Jayne winced as he thought of what Temperance Jones had meant to him, the pain her jilting him had caused. It still hurt, deep inside. For some time afterward he had had trouble trusting anyone, women especially. What good was falling for a member of the opposite sex if all she was going to do was betray you eventually? Better to love 'em and leave 'em. That was his philosophy when it came to intimate relationships with the opposite sex, even now. Dip into that pot of water and jump out again quick before it started to boil.

Unbidden, River's words came back to him. *She wasn't ever yours. She never belonged to you. But you should treat her like she does.*

The girl had been doing that witchy hoodoo of hers. Jayne hated that witchy hoodoo of hers. The way she seemed to know things that others couldn't hear or see, things that others simply couldn't *know.*

Always, though, what River said turned out to be spookily accurate, and in this instance she could only have been talking about Temperance. Who, now that Jayne thought about in retrospect, hadn't ever really been his. There had always been a part of her she kept to herself, out of his reach. They had been together but, even in their most intimate moments, he had sensed her withholding from him. She couldn't seem to commit herself to their relationship as fully as he wished she would and as wholeheartedly as he himself did. Maybe it was the age gap, the distance and disconnect that those few extra years of maturity gave her.

Jayne sat in front of the videoscreen brooding for several minutes. A part of him wanted to turn Temperance down. Send her a wave back telling her to go hump herself. *That'd* learn her.

But, for all that, he already knew what his answer was going to be. *You should treat her like she does.*

He snatched a rifle from the small arsenal he kept in a wall recess above his bed, concealed behind a strip of fabric. Shouldering the gun, a Callahan full-bore auto-lock, he swung up the ladder to re-join his comrades in the cargo bay.

An Old Flame Can Still Cause Burns

"Best not be firin' that thing in here, Jayne," said Mal, "in case it has the unfortunate by-product of you ending up full of bullet-holes."

Mal's gun hand twitched beside the pistol holstered at his hip, known as the Liberty Hammer. Likewise Zoë's gun hand strayed towards the cut-down Mare's Leg lever-action carbine repeater strapped to her thigh. Jayne was a loose cannon at the best of times, and to see him come storming into the cargo bay brandishing his rifle was a cue for extreme caution.

Jayne glanced down at the weapon in his arms as if he'd forgotten he was carrying it.

"Oh, hey, no." He lowered the chunky customized rifle to the deck.

Mal and Zoë relaxed—although not completely.

"No, this is just… Look, I got something I gotta ask you people. Kind of a favor. Now, you can turn me down, or…"

"Or you'll shoot us?" said Simon.

"No, Doc Smart-Britches." Jayne looked about as uncomfortable as any of them had ever seen him, even more uncomfortable than when he had discovered he was idolized as a hero by the mudders of Canton on Higgins' Moon. "I was going to say, 'Or I'll go it alone.' I don't got any right to ask you to accompany me. But there's people who need aidin', and I figure we're the ones best placed to offer that aid."

"There money in this?" Mal enquired.

"Nope. It ain't paid work as such. But there's Vera." Jayne nodded at the rifle at his feet. "She's yours, Mal, if you'll agree to come with me. And the rest of you, you'll get equal shares of whatever credits I got stashed away, which is maybe a bigger sum than you might reckon." This was pure sophistry, since Jayne suspected they thought he had next to nothing stashed away. And they would be correct in that assumption.

"Vera?" Mal could not hide his disbelief. "You'd be willin' to part with Vera?"

"If it comes to it, yeah." Jayne looked pained but resolute.

"But you love that damn gun. More'n life itself, some'd say."

"Should show I'm in earnest, then. Mal, this ain't a thing I'd do lightly, comin' to you cap in hand."

"Don't see no cap. Nor no butt-ugly woolly hat either."

"Figure of speech."

"I did realize."

"I got a friend in need, you see."

"This friend called Temperance McCloud by any chance?"

Jayne nodded. "Old friend. She's in trouble."

Briefly Jayne summarized Temperance's message—Coogan's Bluff, water rights, Elias Vandal, and so on—omitting any mention of his former close relationship with her.

"Well now," said Mal. "You already told us it ain't paid work."

"You'll all still get some platinum." *Just not a lot.*

"And," Mal continued, "paid work is pretty much a priority right about now. Food stores are runnin' low."

"Ammo stores too," said Zoë.

"The compression coil in the steamer keeps acting up," said Kaylee. "It wouldn't hurt to buy a brand new one instead of some reconditioned piece of junk that's been around the 'verse a couple hundred times."

Mal glared at her.

"I'm just saying, Captain."

"The ship's infirmary isn't exactly abounding with medical supplies," Simon chipped in. "We burn through weaves and blood plasma like there's no tomorrow. If only you people would refrain from getting wounded quite so often."

"We'll make a start on that," Jayne said, balling a hand into a fist. "Right after I've done with you."

Simon blinked but kept his nerve. "There could be a little less gunplay around here, that's all I'm suggesting."

"It sounds to me," said Shepherd Book, "as though gunplay is very much in the offing on Thetis. Isn't that so, Mr. Cobb?"

"Mightn't be out of the question."

"Gunplay and more besides. A savage like this Elias Vandal isn't the sort simply to turn tail the moment he runs into opposition. Your friend Miz McCloud must know she is asking a lot."

"I would say she was asking for an army," said Inara. "And, with the best will in the world, the handful of us are hardly that."

"Ain't your fight anyways, Inara," said Jayne. "Thetis ain't no place for a Companion."

"It's up to a Companion to decide where is and isn't suitable for a Companion. At House Madrassa we were taught techniques for fending off aggressive clients. I also know how to use a gun. And a sabre for that matter, as Mal well knows."

"We've done crazier stuff," said Zoë.

"But not stupider," said Mal.

"I'd debate that," said Simon.

Book nodded. "But sometimes there's a moral rightness in stupidity. Ever hear of a holy fool?"

"Hold on, hold on, hold on," said Mal, patting the air with both hands. "How come everyone's started talkin' like this is a foregone conclusion? Like we're already halfway to Thetis?

Nobody's going nowhere 'less I say so, and I ain't said so."

"But Mal," said Inara, "if what Jayne's telling us is true, we can't turn our backs on these people."

"Turning my back on a bunch of folks I've never met is precisely what I aim to do," Mal replied curtly. "I'm sorry for Jayne's lady friend and all, but we don't have a nag in this race. All gettin' mixed up in this will do is bring a passel of trouble down on our heads. This Vandal individual's bad enough, but we face off with him and raise a whole ruckus, we could draw Alliance attention, and you don't need me to tell you that that'd be a whole heap worse. More to the point, it could be a trap. Come on, I can't be the only one thinkin' that. Alliance have pulled tricks just as sneaky in the past. Old flame of Jayne's pops up outta nowhere, flutters her eyelashes..."

"Never said she was an old flame."

"Didn't have to. She wasn't, we wouldn't even be havin' this conversation." Mal's jaw was set firm. "You all need to remember one crucial fact. Last I checked, I'm captain of this ship. And I'm sayin' we ain't going to Thetis and sticking our noses where they don't belong, and that's final."

Mal spun on his heel and strode out of the cargo bay.

"Sir..." Zoë began, in vain.

Kaylee leaned in towards Book confidingly. "You know how I sometimes call him Captain Tightpants? Occasions like this, I wonder whether Captain Tightass wouldn't be more accurate."

The Shepherd feigned pious disapproval. "I would call that comment highly disrespectful." His scowl eased. "If I didn't agree with it."

Zoë patted Jayne's shoulder. "Leave this with me, Jayne. I'll go talk with him."

Jayne tried to say, "Thank you." What came out was a grunt that sounded like, "Okay."

Inara moved to intercept Zoë. "Listen. With your approach, Zoë, you can sometimes back Mal into a corner, and that's where he becomes least receptive. I like to think I'm a little less blunt. No offense."

"None taken," said an offended Zoë.

"I know you two go way back. But he and I don't have your shared history. So it's less complicated for us."

"Keep telling yourself that, Inara."

The Companion gave one of her gracious smiles, something she often did to deflect barbs. "Can I at least have first try?"

Zoë mulled it over, then made an ushering gesture. "Ladies first."

The Scent of a Companion

"Mal?" said Inara, entering Mal's bunk in a shimmer of flowing patterned silk and a glitter of elaborate jewelry. She was so innately graceful, she made even an everyday action like clambering down a ladder seem a gift to the beholder.

"Am I behind on the rent?"

"I beg your pardon?"

"When I'm behind on the rent, you can enter unasked."

"Oh. That's a thing I said to you once. Now you're using it back against me. Clever."

"Weren't it?" Mal leaned against the washbasin, folding his arms. "I guess you've come to talk me round. The crew thought, 'Send in the Companion. Her wiles'll work on him.'"

"I volunteered. Zoë was all set to tongue-lash you into seeing sense."

"So you're gonna use your tongue some other way. One of them fancy Companion tricks they taught you."

Inara did not rise to the bait. Mal Reynolds was never more ornery than when he was under pressure. Especially emotional pressure.

Calmly she said, "You know deep down that we have to go to Thetis. You've made up your mind. You just can't admit it. Not even to yourself."

"And here was I thinkin' it was River who was queen of not making sense." He bowed elaborately, twirling a hand at his forehead like some minion to royalty. "Your Majesty."

"That woman, Temperance, must be desperate if she's reaching out to Jayne."

"Now there I can agree with you. Anyone who reaches out to Jayne is by definition desperate."

"There's obviously some kind of bad blood between them. You can see it in Jayne's eyes. Whoever Temperance McCloud is, whatever she was to him, she did something that hurt him. He hasn't recovered. Now, out of the blue, she's back, and Jayne doesn't know how to deal with it. Yet it speaks volumes that, in spite of everything, she's been able to touch something inside him, something noble."

"You're still talking about Jayne Cobb, right?"

"Yes."

"Only you used the word noble."

"He has nobility. Buried deep but it's there. And the same is true of another man I know."

"You know a lot of men."

Inara took a couple of steps across the narrow room. She wore a fragrance that was like some sort of floral incense—could be it *was* the incense she regularly burned in her shuttle—sweet, with just the right amount of sharp notes. Kaylee was forever saying how great Inara smelled. Mal could not disagree with that. He associated Inara's perfume with everything that was right and perfect. Unconsciously, unwillingly, he half-closed his eyes and breathed it in.

"Mal," she said, laying a hand softly, tentatively, on his chest. "Jayne is your friend. He's stood by you through countless tough situations."

"Ratted me out in a number of 'em, too."

"But when it counts, you know you can rely on him."

"Rely on him to do what's best for Jayne Cobb."

"This rescue operation, or whatever it turns out to be, means a lot to him. It took courage for him to stand before us all and humble himself the way he did. All that pride he had to swallow. Can you imagine how hard that was? I reckon you can. I've seen you do it more than once."

"This still ain't winnin' me over, Inara."

"No? How about this, then? Not so long ago there were those whores who needed our help. My friend Nandi. The Heart of Gold bordello. Ring any bells? You didn't need much convincing to step up then. The situation on Thetis isn't so different. Maybe it's on a larger scale but the essentials are the same: big, bad aggressor taking advantage of the vulnerable. And if there's one thing I know about Mal Reynolds, he hates aggressors, whether it's gangsters or the Alliance."

"You say that like gangsters and the Alliance are two different things."

"Exactly. You can't stand them, so you stand up to them."

"If you think I'm just gonna—"

"I think, Mal, that you can do the right thing, and you will. Usually you need time to get to that point, but time's something we don't have much of. How far is it to Thetis?"

"From here? Three days' flyin'. Two if we push the engine to its limit. Kaylee'll be cussin' every step of the way, but two's doable." Mal said this, not able to believe he was even considering making the journey.

"According to Temperance, Coogan's Bluff doesn't have long. If we're to get there in time to make a difference, we'd have to leave straight away. So you need to decide now. No pondering. No leaving it to your conscience to catch up with the rest of us. Listen to what's here."

She pressed her palm more firmly onto his chest, in such a way that she had to be able to feel his heartbeat through his ribcage.

Mal looked deep into her dark eyes and hated himself for thinking how beautiful they were. Inara would be leaving the ship soon. She had told him that was her intention and he had no doubt she meant it. And this had come just when he'd finally screwed up the nerve to try to tell her how he felt about her. Now any interaction between him and Inara bore a tang of bitterness— bitterness directed at himself, mostly.

He tore his gaze away.

"If," he said, and he repeated the word with emphasis, "*if* I go along with this entirely hare-brained idea, which'll most likely end up gettin' us all killed, Jayne'll be in my debt."

"That he surely will."

"And I'll have this to rub his nose in for months to come."

"Again, yes."

Mal crooked one corner of his mouth. "Then what the heck? I'm in. Just tell me this: when did a shipload of criminals, desperadoes, and fugitives become such a bunch of do-gooders?"

Inara had the answer. "When their captain showed them how."

But Mal was already halfway up the ladder and seemed not to hear her.

Up on the bridge, Mal rested an elbow on the back of Wash's seat.

"Thetis," he said.

"Already got the coordinates locked in," said Wash.

"*Et tu*, Wash?"

"Zoë came up and told me to."

"You do everything your wife says?"

"If I want to live, yes. All I'm waiting for is the 'go.'"

"Go."

Wash hit a series of buttons, then grasped the steering yoke and threw *Serenity* into a tight turn. As the engine increased power output, the plastic dinosaurs on the console in front of him began to vibrate, much as if they were alive and growling.

Mal looked at the toys and tried not to think about what they represented.

Extinction.

A No-account World at the Ass-end of the Galaxy

Temperance McCloud, née Jones, stepped outside the front door of her homestead into the ferocious heat of the day. Before her stretched a dozen acres of meager corn and a dusty corral where twenty head of cattle stood listlessly, flicking their ears to keep off the flies and lapping up brackish water from a trough. In the distance lay the huddle of buildings that was Coogan's Bluff, five klicks away down a rough, rutted track. Further off there was a line of low, jagged hills dotted with sage and cactus. The sun shone white on a landscape that was mostly shades of brown.

Time was she would have laughed at the idea she might end up like this, running a smallholding on a no-account world at the ass-end of the galaxy. The last thing Temperance had ever thought she might become was a farmer. As the successful "legitimate businesswoman" she'd once been, she had envisaged a future living large somewhere in the Core, on Osiris, maybe, or another planet just as swanky, or else swanning about space in a private cruiser.

Life had a funny way of kicking out the legs from under your plans.

Temperance shaded her eyes scanning her property. Faintly she could hear the drone of a pest-control unit. She looked for the plume of dust that betokened the activity of a remote-controlled corkscrew drill extracting devilworms from the soil. The verminous insects were a plague on every farmer on Thetis. They loved nothing more than burrowing under arable fields and feasting on the roots of crops. Digging up devilworms was a never-ending task. Just when you thought you had got them all, the next swarm appeared.

The only bonus about devilworms was that they could be dried, ground up and turned into meal, which could then be baked into cakes. Devilworm cakes, even when sweetened with honey, were far from delicious, but protein-wise, boy, were they nutritious.

There. A skein of ocher vapor rising to the south.

Temperance hit the transmit button on the shortwave communicator in her hand.

"Honey?"

"Yeah?" came the reply.

"You've been out working all morning. Sun's nearing zenith. Mercury's closin' in on forty. You don't want to be outdoors when it gets there."

"Sure. Gimme another five minutes and I'll have all the rows down here done."

"Lunch'll be on the table when you get in."

"Check. See you shortly, Ma."

True to her word, Temperance had the meal ready when her daughter ambled in; but it wasn't five minutes later as promised, more like half an hour. Temperance rolled her eyes but said nothing. *Choose your battles.* The pair of them sat opposite each other and wolfed down corned-beef hash, biscuits, and gravy, washing it down with a precious half-glassful of water each. For afters? Devilworm cake, of course.

This, across the dining table from her, was the girl for whom Temperance had given up everything. This was the reason she had jettisoned her old life and wound up on Thetis. This blue-eyed young teen—strong, diligent, determined—was now the epicenter of Temperance's life, the sun around which she orbited.

Temperance had sworn to protect her daughter to her dying breath. Elias Vandal and his Scourers wanted Coogan's Bluff's water supply, and if they got it, she had a good notion that the trouble wouldn't end there. Vandal and his men were takers. They took everything they could get their paws on. And they had certain predilections. Reports from other towns that they now controlled all said the same thing. The Scourers liked young women. Especially girls who were barely yet women. They abducted them and subjected them to all manner of depravity, day and night, using them up until there was nothing left of them.

If you had a daughter, she was better off dead than in the clutches of the Scourers.

But it would not come to that, Temperance thought. Not if Jayne Cobb came through for her.

She wondered what it would be like, Jayne meeting her daughter for the first time. If it happened.

They were similar characters, the two of them. Both could be headstrong. Both had a stubborn streak a mile wide. Both, too, were the sort to always finish what they started and never back down from a challenge.

She wondered what Jayne would say when she introduced them to each other.

How he would react when he learned that she had a daughter.

How he would react when he learned that the daughter's name was Jane.

Welcome to Thetis

Serenity hit Thetis atmo a little over forty-eight hours later. Wash had flown her hard, maintaining a near-continuous vigil on the bridge. He had eaten his meals at the controls, even slept at the controls. You could not drive a ship at maximum burn and leave everything to the autopilot. Now *Serenity* soared across Thetis's undulating, endless vistas of scrubby desert, steep bluffs, and meandering canyons, making a beeline for Coogan's Bluff. Wash was looking forward to setting the ship down, taking a well-earned shower and hitting the sack.

If his wife cared to hit the sack along with him, that would not be the worst thing imaginable.

Kaylee, meanwhile, was no less exhausted. She too had been working almost without rest. *Serenity*'s engine was basically held together with string, chewing gum, and a whole lot of wishful thinking. Sometimes Kaylee reckoned that it was her willpower alone that was keeping the ship aloft. Really, though, it was her skills as a mechanic. Machines, especially spaceship engines, spoke to her. Each had a story to tell, if only you cared to listen to it. Kaylee often likened herself to a doctor, able to diagnose ills simply by identifying symptoms and asking the right questions. Her patients complained of things such as an ailing gravity ring or a faulty trans-warp drive, and it was her job to empathize, diagnose, and cure.

In that respect, she felt she had something in common with Simon Tam.

She liked to think it wasn't the only thing she had in common with Simon Tam.

At any rate, she was relieved they had made it to Thetis without a major blowout.

"Attagirl," she said to the engine as its thrumming note altered pitch, becoming bassier and more reverberant, an indication that *Serenity*'s thrusters were now sucking air rather than vacuum. "You did good."

Serenity was narrowing in on Coogan's Bluff when Wash saw the flash of light.

It came from the mouth of a gorge a thousand feet below. It was a bright orange twinkle, there then gone in an instant.

He might not have thought anything of it, had he not then glimpsed a tiny, needle-like object hurtling up from the ground.

A tiny object that was getting rapidly larger and less needle-like.

A siren began blaring throughout the ship as the proximity alert sensor was triggered, but Wash was already taking evasive action. He swung *Serenity* hard to port, feeling the ship groan beneath him. This wasn't the first time he'd put the old girl under sudden strain. She could take it. Fireflies were built strong. Still, there might yet come a day when something gave, unexpectedly and catastrophically.

Wash hoped that that day would not be today.

The proximity alert siren kept up its shrill warning. Wash threw *Serenity* to starboard and poured on speed. Back to port. Starboard again.

Mal stumbled onto the bridge.

"We're veerin' all over. Why are we veerin' all over?"

"Can't talk. Flying."

"One-word answer."

"Heat-seeking missile."

"That's two words. Maybe three. But all right." Mal peered out through the viewing ports. "Where?"

"Our six."

"Who?"

"How should I know? Someone who mistook us for a turkey?"

Wash tried to nudge a little more speed out of *Serenity*, even though she was already going pretty much flat-out. She responded grudgingly. After two days' hard travelling the ship was, like its pilot, in need of rest.

"Just stay with me, baby," Wash murmured. "You don't want that nasty missile up your rear any more than I do."

Zoë, Jayne, and Simon were now on the bridge too.

"Did someone just say 'missile'?" said Simon.

"Why the hell aren't we getting out of its way?" said Jayne.

"What do you think all this jigging about has been for?" Wash snapped. "Anyone else got any dumbass suggestions they can waste my time with?"

"We can outrun it," said Mal. "We're faster."

"Hate to break this to you but we're not." With a jerk of his head Wash indicated the radar screen. The red icon that was the missile was inching towards the central green icon that was *Serenity*. "Might be, were the engine fresh, but we're at the end of a long haul. Things're clogged up. The old girl's fighting me. It's going to be touch-and-go."

"Launch chaff," said Jayne.

"Golly gee, where would I be without you?" Wash would never have dared be so snitty with Jayne under normal circumstances. "I'm waiting till the missile's near enough."

"Too soon and the chaff'll disperse," said Mal. "Won't fool the missile's targeting lock."

"I knew that," said Jayne, unconvincingly.

"Honey." Zoë put a reassuring hand on the back of her husband's neck. "Just ignore them and fly."

"That's what I'm trying to do, only the bridge has turned into a mother-humping coffee klatch."

Wash cast an eye at the radar screen, then flipped the security lid off the chaff initiation switch.

"Okay. Launching chaff in three, two, one…"

He threw the switch.

At *Serenity*'s aft, a canister popped up from its housing. A half-second later the canister detonated, evaporating into a cloud of smoke and metallic flakes.

The missile deviated towards the chaff cloud…

Then darted around it and resumed its pursuit of *Serenity*.

Wash swore violently.

"Try again," said Mal.

The second chaff canister was no more effective than the first.

"Missile must have gorramn distraction-override software," Wash said.

"Meaning…?" said Simon.

"Meaning it's down to me to stop us getting blown up by it."

In the engine room, everything was warning lights and hideous grinding noises and small explosions.

Kaylee sprinted back and forth, fixing each problem as it arose. When several arose at once, she assessed which most demanded her attention and tended to it first, a kind of mechanical triage. She barely registered the still-blaring alert siren, nor did she care exactly what the nature of the threat was. All she knew was that *Serenity*'s

52

engine was sorely overtaxed and she had to keep the ship airborne. The crew were counting on her as much as they were on Wash, even if they didn't know it just then.

"Oh come on!" she said through gritted teeth as a cluster of cables fell free from their support mounting. One cable snapped in half and started writhing and flexing across the floor like an angry snake, spitting sparks. Kaylee ran to the circuit-breaker board and isolated the current, then began patching the broken cable back together.

Serenity was distressed and in pain. Kaylee Frye put all her energy into making the ship well again.

"Okay, everyone's going to need to hold on to something now," said Wash. "And if you're prone to airsickness, please try to find somewhere that isn't here to throw up."

He guided *Serenity* into a steep descent, sweeping her into a canyon not much wider than her own wingspan. The missile followed suit.

Immediately Wash embarked on a series of yawing, seesawing maneuvers. He was playing a risky game. Each lurch, whether to port or starboard, brought the wingtip on that side hazardously close to the rock-face. The slightest miscalculation, there'd be a collision and *Serenity* would ricochet along the canyon like a billiard ball, disintegrating into a blaze of incandescence and debris as she went.

All the while the heat-seeking missile zeroed in, closer and closer.

But Wash's wild, precarious aerobatics were taxing its guidance system. The missile followed its target faithfully but that meant it too was careering from side to side.

What Wash was hoping for—praying for—was that it would hit some projection of rock that *Serenity* had just narrowly missed.

His prayer was answered.

If not wholly as he might have liked.

With only a few yards separating the missile's nosecone and

Serenity's tail, the ship passed beneath an overhang with inches to spare.

The missile failed to do likewise.

It struck rock.

It became a fireball.

But there were repercussions. The shockwave from the blast engulfed *Serenity*, buffeting her mercilessly.

Wash struggled with the yoke but could not compensate. *Serenity* caught herself a glancing blow against the canyon wall. The impact juddered through her from stem to stern.

Wash hauled back on the yoke, putting *Serenity* into a steep climb. He knew they were going to crash. Nothing he could do now would prevent that. He just didn't want to crash inside the canyon. Outside the canyon lay an expanse of flat plain. There was room to control the ship better there. Mitigate the inevitable disaster. Maybe even get them all through this in one piece.

These thoughts went through Wash's mind in a flash. His training had kicked in. He was no longer consciously thinking. He was operating on instinct alone. He had run scenarios like this in a simulator dozens of times.

The words of his Zen Buddhist flight instructor echoed in his head: *You are a leaf on the wind.*

As *Serenity* roared up over the canyon's rim, she felt more like a brick in freefall. But no matter.

Wash flattened her out as best he could. The ground was rushing by below. Her belly was going to hit in about—

WHAMMM!

Sooner than Wash had anticipated, *Serenity*'s underside scraped soil. She was hurled into a spin. She skipped along a few meters above the landscape, revolving through repeated 360-degree turns like a cartwheel on its side. Wash fought to keep her from flipping. A pancake landing was survivable. Rolling ass-over-apex at this speed? Nobody would be walking away from *that*.

Finally Thetis's gravity claimed her. *Serenity* slewed across the ground with a screech of tortured hull metal and a rumble of churned-up earth. She made one last slow, slithering revolution before coming to rest. She fetched up lying canted at a shallow angle, a cloud of kicked-up dust drifting over her.

On the bridge, no one spoke.

Then, grimly, Mal said, "Well, ain't going to be me who fills out the insurance claim form for *this*."

Wash looked round at him. "We have insurance? Why didn't you tell me? I'd known, I'd have totaled her and we could buy ourselves a new ship with the payout."

Zoë kissed the crown of Wash's head. "You did great, dear."

"Crashed the boat. Pretty much wrecked her. *Serenity*'ll maybe never fly again. Yeah, great."

"You're too hard on yourself. We're alive, ain't we?"

"There's that, I guess." Wash waggled both fists in the air. "Yay me."

The cargo ramp was lowered. All nine of the crew tottered outside. River, bewildered, clung to Simon's arm. A visibly shaken Shepherd Book knelt on the ground, crossed himself and bent his head to send up a prayer of thanks to the Lord for bringing them down safely—or at any rate for granting Wash the piloting skill to bring them down safely. Inara Serra gazed around her, reflecting on the small details of the landscape and cherishing them for their stark, simple beauty. Her faith, Buddhism, was somewhat more complex than Book's Christianity. Divine grace, which could be given or withheld according to God's will, had no part in it. Inara was content to believe that if she had died just now, it was meant to be. Because she hadn't, that was also meant to be, and she should enjoy this moment to its fullest in the light of that awareness.

Wash, Kaylee, and Mal strode around the ship, inspecting the damage.

"Verdict?" asked Mal.

"Could be worse," said Kaylee. "I won't say everything's shiny. We're going to need some new hull panels, and that dent in the heat exchanger will need beating out. Brace manifold's gone. The gravity drive is going to have to be recalibrated from scratch. There's probably five or six basic engine parts that have burned out and are going to have to be replaced, and I don't like how the power conduit's looking."

"Long and the short. She gonna get aloft again?"

"Yes."

"How soon?"

"I can have her up and running in a week. Provided I get those parts."

"A week."

"You want it quicker, you'll have to hire a team of mechanics," said Kaylee. "As it is, you've got just me, so…" She smiled brightly, so as to soften the bad news.

Mal surveyed his ship, then turned towards the west, in which direction a small town lay, glimmering in the distance, low on the horizon.

"That's Coogan's Bluff, right?" he said.

"According to the nav computer," said Wash.

"So we're where we want to be."

"Near as dammit."

"Grand. Because somebody just tried to blow us out of the sky, and I'm itchin' to know who and why."

"It was the Scourers, surely," said Zoë.

"More'n possible, but I want to know for certain. And if I have to bust some heads to obtain the information I'm after, so be it."

"What if no one in Coogan's Bluff has that information?"

"Still get to bust some heads."

Jayne grinned wolfishly. "*Now* we're talkin'!"

The Inevitable Bar Brawl

Mal, Zoë, and Jayne broke out the ship's Mule bike and drove off towards Coogan's Bluff. Mal had bought the bike as a replacement for the one destroyed during the assault on Adelai Niska's skyplex, from a second-hand dealer at Eavesdown Docks on Persephone who had spun the usual yarn about "one careful owner" and promised "years of trouble-free usage." So far its performance had not disappointed, but that was probably due more to the care and attention Kaylee lavished on it than anything else.

The other crewmembers stayed behind with *Serenity*, Wash and Kaylee to start work on the repairs, the rest to set right all the furniture, utensils, and loose cargo that had been scattered about during the crash landing.

Mal, perched beside Jayne on the back of the bike, took in the surroundings. He had visited some hardscrabble places in his time. Resided in a fair few of them, indeed. But he couldn't recall being anywhere quite as miserably run-down as Coogan's Bluff.

Poverty radiated from the ranches and plantations dotted around the outskirts. Farmhouses that were little more than shacks. Fields sprouting stunted crops. Skin-and-bone livestock, the cows with shriveled-up udders, the bulls looking hangdog and browbeaten. Pieces of broken-down agricultural equipment that were more rust than steel.

In the town itself, things weren't a whole heap better. The buildings were either prefabricated units on their second or even third lease of life, or else they were homespun cabins with roof shingles missing and poorly joined planks, silvery reflective material patching some of the holes. There was dust just about everywhere, silting up at the roadside, coating windowpanes.

A dog that took the word "mangy" to a whole new level plodded across the street in front of the approaching bike. Zoë, at the controls, had to decelerate to dead slow in order to avoid hitting it, but the dog didn't seem to mind much whether it lived or died. It halted and stared at the four-wheeled all-terrain vehicle, almost asking to be run over.

"Shoo!" Zoë yelled, and the dog dropped its head and slunk off.

Jayne looked around at the town, and his expression said it all. *This is the place we've come to defend?* Coogan's Bluff seemed to have about as much intrinsic value as a sandcastle.

Mal told Zoë to pull up outside Billy's Bar. "Figure if we want to find locals that are talkative, a bar's the place to go."

"And a slug of whisky after our near-death experience earlier wouldn't go amiss."

"Also that."

As bars went, Billy's was unimpressive. It didn't even have holographic windows, let alone a holopool table. Mismatched wooden tables and chairs were arranged randomly around the premises, and there were about a dozen patrons drinking in a desultory fashion, hardly any of them speaking.

Those that were speaking fell silent as the three strangers walked in. Mal could sense tension in the air. It had been present before he, Zoë, and Jayne entered. Now it thickened.

Glasses were set down on tabletops. Eyes swiveled. All at once the new arrivals were the center of attention.

"Howdy, all," said Mal.

No reply.

"Okayyy. Well, we're just three out-of-towners, stopping by at this fine drinking establishment. Don't want no trouble."

"Yeah," Jayne rumbled menacingly. "No trouble."

"Just gonna slake our thirst and maybe have a word or two with anyone who cares to be amiable."

"Amiable," Jayne said.

Mal rounded on him. "There an echo in here?"

"What my friend is saying," said Zoë, "is that we only want to chat with you folk, and there's a drink in it for anyone who's interested."

Nobody moved. Nothing radiated from the townspeople's faces except mistrust and hostility.

Mal went to the bar. "Three of whatever you'd recommend."

Billy Kurosawa had been polishing the same glass since they'd come in. Now he placed it down on the bar and flung the drying cloth over his shoulder. He sidled over to the shelves behind him and selected a bottle of some greasy, tea-colored liquid which may have been whisky. Equally, it may have been industrial lubricant. He filled three shot glasses to different depths and shoved them across the bar. All without saying a word.

Mal fished in his pocket for coins.

"On the house," said Billy. "Drink up and go."

"Well now, that is more'n hospitable of you. I'm already liking this place. Goin' to leave a five-star review on the Cortex."

As he sipped his liquor, Mal turned to face the room.

"Ladies and gentlemen, here's the thing. Somebody just tried to shoot my ship down. You can't not have noticed. We came down a mite heavily, not so far from here. Tiresome it was, too."

"We heard somethin' of the like," growled one of the locals, a man with a beard so big and bushy it looked like a beaver hanging off his face. "An impact. So?"

"Ah, they can talk. That's ten credits you owe me, Jayne. You said these hicks'd be too dumb to understand plain English. I said no, I'm sure they'd have at least basic vocabulary. Honks. Snuffles. Maybe oinks. You lost the bet. Pay up."

Jayne feigned a look of chagrin. "Aw, man."

The beaver-bearded fella rose to his feet. "Whoever the hell you people are, you should leave. Now. Coogan's Bluff ain't for you."

"Now that seems like sound advice," said Mal. "Only, like I said, we're here to talk. Any of you nice folk have an idea who'd try to destroy an innocent passing spaceship, tell us. We'd love to know."

"It must've been—"

"Shush, Horace!"

The first speaker was a youngish man, the second a middle-aged woman seated next to him who might have been his mother or else his much older wife.

"Hey, Horace." Mal sauntered over to their table. "Anything you want to say?"

Horace glanced at the woman with him, then shook his head. "Nuh-uh."

Beaver Beard piped up again. "For your own good, you really want to get out of town." He sounded sincere, almost plaintive.

Trouble was, Mal wasn't in a mood to listen to anyone even if they were well-intentioned. Zoë could tell by his stance that he needed to let off some steam.

She knew what was going to happen. It was already playing out in her head. Mal would up the snark quotient. He'd goad Beaver Beard, or someone else, until the guy snapped. The other person would throw the first punch. A fight would erupt.

"Here we go," she murmured to herself. "The inevitable bar brawl."

* * *

So it went.

Within a minute Mal and Beaver Beard were toe-to-toe, trading blows. Jayne was grappling with another man. Zoë herself was fending off an attack by both the middle-aged woman and Horace, who was her son or husband.

Billy Kurosawa appealed for calm from behind the bar. Nobody heeded him. Other patrons piled in, joining the fray. Chairs were sent flying. Tables were overturned. Glass shattered.

Mal had a goofy, delirious grin on his face. Jayne likewise. Even Zoë found that she was, in a perverse way, enjoying herself. She was never the sort to start a fight without good reason, but once she became embroiled in one, she committed to it, all in.

The three *Serenity* crewmembers gave a good account of themselves, even though they were outnumbered fourfold. In the end, however, the uneven odds weighed against them. They found themselves being dragged outdoors and tossed into the road dirt.

Billy Kurosawa stood over them, surrounded by irate customers, some nursing bruises.

"You may wish to leave now," he said sternly. "There's plenty more where that came from."

At that moment a smartly dressed man in black suit and bootlace tie appeared, hustling along the street. He was somewhat overweight and had a face that exuded kindliness and perspiration.

"Now what in the name of all that's holy is going on here?" he demanded.

"Nothing, Mr. Mayor," said Billy. "Just showin' these here folk how Coogan's Bluff ain't to be taken lightly."

"That ain't courteous at all."

"They weren't courteous to us."

"Look," said the mayor, addressing all of the townspeople present, a fair proportion of his electorate. "I appreciate we're all on edge right now. That doesn't mean we have to behave like animals."

"They started it," said Beaver Beard, gently touching a swollen lip.

"Technically *you* did," said Mal. "Remember? When you took a swing at me?"

"People, people, people," said the mayor. "I do not know who these three are, but I'm wondering whether they're not from that Firefly that just crashed yonder, out by the barrens. My guess is they are. That makes 'em needy unfortunates, not enemies. God knows we've got enough enemies as it is without making more."

The mayor eyed the three crewmembers.

"I'm also getting to thinking," he said, "that you three may be offworlders and you're here on Thetis by request. Or am I wide of the mark?"

"Not that wide." Mal had by now stood up and was dusting himself off.

"Did Temperance McCloud by any chance send for you?"

"She did."

"Then goodness me, allow me to apologize on behalf of all of Coogan's Bluff for the reception you've just been given." He stuck out a hand. "Huckleberry U. Gillis. He who, as you may have gathered, has the honor of being mayor of this fine burg. And you are...?"

The Cavalry

"Little under a month ago, they came," said Gillis. "We knew they were on their way. Other towns in the county had been falling to 'em one by one like dominoes. Yellow Rock. Pandoraville. Yinjing Butte. You couldn't ignore the news. Couldn't do much about it neither. It was like a plague of locusts. A force of nature."

"A force of nature made of people," said Mal.

"But they ain't just people, the Scourers. They're sadistic and ruthless. You stand up to them, you're going to get knocked down. That's what happened at Yinjing Butte. People there got uppity. Scourers came down hard. Now? Well, there ain't a Yinjing Butte to speak of anymore. There's just a charred ruin."

"Nice."

"And skeletons. Lots of skeletons the carrion birds have picked clean."

"We get the picture."

"The Scourers' ranks swell with every place they take over, that's what makes it worse. They'll pick up a half-dozen, maybe a dozen recruits each time. Folks who fancy being on the winning team. Folks who were perhaps never that popular in their hometown. The dregs, the losers. They see something they like in

65

the Scourers and they latch onto it."

"Power."

"Yeah, or the opportunity for payback for all the rejection they've had in their lives."

Gillis paused, musing darkly.

They were in his office, a cramped single-room annex attached to the side of the one and only hotel in Coogan's Bluff; he rented the space from the proprietor, paying for it out of his measly mayoral salary. A couple of framed images were the only visible testimony to his position of authority. One was a picture of a much younger Gillis taking an oath, hand on Bible. The other was an affidavit, remote-signed by some bottom-rung Alliance functionary, stating that, "By the power invested in me on behalf of the Anglo-Sino Alliance, I hereby certify that the herein-mentioned Huckleberry Ulysses Gillis is solemnly declared civic mayor of the municipality of Coogan's Bluff." The date stamp and the brown paper implied that he had held the post for many years. It would seem that no one else much coveted it.

"So yes," Gillis continued, "we knew it was only a matter of time before the Scourers turned their attention to us. Guess we just lowered our heads and hunkered down and hoped it wouldn't happen. It's Elias Vandal, see. He's the real problem. He's not just a leader. He's a figurehead. An icon. He's charismatic—as charismatic as someone that pug-ugly can be. He's got this kind of outlaw glamour, draws followers to him like moths to a flame. Makes 'em insanely loyal to him. Also, he'll kill you as soon as look at you. That helps whip his gang into line."

"Sounds like a real peach," said Zoë.

"He's a Reaver, what's more."

"What?" Jayne said, sitting bolt upright. His eyes widened in anxiety. There wasn't much Jayne Cobb feared, apart from Reavers. Even the mention of the word could set his pulse racing.

"That's what he claims," said Gillis. "Says he used to run with a Reaver pack, way back when. Spent a few years far out beyond the Rim until his soul was emptied and his heart turned to ice. He stared into the Black and the Black stared back."

"But Reavers," said Mal, "they don't return to civilization. Once a Reaver, always a Reaver. You don't become one and then 'get better.' You stay one till you die. And you die mad. Diseased. And eaten up. Literally eaten up."

Gillis splayed out his hands. "I can't speak to the truth of it. I'm only telling you what he says. He's got the face for it, that's for sure. I mean, I've never personally seen a Reaver, but from what you hear... You know, with the wounds and the scarring, mostly self-inflicted. The whole of one side of Vandal's face is messed up. Badly. Kinda makes me sick even to think of it. Looks like it must still hurt him. Could be that's why he's so mean."

"Okay," said Mal, "so Vandal's a bad hombre. Maybe a Reaver, maybe not. But he's still human. Bullet'll take him out just as it would anyone. We kill Vandal, problem solved. He has such a hold over the Scourers, they'll fall apart without him."

"Possibly," said Gillis. "You'd have a devil of a time getting to him, though. He never goes anywhere without a posse. Men and women, armed to the teeth, who'd die to protect him. And when he comes back to Coogan's Bluff next, you can bet he'll be coming mob-handed, bringing every last Scourer with him."

"How many?"

"Best guess, a hundred. Hundred and twenty. Something like that."

Mal whistled through his teeth. "That's a fair number. But there's more townsfolk than that in Coogan's Bluff."

"In total, yes, 'bout four times as many, but we're talking children and seniors as well as adults. Able-bodied and of age, there's probably a hundred, a hundred fifty."

"Oh."

"But that's okay, because there's loads of you, right?"

Mal, Zoë, and Jayne exchanged glances. *You want to tell him or shall I?*

"You're just the official representatives," Gillis went on. "Your Firefly's only the first ship to arrive. Advance party. More are due."

"Not as such."

"Well then, you've brought a sizeable contingent with you anyways. Cargo bay of a Firefly could sleep at least thirty. People sharing bunk space, doubling up, that's another couple of dozen or so."

"No, Mayor Gillis," said Zoë. "You don't seem to understand. You're hoping for the cavalry? We're it. We're the cavalry."

Gillis's mouth dropped open. "The... The three of you?"

"Nine of us."

"Nine. Oh well, that's all right then. Nine of you." Gillis's usually genial face had soured into a sardonic leer. "That'll make a load of difference, nine people. Yeah, Vandal'll be dampening his longjohns when he learns we've got a whole nine extra people lining up against him."

"You're welcome," said Mal, deadpan.

"Gorramn it!" Gillis exclaimed. "When Temperance told me she knew someone who might help, I assumed there'd be significant numbers coming. A small army. Nine!"

"Some of us ain't even fighters," said Jayne, thinking he was being helpful by being truthful.

"I kinda wish the Scourers *had* blown your ship to smithereens. Then I wouldn't have gotten my hopes up as I did."

"Hey!" Jayne barked. "You're lucky we're here at all. You go on like that, what's stopping us turnin' tail and lettin' the Scourers have their way with you? Show a little gratitude."

"Yes. Yes. I'm sorry, Mr. Cobb. Forgive me. You can't blame me for being a tad disappointed, though, can you?"

"You're sayin' it was the Scourers fired that missile at us?" said Mal.

"Can only have been, Mr. Reynolds."

"Captain Reynolds, if you please."

"I'm sorry. Captain. They have rocket launchers and stuff. They're well supplied, for a bunch of bandits. They've got resources. They can afford it, the money they make ripping off folk for their water. Where were you when they shot at you?"

"About twenty klicks north."

"Sounds right. They have a camp up there in a ravine called Brimstone Gulch. Must be their scouts spotted your ship and Vandal put two and two together. Thought he'd take you out so you couldn't cause him grief. Nipping the problem in the bud, as it were. Either that or Scourers just like taking potshots at passing spacecraft. That's not out of character for them."

"Twenty klicks. Not far."

"No, and they're scheduled to return here tomorrow."

Mal grimaced. "Tomorrow."

"At dawn."

"So we have less than a day to prepare for their arrival. Ain't long. Ain't nearly long enough. Okay. First and foremost, I need to know what level of support we can count on among the locals. Seems like the people of Coogan's Bluff do have a bit of sand, judging by how they acquitted themselves at that bar. We tap into that, place could have a fighting chance."

"I don't know. Tackling three out-of-towners, that's one thing. The Scourers? That's quite another."

"Still and all, it's worth a shot. I have a favor to ask, Mr. Mayor."

"I'll do what I can. You are at least sounding like you're going to pitch in. What do you want?"

"I want you to call a town meeting, soon as possible. Get everybody together. I mean everybody. Beat the drum. Rally the troops. Give us something we can work with. Reckon you can manage that?"

Me Jayne, You Jane

Huckleberry U. Gillis stood on a crate in the Coogan's Bluff's main square. Around him were assembled fifty townspeople or thereabouts, as many as he had been able to rustle up in the space of an hour. They were a ragged, weather-beaten lot, scrawny and ill assorted. They didn't look much.

It was up to Gillis to make them more.

This was, he knew, the speech of his life. He had never and probably would never make a more important oration. He tried to channel the spirit of the greats. Abraham Lincoln. Winston Churchill. Martin Luther King. Madame Xiang, principal architect of the exodus from Earth-That-Was. That was what people were expecting.

Grasping one lapel, he puffed out his chest and began.

"Folks. I don't need to tell you that things are not looking rosy for us right about now. Barbarians at the gates, in a manner of speaking. When next the Scourers are here, they'll be here to commandeer off us the one thing we truly rely on: our water. They'll steal it and they'll sell it back to us at what will no doubt be an extortionate rate. It may seem there's not a lot we can do to change that outcome."

The faces upturned before him were a sea of scowls—although

that could have been because the sun was so bright and everyone was squinting.

"I say to you that there is." Gillis gestured at Mal, Zoë, and Jayne, lined up beside him. "These three offworlders—Captain Reynolds, Miz Washburne, Mr. Cobb—have come to organize a resistance. They are giving of themselves freely in order to stand in the Scourers' path. They assure me they have experience and expertise. They are, in short, the answer to our prayers. But… they cannot do it alone."

He gazed from one person to the next, trying to catch as many eyes as possible during this dramatic pause.

"They need you. They need *us*. They can lead a counterattack against the Scourers but without you backing them up it'll be meaningless. I am asking you good gentlefolk—begging you—to provide that backup. Together, we are capable of anything. United, we can make all the difference. With guns, farming implements, heck, even garden forks and kitchen knives, we can stand together, present a unified front, and show Vandal and his band of no-good varmints that we are not to be trifled with."

His voice rose in pitch and volume. The speech was approaching its climax.

"Where other towns on Thetis have rolled over and shown the Scourers their bellies, we can say a loud, resounding no. We can draw a line in the sand. We can tell them, 'This goes so far and no further. Enough is enough. Your campaign of terror ends, here at Coogan's Bluff.'"

He was quite pleased with that rhyming couplet. He thought it a nice rhetorical flourish.

He lofted his arms. "So what do you say? Will you stand shoulder to shoulder with me and our three new pals here, and their pals? Will you make this the turning point? Will you put the Scourers in their place once and for all? Are you with me? Let me hear you say it. Let me hear a roar from you all. Let your voices carry to the heavens.

'Yes, Mayor Gillis, we're with you!' Come on! All together now. 'Yes, we're with you!'"

Silence from the crowd. Eyes darted uneasily around. Feet shuffled. A discreet cough. Everybody was waiting for somebody else to step up.

Gillis went for it one more time. "'Yes, we're with you!'"

The same non-reaction.

Gillis was crestfallen. "Really?"

Gradually the townspeople began drifting away. First in ones and twos, then groups. Within a minute the meeting had dispersed. Gillis was left standing alone, save for Mal, Zoë, Jayne, and a couple of crowd members who hadn't yet decided to go.

Mal slow-handclapped. "Mighty inspiring speechifying there, Mr. Mayor. Sure got everyone's dander up."

Gillis stepped glumly off the crate. "I truly thought..."

"What?" said Jayne. "That your town is full of cowardly pissants?"

"They're scared," Gillis said defensively. "They have every right to be. I just hoped I could get past that. Dig into some kind of reserve of courage."

"Jayne Cobb."

This came, softly uttered, from one of the two members of the crowd who had remained behind.

Temperance McCloud removed the broad-brimmed hat that had been shading her face from view. Her smile was hesitant, a smile that was uncertain whether it would be reciprocated.

Beside her stood a teenaged girl who was in many ways the spit of Temperance, apart from the piercing blue eyes.

Jayne moved towards Temperance. His arms were extended half out, as if he was considering embracing her.

She strode up to him.

The slap was so loud, it echoed all the way across the square.

Jayne recoiled. "Ow!"

"You dumb son of a bitch!" Temperance thundered.

Jayne put a hand to his face. He looked as much surprised as hurt.

"Nice to see you again too," he said.

Temperance slapped him again, on the other cheek.

Jayne clenched a fist. "Do that to me one more time, I'll forget I'm a gentleman."

"You never were a gentleman," Temperance said, "but you're certainly a moron."

Mal said to Zoë, in an aside, "She's sure got the measure of him."

"I'm rooting for her to slap him some more," Zoë said. "I could watch her do it all day."

"You came," Temperance said to Jayne.

"Yeah, I did. Though I'm asking myself now why I bothered."

"You came with just two other people."

"Eight, as a matter of fact. But who's countin'?"

"I am! I'm counting! Nine of you in total. That's it?"

"It's the best I could do."

"Moron."

Temperance's expression lightened just a fraction.

"But thank you."

Now she leant forward and kissed him on the same cheek she had just clouted, where a red handprint was starting to appear, mirroring a similar handprint on the other cheek.

Jayne, thoroughly nonplussed, turned to the girl beside her. "So who's this?"

Temperance slipped an arm around the girl's shoulders. "My daughter."

"Huh," said Jayne. "Didn't know you had one."

"I didn't say. Jayne Cobb. Jane McCloud."

"Hi," said Jane diffidently.

"Hi."

"She's Jane without the 'y,' in case you were wondering," said Temperance.

"I wasn't, but still."

"She's thirteen."

"Nearly fourteen," said Jane.

"Oh. Okay. Nice to meet you, Jane."

"Sure. Likewise."

Mal nudged Zoë in the ribs with an elbow. "You don't think…?" he whispered.

"Couldn't be," said Zoë. "Could it?"

"How long ago did Jayne say he and Temperance were a thing?"

"He didn't."

"A few years, though. Maybe fourteen?"

"Sir, I don't know what to make of it. But the color of her eyes… It's possible."

Oblivious to this exchange, Jayne said to Temperance, "You're looking good."

"You too. My boy named Jayne is now a man named Jayne."

"I was that, even back then. A man, I mean."

"Not to me. What a difference fourteen and a half years makes."

"See?" said Mal to Zoë. He was equal parts amazed and gleeful. The name. The eye color. The timing.

Jayne seemed blissfully unaware of it, but Mal and Zoë were convinced that the girl standing in front of them was Jayne's daughter.

The Path of Least Bloodshed

Coffee was being brewed on the hob. Much coffee. The delicious smell of it filled Temperance's kitchen.

The room was crowded, with Mayor Gillis and almost the entire crew of *Serenity* congregated around the dining table.

Missing from the gathering were Jane McCloud, who was giving the cattle their evening feed, and River. As soon as the party from the ship had arrived at the farm in the Flying Mule, River had leapt down from the land speeder and skedaddled out into the cornfield. She was now wandering up and down the crop rows, brushing her fingertips over the brittle leaves and the drooping ears. It was as if she was seeing these things for the first time, or else was seeing them in ways nobody had ever seen them before.

"That girl all right?" Temperance had enquired as River headed off.

"Short answer, 'No,'" Jayne had replied. "Long answer, 'Really no.'"

"Hey!" Simon had objected.

"Aw, come on," Jayne had said. "You're her brother and even you pussyfoot around her, like she might blow up in your face."

To that, Simon had had no answer.

Now Temperance began filling enamel mugs with steaming

coffee and distributing them among her houseguests.

"Hope you people appreciate what a privilege this is," Gillis said. "That's a whole day's ration of water Temperance is using to give us all a drink. She wouldn't do it for just anyone. *That's* hospitality." He turned to Inara. "It's kind of like the tea ceremony you Companions put on for your clients, in a way. A token of respect."

"You've identified my profession, Mayor. How astute of you."

"Wasn't too hard. What puzzles me is what a classy lady like you is doing hanging out with a motley bunch like this. Doesn't seem a natural fit, you and them."

"Oh, motley or not, they're fine company," said Inara. "They let me be. You can't put a price on that. Besides…" Her dark eyes flashed furtively in Mal's direction. "They have a certain obscure couth."

"I'm happy to use some of my water on these folk," said Temperance. "Figure if they can send the Scourers packing, they're worth it. 'Course," she added, "if they can, it'd be a gorramn miracle such as would impress Jesus Himself. Begging your pardon, Preacher."

Shepherd Book shrugged off the mild blasphemy. "You've set the bar rather high, Miz McCloud. If we can even approach Our Savior's level of wonder-working, that would be something."

"Fact of the matter is," said Mal, taking a sip of coffee, "since it looks like it's just us versus the Scourers, we're never going to be able to beat them in a straight-up fight. We're going to have to be sneaky. We're also going to have to buy ourselves some time somehow. No way we can build barricades and organize a halfway decent defense overnight. If the Scourers have the numbers Mayor Gillis says, they'll just plough straight through anything we set up." He looked around the table. "I'm open to suggestions."

"I thought you were about to reveal some amazing plan, sir," said Zoë.

"Since when have my plans been amazing?"

"Or even *plans*," said Wash.

"I say we ambush 'em," said Jayne. "Set up a couple sniper nests, catch the Scourers in the crossfire as they ride in."

"From where?" said Mal. "You'd need high ground, and there's none in the vicinity."

"Rooftops."

"Practically every building in Coogan's Bluff is single-story."

"Tree, then."

"Rooftop, tree, up on a flagpole, a sniper'd last maybe a minute, two minutes at most, before the Scourers got him surrounded and took him out. These people have rocket launchers, don't forget."

"What about their camp?" said Jayne. "According to the Mayor, it ain't far from here."

"It's well guarded, by all accounts," Gillis said.

"And going in there all guns blazin'?" said Mal. "Right into the lions' den? It'd be a suicide mission."

"They're bullies," Simon said.

"Oh hey!" Jayne slapped his forehead mockingly. "That never occurred to us. Thanks for the insight, Doc. Graduated top three percent in your class, wasn't it? I can see why."

"No." Simon stifled an exasperated sigh. "Bullies are used to getting their own way. They don't like it when things don't run smoothly for them. Tends to be, if you stand up to them even a little, they fold. There was a guy I knew at Medacad in Capital City, another student in my year, Murray Featherstone. He kept getting pushed around and abused by one of our professors, Dr. January. Dr. January just took against him for some reason and picked on him every chance he could. Asked Murray questions he knew he couldn't answer. Scoffed at him when he got the answer wrong. Made him retake tests if he didn't get the absolute highest grade. Apparently Dr. January did this with every group of new intakes. There'd always be one victim, somebody he'd single out for special punishment. I guess he thought it would impress the rest. Show them he meant business."

"This dumb anecdote better be goin' somewhere," said Jayne.

"The day came when Murray had had enough. It was during an anatomy lecture. Murray just laid into him. Called him all manner of names. Told him a few home truths. Nobody had spoken like that to Dr. January before. No student, at any rate. You could see how shocked he was. He simply hadn't been expecting it."

"And?"

"And, Jayne, Dr. January never picked on Murray again. He was as sweet as can be towards him from then on."

"Awww," said Kaylee, delighted that the story had had a happy outcome.

"So," said Jayne, "you're telling us we can beat the Scourers… with loud cussin'?"

"No," said Simon. "But maybe if their leader—what's his name? Vandal. Maybe if Vandal meets his match, gets his comeuppance, that'll be it. Vandal's the arch-bully. It's likely he's never encountered someone who's as tough as him, if not tougher. Someone who can put him down on the ground. It might be so surprising to him when he does, he loses his nerve and cries off."

"One of us should butt heads with Vandal, is that what you're saying, Simon?" said Book.

"Who?" said Jayne to Simon. "I don't see you volunteerin'."

"I reckon our captain is a match for any man."

Mal spluttered into his coffee. "I'll take the compliment, but you're askin' me to challenge Vandal to a duel? Is that where you're going with this? This ain't no snootsome society ball on Persephone, Simon. Swords at dawn ain't going to cut it."

Simon looked vaguely embarrassed. "I just thought it'd be the path of least bloodshed."

"Except for the person whose blood might get shed," said Jayne.

"Well, *I* like your idea," Kaylee said, patting Simon's arm. "And seeing as you haven't come up with a better one, Jayne, maybe you should at least consider it. We all should."

Meanwhile, out by the corral, Jane was pouring the last sack of cattle feed over the fence into the trough. The cows jostled to get their noses into the mixture of grain, soy, and protein, munching hard. Pasturing a herd was out of the question on Thetis. There just wasn't any grass.

"They're so slow."

Jane jumped. The girl from the ship, River, had stolen up on her stealthily from behind. She hadn't heard her coming.

"Yeah, well, they're cows," Jane said, trying to mask how startled she'd been. "Kind of goes with the territory."

"No. Their thoughts," said River. "Their thoughts are so slow. Like molasses. So peaceful, too. They're just content with everything. They know that they're hot and thirsty most of the time, but they don't mind. They accept it."

"You can read cows' thoughts?"

River blinked at her. "Can't you?"

Jane didn't know whether she was joking or not. "I've never tried."

River clambered up onto the corral's three-rail fence and surveyed the feeding beasts.

"They love you," she said to Jane.

"Uh, good?"

"Do you love them?"

"Never really thought about it. I look after them. Sometimes, when Mom's slaughtered one, I'll feel sad. But it means we can eat. We can live. It's just how it has to be."

River straddled the fence. "Can I stroke them?"

"What? Oh. No. Don't do that. They're not pets."

Too late. River had slipped into the corral and was padding

81

towards the nearest cow, hand outstretched.

"River," said Jane. "That's your name, right? River, get out of there. Come back this side of the fence. It's not safe."

River did not heed her. She placed a hand on the cow's rump. The animal swiveled its head to look at her. It lowed uneasily, menacingly. It did not like being interrupted during its meal.

Jane knew that the cow, if it got really spooked, might turn on River and charge at her. And if one cow did that, the others might panic and follow suit. The herd would stampede the strange young woman and trample her to death.

And if Jane climbed over the fence to try to rescue River while that was happening, they would do the same to her.

"River!" she said, waving an urgent arm. "Back away, nice and easy. Leave them be. You're in danger."

River had her head cocked to one side, as though she was listening to something, her face alight with curiosity.

The cow lowed again. It reared away from the trough, snorting. The rest of the herd, sensitive to any disturbance in their routine, did likewise. Together, the cows moved to form a semicircle around the human interloper. An array of sharp horns faced towards River like drawn daggers.

If River was perturbed by this behavior, she gave no sign. Rather, she smiled in a weird, loopy sort of way. Amused, apparently.

"River!"

Jane climbed up onto the fence. She wasn't sure what to do. She was reluctant to risk her life for a person she barely knew. But she couldn't simply leave River to face the cows alone, could she?

She was about to slide over the fence when she noticed something odd.

The cows weren't moving. They were eyeing River calmly. They seemed to sense she posed no threat. They might have acted that way towards Jane herself, but with a complete stranger? Somebody who had tried to come between them and their eating? It was unheard of.

River started laughing as the cows swished their tails and gazed at her through their long, luxuriant eyelashes.

"We had some of your friends aboard *Serenity* once," she said to them. "Cows in space. Cows that jumped over the moon."

She touched the head of each cow in turn, rubbing the scrubby topknot between the horns. Then she skipped back towards the fence and vaulted over it nonchalantly, all as though she had just been petting a basket of puppies, not a cluster of unpredictable 600-pound longhorns.

"You," Jane said to her, "are either the bravest or the craziest person I've ever met." She added, "I like you. Will you be my friend?"

"Don't be silly!" River replied, chuckling. "We're friends already."

"Now, this may be the most ridiculous thing I've ever said..." Mal began.

"There's some fierce competition for that," Inara quipped.

Mal shot her a look. "But I'm thinkin' the doc may be on to something. One on one, do you think I could take Vandal, Mr. Mayor?"

"It strikes me that you were a soldier once," said Gillis. "Would that be correct?"

"What gave it away? The impressively fierce demeanor? The impeccable straight-backed posture?"

"The brown coat."

"Or that."

"You were an Independent. Independent troops fought hard and they fought dirty. A ragtag band, but you held out against the full might and panoply of the Alliance forces. Nobody can do aught but respect how your side conducted themselves during the war, even if the rightness of your cause is open to debate."

"Our cause made every Browncoat worth a dozen Alliance soldiers."

"I'm sure you are a resourceful and accomplished combatant. I imagine you've held your own against many an imposing foe." Gillis's face tightened. "Believe me when I say this to you. Even someone of your caliber does not stand a prayer against Elias Vandal."

"Oh. That was quite a build-up. Didn't much like the punch line, though."

"Vandal is as big and mean and tough as they come, Captain Reynolds. Next to him, your burly friend Mr. Cobb here is a mere pantywaist."

Jayne tapped Wash on the shoulder. "Did he just insult me or say somethin' nice? I can't tell."

"I think it was both," said Wash.

"You're sayin' I'd be mad to challenge him?" said Mal.

"I'm saying," said Gillis, "that you could do so, but you'd surely be needing the services of your Shepherd afterward."

"Huh." Mal squared his jaw. "Well, that kinda makes my mind up."

"You'll come up with some other way to defeat the Scourers?"

Inara shook her head sorrowfully. "No, Mayor Gillis. You clearly haven't grasped what sort of a man Malcolm Reynolds is."

"Me an' Mr. Vandal are going to have us a little showdown tomorrow morning," Mal said with finality. "Reaver or no, he's going to find out—maybe for the first time in his life—how it feels to have his ass handed to him."

Piecing it Together

Thetis's sun was perched on the horizon, sending out shafts of red light in all directions like distress flares. It was an ageing star, running low on inner fuel. Soon it would commence the millennia-long process of dying, expanding as it consumed the last of its own thermonuclear energy, then collapsing in on itself. That was "soon" in astrophysical terms, of course. Centuries from now. The 'verse never did anything in a hurry.

Jayne and Temperance were out on the stoop, side by side in rocking chairs, facing the sunset. Everyone else was indoors, save for River and Jane. Jane was showing River around the farm.

An awkward silence hung between the former lovers. Jayne, never good with words, hoped Temperance would say something. Temperance, for her part, was waiting to see if Jayne was going to volunteer to speak. Both would exchange glances now and then and pretend they were just two old friends having a pleasant, companionable time watching the day end.

Jayne was the one who finally broke the impasse. "So. It's Temperance McCloud now, huh? There a Mr. McCloud?"

"Nope," replied the woman he used to know as Temperance Jones. "I just thought, 'New planet, new surname.'"

85

"And maybe you're hiding from your past," Jayne said. "Runnin' from something you don't want catching up with you."

"Past like mine, you surprised by that?"

"Not really."

"I'd take it as a kindness if you wouldn't mention to anyone as how I used to be Jones. 'Specially in front of Jane. She doesn't know about any of that stuff, and doesn't need to. Far as she's aware, I've always been a farmer."

"Got it. Your shady days are behind you."

"You still mad at me, Jayne?" Temperance said. "After all this time?"

"No," Jayne lied.

"You'd have every right."

"All right then. I am. You just lit out, Temp. I woke up one morning, expectin' to find you next to me in bed. There was just an empty space. No note, no nothing. For a whole day I kept thinkin' you'd be back any moment and I'd be all, 'Oh, where were you?' and you'd be all, 'Oh, something came up,' and that'd be that. A week went by, and I was still hopin'. Like a fool."

"I should've given you some sort of reason, I guess."

"Ya reckon? I was outta my mind trying to figure out where you might have gone to. Tore up half of Bellerophon lookin' for you. We'd just pulled a nice little switcheroo with some iffy Earth-That-Was artifacts, hadn't we?"

"Couple of jazz long-players, as I recall," said Temperance. Her smile was wistful but had a certain cold edge.

"That was a good dodge, that one," Jayne said. "We printed up Miles Davis labels and sleeves and stuck 'em on Kenny G vinyl. The mark... What was his name?"

"Cain Stephenson."

"Yeah. Him. He was such a dumb sack of *niú fèn*, he played them on his gramophone and couldn't tell the difference! Threw his cash at us like we'd just handed him the Holy Grail, and it's not like the two men even play the same *instrument*. Rich idiots and their dough—they deserve to be parted. Don't get me wrong," he added. "I like money as much as the next guy, but only if it's properly earned, not if it's inherited or got from doin' somethin' soft-handed like lawyering or politicking. That sort of money don't count. The sort of people who have it don't count either. They make my skin crawl."

"Yeah," said Temperance vaguely.

"What I still can't figure, though, is what made you up and leave. It was all going so well, and then suddenly…"

Temperance looked away towards the sinking sun. Its rim was now touching the peaks of the hill range to the west. Nearer by, Jane was demonstrating to River how the corkscrew drill worked. When she showed River the devilworms squirming inside the machine's collection chamber, River squealed—although it was hard to tell whether in delight or disgust. Perhaps both at once.

"It was… complicated," Temperance said. "It wasn't that I was unhappy being with you, Jayne. Far from it."

"But you were gettin' itchy feet."

"Wasn't that neither."

"I didn't give you any reason to hate me. I was nothin' but good to you."

"I know!" Temperance sounded frustrated. "We were great together. Maybe perhaps that scared me a bit, but in a good-scary kinda way. No, Jayne, it was…" Her voice trailed off. "I can't explain."

"Can't or won't?"

"Little of both. I'm hoping you might be able to piece it together."

Jayne rose to his feet. He was angry but doing his best to restrain his emotions.

"Piece it together?" he said gruffly. "How? You ain't tellin' me nothing, Temp. Give me something to work with, some clues, then yeah, I can piece it together. Don't give me anything, I'm in the ruttin' dark!"

He strode off, stalking away into the gathering dusk, shoulders hunched, fists clenched. He passed a tree and looked as though he might punch it, before thinking better of the notion. On he went until he was lost from Temperance's sight.

A few moments later, Shepherd Book stepped out from the house onto the stoop.

"You aren't being fair with him, are you, Miz McCloud?" he said.

"Were you behind the door eavesdropping, Preacher? Mighty unchristian of you, if you were."

"Not at all. I only came out for a breath of air. I saw Jayne stomping off. Saw your face. It wasn't hard to come to the conclusion I did. I'm good at reading people, you see."

"Because you know scripture?" Temperance said sharply. "That's what gives you such a powerful insight into folks' hearts?"

"May I?" said Book, pointing to the chair Jayne had just vacated. It was still rocking from his abrupt departure.

"Free country," Temperance replied with a shrug.

"Now, I don't pretend to know everything that's going on between you, or that *has* gone on," Book said, seating himself. "But Mal and Zoë have said a couple of things back there just now." He jerked a thumb towards the kitchen. "Veiled comments. Unsubtle hints that have enabled me to make certain inferences. Really, though, it's as plain as plain can be. To everyone except, it seems, Jayne Cobb."

"What is?"

"Who Jane—your Jane—is."

"And who is she?"

"Please don't mistake me for an innocent, Miz McCloud. The clothes may suggest I am. My past says I am not. There's many a

Shepherd who's guileless and naïve. I am not one of them. Jane is Jayne's, isn't she?"

Temperance did not reply.

"And she is the reason you ditched him," Book went on. "You were pregnant with her—his child—and for some reason you had a problem with that. You couldn't tell him. You couldn't bring yourself to 'fess up. So you fled."

"Calling me a coward?"

"An aggressive response there. Could it be I've struck a nerve?"

"I just don't take kindly to people insinuating things, least of all men of the cloth."

"Miz McCloud… May I call you Temperance?"

"If it pleases you."

"Temperance," Book said. His tone was gentle. Compassionate. "The prospect of motherhood is daunting at the best of times but never more so than if the baby is conceived by accident and you are not in a committed relationship. And Jayne as a father? Trust me, I have difficulty getting my head around the notion, let alone considering it an alluring prospect. Moreover, you were young. No one could blame you for running. I simply wonder whether it would have been better to be honest with him. He might have surprised you."

"I couldn't," said Temperance. "Not then."

"And now?"

She directed her gaze towards her daughter. "No less hard now. Jayne mightn't be ready for the truth. He might freak out."

"I must say it's a source of some perplexity among the crew that he hasn't cottoned on yet."

"Jayne was never what you'd call a towering intellect."

"It may not dawn on him at all unless someone tells him," Book said. "Surely it would be preferable if the revelation came from you, rather than Mal, for instance, letting it slip. Because sooner or later, you mark my words, one of the crew is going to say *something*.

They're like children in a way. They can't control themselves. Especially if there's a juicy secret begging to be spilled."

The daylight was almost gone. Coogan's Bluff lay not far north of Thetis's equator. In these latitudes, when the sun got itself a mind to go, it went fast.

"Preacher," said Temperance, "I don't hold much with religion."

"Few do, and of those who profess faith, some take it far too seriously and others consider it a license to misbehave."

"I guess you're used to acting as spiritual counselor to your shipmates."

"Among other functions I fulfill."

"Probably they listen to you."

"If only," Book said, smothering the remark in a rueful chuckle.

"Well," said Temperance acerbically, "I ain't one of your shipmates, and I'd consider it a favor if, in future, you keep the spiritual guidance to yourself when you're around me. Do I make myself clear?"

"Abundantly so." Shepherd Book stood, his manner all at once somewhat stiff. "I apologize if I have upset you in any way."

He headed back indoors.

The sun had disappeared. The western sky was purpling. A smattering of stars were twinkling into life.

Temperance felt ashamed of herself for turning on the Shepherd. He had only been trying to help. She should have been more forgiving.

But tell Jayne the truth about Jane? The whole truth?

If she did, Jayne might never forgive *her*.

Stop the Mule, I Want to Get Off

Before daybreak the next morning, there were two departures from *Serenity*.

One was Inara and Kaylee setting off in Inara's shuttle. Their destination was Whiteplains Edge, the largest town on Thetis, to all intents and purposes the capital city. It lay a quarter of the way round the planet, a good half-day's travel, and according to Temperance it boasted several scrapyards where spaceship parts could be bought. Kaylee had a shopping list as long as her arm and was looking forward to haggling over prices. There wasn't a parts dealer in the 'verse who knew more about astronautical engineering than she did, and nobody could fob her off with a cobbled-together piece of garbage pretending it was top quality. She was no rube. She would not be taken advantage of.

Inara was with her not only as pilot but as escort and friend. Her role was to protect Kaylee and keep her out of trouble. At the scrapyards Kaylee would need no assistance, but in the wider environs of the city she might well benefit from having an experienced, older person present. Just in case.

* * *

Kaylee was full of enthusiasm as the shuttle embarked on the journey to Whiteplains Edge. Inara was happy to accompany her. Their departure could be described as optimistic. Shiny, even.

Not so the morning's other departure.

Mal, Zoë, Jayne, Simon, and Shepherd Book were making their way to Coogan's Bluff in the Flying Mule. There, Mal would be throwing down the gauntlet to Elias Vandal.

Mal was not exactly thrilled about this.

But in the absence of a viable alternative, he accepted it was what he had to do.

As far as he was concerned, there was one small chink of light in an otherwise dark situation. Temperance was paying for the repairs to *Serenity*.

"Partly my fault your ship was brought down, Captain Reynolds," she'd said. "It'd never have happened if I hadn't asked you to come to Thetis. So I should be the one to make it right financially. I've money squared away. I can afford it."

True to her word, she'd set up a transfer of credits from her account to Mal's. Kaylee found she had more cash to play with than she'd been expecting—although the total figure Mal had told her she was allowed to spend at the scrapyards was somewhat lower than the sum Temperance had handed over. He was keeping a bit back for, you know, expenses and suchlike.

Of course, no amount of money was going to be any good to him if he died today.

"Generous woman, your ex," Mal said over his shoulder to Jayne as the Mule skimmed towards the town through the pearly-gray light of predawn. Jayne, Simon, and Book occupied the back seat while Zoë rode up front with Mal.

"Yeah. Regular saint," Jayne mumbled.

"You'd be sitting pretty right now, I reckon, if you and she were still an item."

"And you'll be yappin' through a busted jaw if you don't stop going on about her."

"Raising Jane together. Maybe a heapin' of other kids as well."

"Seriously, keep this up and I'll rip your arm out of its socket and beat you to death with the wet end."

"Touchy," said Zoë.

"Well," said Mal, "he *has* had overnight to think about it."

"Think about what?" said Jayne.

"Mal." Shepherd Book, leaning forward, laid a hand on Mal's shoulder. It gripped like a clamp, meant to stem a flow.

But Mal was in a reckless mood. The imminent possibility of death did that to a fella.

"I mean, come on," he said. "Temperance couldn't be making it more obvious with the name. It's practically a neon sign."

"Captain," said Book, "this is neither the time nor the place. It should come from Temperance, not from you, not from any of us."

"All right!" Jayne growled, thumping the Mule's bodywork in agitation. "That's it! What the gorramn hell has got everybody so all fired up? You're all yammerin' like you're in on some big joke and I ain't. Somebody better tell me what this is about or I'm gonna start bashin' heads together."

"I figure I should be handing out cigars," Mal said. "Roughly fourteen years too late, but better late than never."

"Cigars?"

"And you're due all those Father's Day cards you didn't get."

"Father's Day..."

Jayne flicked an ear as though a gnat was buzzing him. His brow furrowed and his eyes lost focus as he pursued a train of thought.

"Penny's dropping," said Mal.

"Well, I'll be a *qīng wā cāo de liú máng*," Jayne muttered. "It can't... She ain't... Is she?"

* * *

Shepherd Book slumped back in his seat with a disgruntled expression. This was precisely how he'd hoped it would *not* turn out. Jayne discovering he was Jane McCloud's father should have happened at a time of Temperance McCloud's choosing. It was Temperance's truth to share, not Mal's or anyone else's. Mal had not had the right.

Nor could Mal have chosen at a less opportune moment. They were on their way to confront a gang of bandits. Everyone needed to be focused and on top of their game. The last thing they wanted was Jayne distracted and off-beam.

Mal Reynolds had a real knack of making bad situations worse.

While Jayne struggled to process the information he had just received, Inara Serra was similarly subdued and preoccupied. Kaylee noted the Companion's somber air. Inara had hardly spoken since they'd left *Serenity*. At first Kaylee had put this down to her concentrating on piloting the shuttle. Then she wondered if it might have something to do with the fact that Inara had recently announced she would be quitting the ship at the first available opportunity, most likely when they next passed by New Melbourne. Was she brooding on that decision? Kaylee sincerely hoped that it wouldn't come to pass and that Inara was even now rethinking the whole idea.

Eventually she decided that the source of Inara's anxiety could only be one thing. "You're worried about Mal," she said.

Inara pursed her lips. "Worried? Yes. Worried sick. I'm also furious with him. Such a damn-fool thing he's doing."

"Why haven't you said anything about it to him?"

"What you may have noticed about our esteemed captain,

Kaylee, is that the more you warn him something's a bad idea, the more he's apt to think it's a good one."

Kaylee laughed, not because it was funny but because it was true.

"But you don't reckon he's going to wind up getting killed today," she said. "Do you? I mean, it's the captain. He'll find some dopey, half-assed way to get himself out of trouble. It's what he does."

"I don't know." Inara looked pensive. "I'm just relieved I'm not going to be around to watch."

"That the reason you offered to come with me?"

"I couldn't in all conscience let you go off on your own without someone backing you up. I'd rather that someone was me."

Kaylee felt a warm, fuzzy glow inside. She had been an only child, and Inara was the older sister she wished she had had when growing up. Inara was the perfect blend of love and beauty, stateliness and steeliness. There were times when Kaylee wanted to *be* her, only without the whole sleeping-with-people-for-money thing. Mostly, though, she just felt blessed to have Inara in her life.

Growing up, Kaylee had been close to her father. A mechanic himself, he had given her a thorough grounding in engineering and encouraged her to pursue her dream of becoming a mechanic too. With her mother, though, she had had a more strained relationship. Mrs. Frye had not been enamored of her tomboyish daughter, nor of the fact that Kaylee and Kaylee's father had such a major interest in common.

Maybe that, more than anything, was why Kaylee found the prospect of Inara leaving so dismaying. She was sensitive to the fragility that existed within a family unit and how tricky it was holding together even people who loved one another—and what was the crew of *Serenity* but a makeshift, mismatched family?

This train of thought provoked another train of thought: Jayne and his newly discovered daughter.

"It's crazy, huh?" she said to Inara.

"What is?"

"Jayne a dad. Who'd have thought?"

"I only hope, when he finally realizes, he doesn't overreact," said Inara. "Last thing Mal needs right now is Jayne Cobb going off at the deep end."

"STOP THE GORRAMN MULE!" Jayne bellowed. "I wanna get off."

Zoë shook her head. "Look. We're nearly at the town. Just be calm, Jayne. Head in the game. We can sort this all out later."

"I said stop!" Jayne shouted. "I need to see Temperance. I'm gonna have words with that *bù huǐ hèn de pō fù.*"

Book felt moved to lean over and address Jayne in his calmest, most soothing tone. "Son," he said, "it's a lot to take in, I understand. But you have to concentrate on what's important right now, and that is Mal and Elias Vandal. There'll be plenty of time later for reproach or, preferably, reconciliation. Should things go awry in Coogan's Bluff, we need to know we can rely on our strongman."

"Due respect, Shepherd, you ain't just learned you got a kid you never knew you had. Being as you're a priest, chances are you never will."

"You might be surprised."

"I've got me a powerful urge to tell Temperance what I think of her keeping this a secret from me, and that urge wants satisfyin' now, not later."

"All the more reason to delay," said Book. "Temper like yours, Jayne, you won't be at your most amenable with her. You may say or do something you'll regret. Let your anger settle. Let it cool. Better still, let it simmer and, if the need arises, take it out on the Scourers. I imagine knocking a few of them around would be cathartic."

Jayne's scowl said he wasn't sure what cathartic meant.

"It means 'cleansing,'" Simon chipped in obligingly. "'Promoting the release of strong, pent-up emotion.'"

"Huh," said Jayne.

Looking at the tension in Jayne's posture—the clench of his fists, the set of his jaw—Book set to wondering. Of late, he had been having the feeling his time aboard *Serenity* was nearing an end. Increasingly he was getting the sense that the crew were fracturing, drifting apart from one another, the more so since Inara had revealed her intention to leave. Often Book was the one who held them together when they began to crumble—as Jayne was now—and he was finding it harder and harder to muster up the strength, or the will, to do so. He could think of various communities where he might be able to do more good and where, too, there would be a whole heap less strife and conflict in his life. One sprang immediately to mind. It was on Deadwood's moon, Haven. The name itself spoke of refuge and peace, and was very close to "heaven."

Yes, maybe, in the not too distant future, Book would be making a departure himself.

The prospect filled him with regret, but a man had to tend to his own garden first before he could tend to the gardens of others.

All of a sudden, right before Book's eyes, Jayne seemed to relax. His outrage had subsided and all that was left was a small, residual frown. He had come to some sort of decision, it would appear.

Shepherd Book would have liked to believe that Jayne had managed to get a grip on himself. That he had his feelings under control.

He wasn't so sure this was the case, however.

Jayne Cobb was like an active volcano. He rumbled and fumed, but if he went quiet, that was when you should be concerned. That was when he was liable to erupt in fire and fury.

Hair Triggers

Coogan's Bluff was quiet.

Too quiet.

Not completely quiet, though. An early morning breeze was scattering the dust around. Particles ticked and tapped against windows and woodwork.

Then there was the slow, lazy revolution of solar-powered well pumps, each extracting a trickle of water up from the bowels of the earth. On some of them, the bearings creaked rustily.

An unseen dog—maybe the same one Zoë had managed not to run over last time they were in town—offered a few listless barks to the rising sun.

Somewhere, a loose window shutter rattled.

The distant hum of a generator.

And, finally, the hiss-sigh of the Flying Mule's directional turbofans as they powered down and the land speeder sank to earth.

Mal stepped out into the town square.

There to meet the crew was Mayor Huckleberry Gillis.

"No one else?" Mal said, looking about.

"No one else," said Gillis. "I'm the reception committee."

"And no Scourers yet?"

"Not as yet. I'd wager they're on their way."

"I was kinda expectin' some of your people might turn out," said Mal. "You know, to show willing. Cheer on the home team."

Gillis ducked his head apologetically. "They'll appreciate what you're doing for them, Captain Reynolds. Afterwards. Right now, keeping a low profile's their priority. Don't want to be seen supporting any kind of opposition to the Scourers, 'case it comes back later to bite 'em on the backside. I presume you're still going ahead with this *bù tài zhèng cháng de* scheme of yours?"

"Were you thinking I might not show?"

"Did occur to me. Wouldn't have blamed you."

"Captain Reynolds is a man of his word," said Shepherd Book.

"Even if that word is 'lunatic,'" said Zoë.

"Good morning, all."

The voice came out of nowhere, catching everyone by surprise. Mal, Zoë, and Jayne all spun on the spot, drawing, cocking and leveling their sidearms in a single swift motion. They, as much as their guns, were on a hair trigger.

Temperance McCloud put her hands up, more a gesture of pacification than of surrender.

"I'd rather you put those irons away, if you don't mind," she said. "Drilling me full of holes isn't going to help none."

"Don't be so sure," Jayne said, keeping his pistol aimed even as Mal and Zoë holstered theirs.

Temperance held his gaze, her eyes steady beneath the broad brim of her hat. "I see you're still nursing that grudge."

"And a lot more besides. You played me for a fool not once but twice, Temp. I surely do not appreciate that behavior."

"To the point where you'd shoot me?"

"Not rulin' it out."

"And leave my daughter motherless?"

"Like you left her fatherless all these years?"

"I had to do what I had to do," Temperance said. "For Jane's benefit."

"What's that supposed to mean? I wouldn't have been to her benefit?"

"'Tain't as simple as that."

"So you keep insistin', but it seems pretty simple to me. I'd have looked after that girl. I'd have looked after the both of you. Instead, you vanished and left me twistin' in the wind, not knowing what was what. You think I wasn't mature enough? Responsible enough? You think I'd have panicked and run a mile?"

"I think maybe you would have."

Jayne acknowledged this. "Yeah, well, maybe I would have. But maybe I *wouldn't*. That ever occur to you?"

"A lot's occurred to me over the past few years, Jayne. A lot of regrets. A lot of recriminations. I can't change the decision I made, however. I can only live with it. I hope you can too."

Whatever Jayne might have been about to say in answer to that was interrupted by a far-off rumbling.

The sound of hoofbeats.

Dozens and dozens of sets of them.

A horde of riders were coming this way.

The Scourers.

Riders of the Post-Earth Age

Some were on motorcycles. Some were on quad bikes. One had a dune buggy. Another rode a narrow-bodied vehicle purpose-built for desert terrain with caterpillar tracks strapped around four triangularly configured sets of wheels.

But most—by far the majority—were on horseback, old-style.

They rode across the plain in a throng. A dust cloud amassed in their wake, purling up to the heavens. Engine roar added to the general ruckus they made, but the thunder of galloping hooves predominated.

Fat, thin, tall, short, male, female, they were an assortment of types but all had two factors in common: a love of Elias Vandal and a hatred of anyone who was not one of them. They thought of themselves as pure and righteous. They had a kind of holy fervor about them, despite which—or perhaps because of which—they were capable of unholy atrocities. They favored ragged clothing and wild haircuts. Each was armed to the teeth.

The notorious Shan Yu would have looked on an assemblage like this and smiled in recognition and approval. So would any other tyrant or conquering general. These people were ideal for their purpose. They were loyal enough to keep discipline, vicious enough to be merciless, and unintelligent enough to do whatever was asked of them. In the overlap between army and rabble, there lay Elias Vandal's Scourers.

Vandal himself was at the vanguard, leading from the front. He spurred on his jet-black stallion, the tails of his ankle-length duster coat flaring behind him like demonic wings. His half-ruined face was set in a leer of anticipation. Yet another town was about to fall to him, and whatever resistance it put up would be so feeble as to be inconsequential. It would be crushed like a bug underfoot.

A swift glance over his shoulder was all the confirmation Vandal needed. He was spearheading an unstoppable, overwhelming force.

"Zoë," said Simon. The tiniest of trembles could be detected in his voice as the distant sound of hoofbeats grew in volume. "I hate to ask, but what happens if things don't go according to plan?"

"We shoot our way out," came the resolute reply.

"And we'll survive that?"

"When shooting's involved, all bets are off. I reckon we have a chance."

"A good one?"

"I didn't say that."

Simon's mouth felt dry. He licked his lips but his tongue had little moisture to spare. He still wasn't sure why either he or Shepherd Book had agreed to come along to this rendezvous. Perhaps it was merely to give Mal moral support, although Simon might well have to make himself useful if Mal sustained wounds that needed patching up. Book might have to make himself useful too, if the worst came to the worst. Administering the last rites.

Simon felt a small pang of guilt for having proposed the whole idea in the first place. Mal hadn't had to agree to it, though. That was on him.

At least River wasn't here. She was helping Wash back at the crash site.

Small mercies.

Simon hoped he was not about to leave River without her older brother. He was all she had.

He braced himself for what was coming. He couldn't quite believe it. The young man from Osiris, who'd grown up cocooned by wealth and privilege and had sacrificed it all to save his sister, was now about to face a bandit army on a planet so remote, most people had never even heard of it.

And this was only the latest in a long line of scrapes and escapades, some near-fatal, most borderline criminal.

Life could sure take some bizarre turns.

Arriving on the outskirts of Coogan's Bluff, Vandal waved a hand in two directions and some of the Scourers fanned out. Quickly they formed a cordon around the town. All roads in and out were covered. Nobody was entering, nobody was leaving.

This task accounted for a quarter of the total number of Scourers present. The remainder, Vandal still to the fore, rode on into the town itself.

In no time they were pulling into the town square.

Vandal slowed his steed from a trot to a walk, and his Scourers did likewise. There was a small representation in the square, a half-dozen or so folk. Vandal recognized Mayor Gillis, drew a blank on the others. Townspeople? He suspected not. More likely, judging by the Flying Mule parked nearby, they were from that Firefly the Scourers had brought down yesterday.

That intrusive, in-no-way-welcome Firefly.

Reining in his horse, Vandal eyed the modest gathering in front of him. At least three of the strangers looked dangerous. They had a wary, tense air. Something catlike about their confident stances, their alertness. Something that told him they were not to be underestimated.

Plus, they had come strapped. Gunslingers.

Vandal found this almost amusing. Here he was with forty-odd men and women at his back, their bodies bristling with weaponry. Before him, as adversaries, a mere three individuals.

Dangerous-looking or not, they were a joke. Surely they could not think they were somehow going to repel him and his Scourers.

Delusional.

"Mr. Vandal."

Mayor Gillis stepped forward. He, it seemed, was the spokesman for the occasion. He was going to negotiate.

"Mayor," said Vandal, tipping the brim of his hat. His horse pawed at the dirt with its front hooves.

Gillis craned his neck to look up at the Scourers' leader. "I see you left a few of your number behind."

"Some back at camp, others ringing the town."

"But still, you're prompt and on time. That is an admirable quality in a man."

"So is forthrightness, Mayor. Tell me about these here people you have with you. What is their purpose? They don't look local. Some kinda hired help? Mercenaries, maybe?"

"Allies," said Gillis. "Allies with a proposition for you."

Mal strode over. If he was feeling any trepidation right then, it didn't show. His face was open, his eyes warm and easygoing.

"I'll speak plain," he said.

"Kindly do."

"You and me, Vandal. We do battle. Right here, right now. Just the two of us. Winner gets to dictate terms to the loser."

"Battle? As in, we fight?"

"That is the customary definition of battle."

"To the death?"

"Well now, I'd rather that wasn't on the table, but if we have to, yes."

"You?" said Vandal, pointing at Mal. Then he pointed at himself. "Versus me?"

"Am I not making myself clear?"

"With weapons?"

"Don't see why not."

"Like a duel?"

"Exactly like."

Vandal burst into raucous laughter. The laughter was picked up by the Scourers, spreading from one to another like an infection. Soon they were all roaring and hooting, slapping their own thighs or one another's backs.

Mal grinned around at them, a little puzzled. "Is it really so funny? Guess it must be."

"You're serious?" said Vandal. "This ain't some kinda prank?"

"Serious as an undertaker reading the obituary column."

"But if I win—which I will—all I'll be gettin' is what I'd be gettin' anyway. Namely water rights to this one-dog town. What's in it for me?"

"I don't know," said Mal. "Proving to your followers that you're not a snivelin', limp-*diǎo* yellowbelly?"

Vandal's face darkened. "What did you just call me?"

"Sorry, was it my pronunciation of *diǎo*? Those down-up intonations. Never quite mastered 'em."

Vandal's sidearm was out of its holster and trained on Mal in a flash.

Zoë and Jayne both drew too.

So did the Scourers. A great rippling array of ordnance.

Mal spread out his arms. "You'd kill a man in cold blood, Vandal? When he's not got a gun in his hand? Hasn't even slapped leather? Kind of proves my point, I'd say."

Vandal thumbed back the hammer on his pistol. "I don't have no scruples about such things. Fella insults me, he gets what's comin' to him."

"These fine folk behind you, I doubt they're gonna be impressed by that. I imagine they seen you make plenty of corpses. People who've surrendered, most like. People in no position to do you ill. Probably they're bored of it now. 'Oh hey, there's Vandal, shootin' another unsuspecting innocent in the back. *Yawn.*' Whereas Vandal in single combat with a man who'd just challenged him right to his face—now *that's* a novelty. What do you say, Scourers? You want to see big bad Elias Vandal mixing it up with some nobody he just met who's had the nerve to call him nasty names? Ask me, that's a morning's entertainment no one in their right mind would want to miss."

The Scourers muttered amongst themselves. The consensus seemed to be that they would rather enjoy seeing their leader get into a no-holds-barred scrap.

Vandal was sensitive to their mood. Leading was as much about setting an example as it was about controlling and guiding. It wasn't enough simply to be the alpha wolf of the pack. Every now and then you had to demonstrate why you were deserving of the position.

Besides, this fella didn't look much to speak of. Tallish, well built, but he didn't have anything like Vandal's bulk and musculature. Bit of a pretty-boy, to be honest.

Vandal reckoned he would crumple after a few solid hits.

And then Vandal could really go to town on him. He would teach him how he dealt with upstarts. He would show everybody that Elias Vandal was not to be trifled with. There would be blood. And screaming. A right goodly amount of both.

"So be it," he said, holstering his gun and dismounting from his horse. "You, sir, have got yourself a showdown. You've also earned yourself more hurt than you can possibly imagine."

As Mal shrugged off his coat and began rolling up his shirtsleeves, he was aware of Jayne sidling up to him. He assumed Jayne had some fighting tips to impart. Maybe he had spotted some physical weakness in Vandal that Mal hadn't observed, some vulnerability Mal could exploit.

"Captain…" Jayne said.

Mal turned.

He didn't see the punch coming.

All he knew was that suddenly he was sprawled on the ground, his jaw was throbbing and the world was spinning.

Jayne bent over him. "Sorry about this, old buddy."

The next punch had Mal seeing stars.

The third had him seeing nothing.

Boss of the Boat

"Ouch! Gorramn it!"

Wash wriggled out of the narrow confines of the bulkhead crawlspace, sucking on his index finger. He had just been fiddling with *Serenity*'s electrics. *Serenity* had seemed to take this personally and had rewarded him with a shock. His fingertip was singed and tingling painfully.

"Zzzap," said River, mimicking the sound of the spark that had jolted Wash.

"Pass me the pliers, would you?" Wash said irritably.

River rooted around in the toolbox and held out a pair of pliers to him.

"No, not those ones," Wash said. "The needle-nose ones."

"But the needle-nose ones don't have insulated handles. This pair does."

"Okay. Good point. Thanks. Now to show this *jiàn huò* of a boat who's boss."

"Mal is."

"I mean, who's boss when it comes to mending her."

"Kaylee is."

"Okay, who's boss whose surname is Washburne."

111

"Zoë is."

Wash gurned despairingly. He had walked into that one. "Am I the boss of *anything* around here?"

"Pliers."

Taking the implement off River, Wash prepared to shimmy back inside the crawlspace and fix the loose connection. Hopefully without electrocuting himself this time.

That was when he heard a clatter of hooves outside.

"Oh crap," he said. "This can't be good."

He straightened up. He and River were in the cargo bay. The ramp was down.

Outside, four people—three men and a woman—were approaching on horseback. They looked rough and ready. They were well armed. Wash would have laid good money on these being Scourers.

"Nice ship," one of them called out to Wash, sliding off his mount.

"For a piece of space junk," said another, and all four guffawed.

"This'd be the Firefly came over our camp yesterday," said a third. "The one we used for target practice."

"Yeah, thanks for that," said Wash. "Brightened our day. Can I help you people?"

The Scourers swaggered up the ramp.

Now that he had a better look at them, Wash reckoned the four of them must be related. They were all redheads and all had the same freckled complexions, the same sea-green eyes, the same knobbly noses, the same underbites that made their mouths look like hooked catfish. Cousins, at least, if not siblings.

"Just you here?" said the female one, whose air of casual authority suggested she was in charge of the group. Her hair was cropped short, irregularly, choppily, like she'd trimmed it herself with a knife and no access to a mirror.

Wash looked around. Of River there was no sign. She had slipped silently off somewhere the moment the Scourers showed.

Wash didn't know whether to be relieved or concerned.

"Yes. Yes, just me. Nobody else. All on my own. By my lonesome. Alone. Me, myself, I."

Wash had a tendency to babble when he was nervous. The harder he tried not to, the more babblesome he became. It was his curse. Stress-induced verbal diarrhea.

"Y'know, we been lookin' for this ship a whiles," said the woman, prowling around the cargo bay. "Knew she came down, just not precisely where. Vandal suggested we follow a radial search pattern in order to find her. Like, a widenin' spiral."

"And here you are."

"And here we are. Vandal thought we'd find just wreckage but there'd maybe be somethin' we could salvage. Turns out she's pretty much intact, so that's a win for us. Can sell her off for parts. You by any chance the pilot?"

"You got me."

"Musta done some fancy flyin' to avoid gettin' hit directly by our heat-seeker. Nice work."

"Ellie-Mae, stop messin' with the fella," said one of the men. "Just get on an' shoot him."

Wash stiffened. The Scourer called Ellie-Mae was behind him now. He didn't dare look round. He had no desire to see the gunshot that was going to end him.

Zoë. That was his first thought. His only thought. He wished she were here. Not for sentimental reasons. He wished Zoë were here because then these four sumbitches would not be threatening him. Because they would be dead.

"Shoot him, Rufus?" Ellie-Mae said. "Kind of a waste of a bullet, don't you think? Guttin' him with a knife'd be more, whatchemacall, economical."

"No one has to gut anyone with anything," Wash said, sounding as reasonable as he could under the circumstances. "I could just go.

In that direction." He pointed to the ramp. "Been cooped up inside a while. Could do with stretching my legs."

"Let's hang him, big sis," one of the other Scourers offered. The "big sis" part confirmed Wash's suspicion. Siblings. "Been some while since we had a good hangin'."

"And lookee here," said the third member of the family, who was shorter than the rest. The runt of the litter. He held up something he had just found looped around a hook on a bulkhead: a roll of half-inch polyester cord normally used for securing loose cargo. "We got us 'xactly what we need."

Wash made a run for it.

He didn't get far.

Two of the Scourers intercepted. There was a brief scuffle, and within moments they were holding him securely, arms pinned. Wash struggled but could not break free.

Ellie-Mae fashioned a noose out of one end of the cord. She did this in a way that suggested she'd had some practice. Then she slung the cord up around a strut in the catwalk balustrade, tying off the loose end on a wall hook.

An aluminum packing crate was dragged beneath this makeshift gibbet. Wash was forced to stand on the crate. His hands were fastened behind his back and the noose was draped around his neck.

Terror and incredulity vied within him. He was about to die. He could not believe he was about to die. Especially not like this, lynched like a common-or-garden sheep rustler.

"Listen," he said to the Scourers. "You don't have to do this."

"No, we don't," said Ellie-Mae cheerily. "That's what makes it fun."

"Nothing I can say will persuade you to reconsider?"

"No, but it's sweet that you think it might."

Amidst his fear, Wash had the presence of mind to wonder where River had gotten to. He trusted she had slipped out of *Serenity*, maybe via the access door to the shuttle airlock, just past the galley, or one of the EVA hatches. She was now running fast and far. The Scourers would not get her.

Especially if he could buy her some more time.

"There's goods aboard," he said. "Hidden about the ship. Valuable items. Medicines, fresh strawberries, and suchlike. I can show you where everything is. It's all yours."

A bluff. A viable one, he hoped.

Ellie-Mae didn't seem convinced. "Well, assumin' what you're tellin' us ain't a crock of horse dung, we can have the stuff anyway. Might take us a while longer to find it without you guidin' us, but hell, we can do with the exercise."

She set her foot against the side of the crate, preparing to kick it away from beneath Wash.

There was a loud *clang* from up by the dining area.

Ellie-Mae frowned at Wash. "Thought you said you was all alone."

"I am."

"Then what was that noise?"

"What noise? I didn't hear any noise. Did you guys hear a noise?"

The clatter came again, louder.

"Ohhh, *that* noise," said Wash. "Ship's cat. Señor Sneaky Paws. We can't keep him out of the butter dish. Loves him some butter, does Señor Sneaky Paws."

"Isaac. Frank." Ellie-Mae waved a hand. "Go take a gander."

The two Scourers shambled off up to the dining area.

Ellie-Mae fixed Wash with a glare. "Know what I can't stand? When a man lies to me. It's an issue I have. My daddy lied to my momma all the time 'bout his gamblin'. My ex lied to me 'bout all his other women."

"Beats me why anyone'd be unfaithful to a peach of a gal like you," Wash said, then immediately thought, *Hoban Washburne, why do you say these things? You and your smart mouth!*

115

Ellie-Mae half laughed. "Know what I did to him when I'd finally had enough of his cheatin' ways?"

"Forgave him, took the noose off, and let him go free?"

"Let's just say he won't be usin' that pecker of his for anythin' but peein' outta the stump of it."

Wash winced.

"Like I said," Ellie-Mae went on. "Trust issues."

She gave the crate a shove.

"No, no, no!" Wash gasped.

The crate went only a short distance, enough that the tips of his toes were still just on it. Wash was teetering at an angle. His toes were all that were preventing him dangling by the neck alone. His feet kept slipping off the crate. He fought frantically to maintain his toehold.

There was a sudden commotion up above, coming from the dining area. Shouts. Yells. Roars of pain. Bangs and crashes.

Then silence.

Ellie-Mae gestured to the third male Scourer. "Rufus. Check it out. Find out what the hell Isaac and Frank are playin' at."

Little brother Rufus, the runt, drew his pistol and did as big sis said.

Wash was a mite preoccupied, what with the whole business of trying to remain in contact with the crate and alive. Nevertheless, he had a strong hunch that whatever was happening in the dining area, River Tam was behind it.

The girl might look fragile, but everyone on *Serenity* knew she could be dangerous. Deadly dangerous.

A minute passed. For Wash, a *long* minute.

Rufus did not return from his investigation. Nor was there any sign of either of the other two Scourers.

Ellie-Mae was looking irritated. And, in Wash's view, disconcerted too.

"Gorramn jackasses!" she spat. "Rufus Hazzard! Isaac! Frank! Any of you! Answer me! What's keepin' you?"

No reply.

Then, from somewhere in the cargo bay, a soft, singsong voice spoke. River's.

"Made a mess of the mess hall. Three guests for brunch. They didn't much care for what I served up."

Ellie-Mae's gun flashed out from its holster. Say what you like about the woman, she was quick on the draw.

"Who's there?" she demanded. "Show your face."

"Terrible table manners," River said.

Wash could not place where River was in the cargo bay. Her voice seemed to be coming from everywhere and nowhere. It was more than a touch creepy.

Ellie-Mae certainly seemed rattled.

"Come on out, darlin'," she said, steadying her nerves with an obvious effort. She stalked across the cargo bay, sweeping her gun from side to side, checking corners, cubbyholes, blindspots. "I'm sure you and me can talk this through like sensible folk. Whatever you done to my brothers, I ain't mad at you. Let me have a chance to prove it."

Nothing from River.

"Sweetheart?" Ellie-Mae called out. "Can you hear me? I said—"

River dropped onto her from on high like a jaguar pouncing on its prey from a tree bough. She had a torque wrench in her hand—one she must have procured earlier from Wash's toolbox—and she struck Ellie-Mae on the head with it as she came down. Ellie-Mae slumped to the floor like a sack of potatoes.

"Click-type torque wrench," River said, standing over Ellie-Mae, hefting the tool in her palm. "Calibrated clutch mechanism. Knurled handle. Designed for a hexagonal bolt with a nominal diameter of seven-sixteenths of an inch."

Ellie-Mae groaned and pushed herself off the floor.

River clubbed her a second time with the wrench.

"I wasn't finished," she said. "Weight is three pounds two ounces. Torque range is twenty to one hundred and fifty foot pounds. Primary function: tightening or loosening bolts. Secondary function: stopping people like you from hurting me and my friends."

Once more Ellie-Mae tried to rise.

River hit her yet again, right in the occipital region, and this time there was a loud crunch, as of bone splintering. Ellie-Mae collapsed and lay still.

She didn't look likely to get up again. Ever.

"But you probably have realized that," River said to her.

"Uh, River?"

Wash was barely keeping his balance on the edge of the crate. The noose was starting to strangle him.

River jerked her head round. It was as though she hadn't been aware he was there.

"Oh, hey, Wash."

"Not ungrateful for the save and all," Wash said, choking. "But I could do with a little help here."

River broke into a broad, beaming smile. She trotted over to where the cord was tied to the wall and undid the knot.

Wash tumbled to the floor, butt first.

"Who's the boss of the boat, Wash?"

"You are, River," Wash said, sitting up awkwardly. "Most definitely you."

A Powerful, Primal Driver

"Jayne, what the hell?" Zoë exclaimed.

"Yeah, Jayne, what the hell?" Elias Vandal echoed. "Wait," he added, bemused. "Your name is *Jayne*?"

Jayne ignored him. To Zoë he said, "Fight ain't Mal's. Not anymore. It's mine."

"What do you mean by that?"

"Hey. Hey!" said Vandal, demanding attention. "Big guy. One, you're called Jayne? What kinda name is that for a fella? And two, why'd you just cold-cock my opponent?"

"One, it ain't none of your business," said Jayne. "Two, 'cause I'm challengin' you myself. You take on me 'steada Mal."

"Well now, that ain't what I agreed to," said Vandal.

"I'm changin' the agreement."

"Not sure as you can do that."

"Just did. You and Mal, that weren't no contest. You and me, on the other hand? That's a damn sight fairer."

Vandal eyed Jayne up and down. "You're a whole lot more sizeable than the other guy, ain't no doubt about that. Whole lot meaner-lookin', too."

"You pussy or somethin'? Don't like it when you ain't gettin' an easy ride?"

Vandal let out a contemptuous laugh. "You can try and rile me all you want, *Jayne*. Don't alter the fact that I settled to fight one particular person and now you're askin' me to fight a different person. Ever hear of bait and switch? That's the stunt you people have just pulled, and it don't incline me to play along."

"Mal is indisposed."

"Ooh. Fancy talk."

"So I'm steppin' up to take his place. 'Less you're scared of me, that is."

Vandal scowled. "'Course I ain't scared of you." He shrugged, as if he had decided he didn't mind who he fought, provided he fought *somebody*. "I'm willin' to make a go of it. Don't know why you're so keen for a whuppin' that you'd knock a man out to get the opportunity. Since you are, though, who am I to disappoint you? Just don't think I'll let myself get sucker-punched the way your buddy did."

Simon said to Book, "I don't understand. What's Jayne up to? What's got into him? It's not like him to... to..."

"To willingly risk himself when he doesn't have to?" said Book.

"Well, yes."

"I think Jayne feels a sudden burden of responsibility." Book looked towards Temperance McCloud. "I think he realizes he has a considerably greater personal stake in the outcome of this fight than Mal."

Simon followed the line of Book's gaze. "Temperance."

"Not just her."

"Jane McCloud," said Simon, his brow clearing as comprehension dawned. "My God, yes. Because she's his..."

"Precisely. A man'll do anything to protect his child. Even a child he's only just learned he has. That instinct is a powerful, primal driver. Jayne is as susceptible to it as anyone."

Simon nodded, even though he knew from personal experience that what Book had just said was not axiomatically true. His own parents had done little to protect River after it became clear that she was being maltreated at the Academy. They had refused to believe anything was wrong and had remained willfully blinkered to her plight even when Simon insisted, with good justification, that her letters home were coded distress signals. They had set their faith in the government above the interests of their daughter, forcing Simon to take matters into his own hands and rescue her. In the event, he had proved to be a better caregiver for River than either their mother or their father.

Simon took one last look at Temperance before returning his attention to the imminent confrontation between Jayne and Vandal. Temperance's gaze was fixed unerringly on the Scourers' leader, and although the brim of her hat cast her face in shadow, he could make out a deep frown corrugating her forehead. He took this as an indicator of concern—a concern he himself shared. Vandal was a brute, as hulking and intimidating as any he'd met. He hoped Jayne knew what he was doing. He hoped Jayne really could take Vandal down.

"Jayne," Zoë hissed as he stripped off his jacket. "You really reckon you can do this? Take Vandal down?"

"Sure. Why not? Odds are better for me than Mal."

"I hope you're right about that."

"I am."

Jayne turned to face Vandal again. "See you got a fancy-ass blade there in your belt." He drew a bowie knife from a sheath attached to his own belt. The knife was approximately a foot long, with serrations along the blunt section of the blade's upper edge. A fearsome beast. "Here's mine. What say we see whose is sharper?"

"Mine's certainly bigger," Vandal said, unsheathing the semicircular weapon.

"Kinda got a kink in it, though."

"Handles just fine, if'n you know how."

"So let's find out if you do."

A space was cleared for the two combatants in the Scourers' midst. Meanwhile, Zoë and Book dragged Mal's inert form over to the Mule, where Simon checked him over and ascertained that he was merely out cold, nothing worse.

Jayne and Vandal stepped into the ring formed by the Scourers.

Two gladiators in the arena.

The Unpardonable Sin of Badmouthing Mama Cobb

Warily, cagily, Jayne and Vandal circled each other. The Scourers jostled around them, showering their leader with encouragement and bombarding his opponent with insults.

Vandal feinted. Jayne sidestepped. It hadn't been an attack, rather a test, Vandal gauging Jayne's reflexes, assessing how serious a threat he posed.

Jayne feinted back. Vandal body-swerved.

For a big man, he was fast.

Worrisomely fast.

Jayne started snaking his free hand around in the air. Vandal did the same. The motion was a distraction, intended to divert your opponent's eye away from your knife hand. Neither of them succumbed to the trick.

Vandal lashed out. Jayne danced around the knife thrust and slashed in riposte. He, too, missed.

"You know, I had a friend once, looked like you," Jayne said to Vandal. "Face all messed up down one side. Stitch Hessian was his name. 'Course, he had only the one eye, not both. But he was still as ugly."

"Funny," said Vandal. "Even without scarring you're pretty damn ugly your own self."

"My mom would disagree with that."

"She would. She told me so, matter of fact, just the other day as I was wipin' myself off on the drapes. Generous woman, your mother. Didn't even ask for payment like she usually does."

Generally speaking, to badmouth Mama Cobb was to commit an unpardonable sin. You were guaranteed to invoke the full, untrammeled wrath of her son. But Jayne knew it was important in this fight not to let a little bit of trash talk get to him.

"Don't know which is worse," he said. "You pretendin' you slept with my mom or thinkin' she'd have such low standards."

Before he even finished the sentence, Jayne lunged. He almost—*almost*—made contact. Vandal just managed to get out of the way.

Vandal's retaliatory swipe was aimed at Jayne's head, a scything blow that would have embedded the knife blade deep in Jayne's skull had its intended recipient not ducked in time.

Jayne, in a crouch, swung his knife backhand at Vandal. He caught Vandal's duster but cut nothing more than oilcloth.

"Dang!" Vandal looked in dismay at the fresh tear in his sleeve. "My favorite coat and all."

"Maybe shoulda taken it off before we got started."

"Now you done gone and pissed me off, man with a girl's name."

"Heh," said Jayne, grinning. "Pissin' people off is my specialty."

"That means I'm gonna do this."

Vandal threw his knife away.

Jayne gaped. He couldn't quite believe it. Vandal had just recklessly tossed aside the only thing that was stopping Jayne moving in close and stabbing him through the heart.

Jayne was so astonished and elated, he failed to mark the deliberateness with which Vandal had thrown the knife. Nor did he notice how the curved weapon was whizzing through the air in an arc, which took it up over the heads of the surrounding Scourers and back down towards the arena.

Zoë did. "Jayne! Look out!" she yelled.

Too late. Jayne pivoted round in time to see the knife hurtling towards him but not in time to evade.

It thudded deep into his ribcage, the blade burying itself right up to the hilt.

Jayne's eyes rolled up in his head and he keeled over.

There was a collective gasp of delight from the Scourers. This was followed by ecstatic cheering and applause.

Simon hastened to Jayne's side.

Before he could get there, however, Vandal bent down and grasped the knife handle.

"Don't!" Simon yelled. He could tell that Vandal was about to yank the knife out: the worst thing he could do as far as Jayne was concerned.

Vandal glanced at Simon, grinned, and pulled.

The knife came free, and instantly blood started jetting from the wound.

Simon slid to his knees. He wrenched off his shot-silk vest, wadded it up and pressed it to the gash in Jayne's side, applying pressure in order to stem the bleeding. The knife blade had been keeping the wound nicely sealed. Without it, the blood could gush freely.

"He's done, kid," Vandal said. "Done and dusted. *Sǐ ròu.*" *Dead meat.* "Ain't nothin' gonna save him."

"I beg to differ," Simon said, wishing he felt as confident as he sounded. Jayne was still breathing but Simon could hear a wet, sucking gurgle that accompanied each inhalation and exhalation. Jayne's lung had been pierced. Blood was gradually filling it, just as blood was seeping out of him. One way or the other, this displacement of blood was liable to end his life.

Simon beckoned to Zoë and Book. "We need to get him back to *Serenity*, stat. The only chance he has is if I can treat him in the infirmary."

Zoë and Book moved to pick Jayne up.

"Say now, what do you two think you're about?" said Vandal. "Don't recall as I told you you can take the fella away. He's gonna stay here and he's gonna die here, just like he ought. I killed him fair and square. I have earned the right to watch him layin' at my feet, breathin' his last."

"With respect, Mr. Vandal," said Zoë, "nobody's asking your permission. Jayne's coming back to our ship with us and that's that."

"Feisty one, aintcha?" Vandal wagged his bloodstained knife at Zoë. "I like that in a woman. Bit of fire. 'Course, you're kinda old for my likin', but I'm willin' to make an exception this one time. What say the two of us, my fine lady, we get it on? Borrow a bed off of someone and make sweet love? Promise me that, and I'll maybe think about allowin' the young gentleman here to give old ugly-puss the medical attention he needs."

"You want me to sleep with you? In exchange for Jayne's life?"

"Can't make it any plainer'n that. You and me, humpin'."

Zoë's lip curled in disgust. "Not while there are dogs on the street."

"Fair enough," said Vandal. "Nobody can say I didn't offer. You just sentenced your pal to death. That's on your conscience, not mine. If you're willin' to reconsider, all you have to do is—"

BLAM!

Vandal recoiled, flopping to the ground.

As the echoes of the gun report rolled away and faded, everyone looked around in consternation. Who had fired? Where had the shot come from?

Aboard the Mule, an ashen-faced Malcolm Reynolds sat slumped in the backseat. His Liberty Hammer was in his hand, smoke coiling up from the muzzle.

"Did I hit him?" he said in a thick voice, blinking blearily. "Somebody tell me I hit him."

Heroic Measures

Zoë sensed they had only seconds in which to act.

She had no idea if Elias Vandal was alive or dead. What she did know was that the Scourers were stunned, frozen in shock. They would soon recover from their surprise, however, and then the bullets would start flying.

"Book. Simon." Her voice was low, urgent. "Get Jayne to the Mule. Now."

Neither man hesitated. Simon took Jayne's ankles. Book slid his hands under Jayne's armpits. They hoisted him up and lugged him across to the Mule, leaving a trail of blood spatters in the dirt.

For her part, Zoë leapt behind the land speeder's controls and fired up the engine. Mal was still in a state of semi-disorientation. He called out to her confusedly but she ignored him. It was a wonder he had managed to aim his gun with any accuracy at all.

As soon as Simon, Book, and Jayne were on board, Zoë rotated the turbofans to vertical and the Mule rose shudderingly off the ground. The vehicle was facing nose-first into the town square, so Zoë had a clear view of what was happening there. Most of the Scourers were clustered around Vandal, peering down at their fallen leader. The rest were jabbering and gesticulating worriedly.

129

Mayor Gillis and Temperance McCloud, meanwhile, were scurrying for cover. Which, thought Zoë, was a wise precaution. The Scourers might be in a state of paralysis, rudderless without Vandal giving them orders, but it wasn't going to last much longer. Any moment now, one of them was going to grasp the fact that the man who had just gunned Vandal down was escaping, along with his friends. Then all hell would break loose.

In the event, it was Vandal himself who incited the Scourers into action. He sprang up off the ground, clutching his shoulder. Mal's shot had only wounded him. Vandal was alive and well.

And royally pissed.

"They're gettin' away!" he hollered. "You buncha lame-brained monkeys! Can't you see? Bastards're gettin' away!"

Zoë threw the Mule into reverse. No time for anything elaborate like an about-turn. They were leaving the town square *now*, backwards, come what may.

A fusillade of gunfire raked the front of the departing land speeder. Zoë hunched down low as bullets smashed into the windshield and whined off the hood. The Mule veered wildly but continued its rearward progress, gathering speed. Zoë came up with her Mare's Leg in her left hand, her right hand still guiding the vehicle. The repeater rifle boomed once, twice, three times in swift succession, Zoë working the lever action one-handed. Three Scourers were hurled backwards by the impact of heavy-caliber rounds, dead before they hit the ground.

The hail of bullets from the Scourers continued unabated, but the Mule was pulling out of range. It skimmed along Coogan's Bluff's main street, turbofans roaring.

"Hang on!" Zoë shouted, and she threw the land speeder into a tight clockwise one-eighty. Centrifugal force bent everyone aboard to the left. Mal lolled drunkenly against Simon, who was busy applying pressure to the wound in Jayne's side. Simon shoved him back.

With the Mule now facing forwards in the direction of travel, Zoë felt free to accelerate fully.

Just as well, because the Scourers were in hot pursuit. Those with horses climbed up into the saddle, dug in their rowels and galloped after them. Those in vehicles gunned their motors and hit the throttle.

"Zoë," said Book, in the passenger seat beside her.

"Not now, Shepherd. Kinda busy."

"Roadblock ahead. In case you hadn't noticed."

"*Jĭng shì hài sú*," Zoë sighed. *Awesome.*

They were already nearing the edge of town, and there were Scourers lined up across the road. They had their guns drawn. Their horses were tossing their heads and stamping restlessly.

"Might I avail myself of your weapon?" Book said.

"Be my guest." Zoë passed the Mare's Leg across. "I'm guessing you ain't about to kill anybody."

"As I've said before, the Sixth Commandment strictly prohibits it in the case of people. Horses, on the other hand, are a theological gray area."

Book took careful aim and shot the mounts from under two of the Scourers.

The rest of the Scourers scattered, returning fire wildly. The Mule scooted through the roadblock unscathed.

But the Scourers giving chase were close behind.

"We can outrun them, surely," Simon said.

"The horses, yeah," Zoë replied. "The vehicles not so much. Mule's built for freight-bearing, not for speed."

Sure enough, the Mule was putting distance between it and the Scourers on horseback. But a dune buggy, a motorbike and a tri-wheeler with ape-hanger handlebars came to the fore of the Scourer pack, keeping pace with the Mule.

By this stage Mal was a great deal clearer-headed than before. He was sitting upright, taking stock of the situation.

"Zoë, get us off-road."

"Planning to, sir," Zoë said tersely. "Only there's saguaros either side, too tall to go over. But not for much further."

Mal loosed off a couple of rounds at the pursuing Scourers. They shot back, their bullets whanging off the Mule's bodywork.

"Any time soon'd be welcome," Mal said.

Past the dense clumps of cactus, Zoë eyed the terrain to the left and right. It was rocky and rugged, far from ideal conditions for a flying Mule.

"Still can't leave the road just yet," she said.

More bullets came their way. One ricocheted off metal just inches from Simon's face. He flinched, but his focus was mainly on Jayne. The pulmonary hemorrhaging was getting worse. Frothy blood bubbled at Jayne's lips. Then Jayne started to go into convulsions. Simon estimated that, without the right drugs to stabilize him, the man's lifespan could be measured in minutes.

"He's going to drown in his own blood if I don't do something," Simon said, mostly to himself.

"Then do something, son," Book advised.

Simon turned Jayne's head to one side in order to drain the blood from his mouth and nose. It appeared that the pressure he was applying on the wound with his vest was no longer enough. The wound had to be made fully airtight, otherwise Jayne's breathing process would draw air through it into his chest cavity. Ideally, Simon would have used a chest seal. Failing that, he could have covered the wound with a piece of taped-down plastic.

None of those things was available on the Mule, so he removed the wadded-up vest and placed the flat of his hand over the gash. The bloodflow helped form a seal, but he couldn't relax the pressure from his hand for one moment.

The makeshift seal wasn't perfect but seemed to work. Now what Simon had to watch out for was a tension pneumothorax—Jayne's lung collapsing, allowing blood to leak into the space between it and the chest wall. Among the symptoms were cyanosis of the lips and fingers, neck veins bulging, and severe shortness of breath. If it went undetected, the build-up of pressure within the chest cavity could lead to shock and potentially death.

He asked himself why he was going to all this trouble for a man whom he didn't much like and who actively despised him.

But then such was the lot of the physician. You saved whomever you could, whenever you could, regardless of their character or their relationship to you. You used heroic measures even for the least heroic individuals.

As Simon did his best to keep Jayne alive, beside him Mal blasted away at the Scourers with his pistol.

The Scourer on the motorbike took a bullet in the shin. Yelping in pain, he jerked the handlebars reflexively. The bike skidded, slewed, and went tumbling end over end, jettisoning its rider. He hit the dirt head-first, with neck-snapping force.

Book planted a round neatly in the engine cowl of the tri-wheeler. Smoke billowed and the vehicle ground to a halt, stranding its occupants.

That left the dune buggy, and it was gaining on the Mule. The man at the wheel was a skilled driver, expertly negotiating the deep, criss-crossing ruts in the road. Meantime its passenger had a high-velocity rifle in his hands and was drawing a bead on the Mule. He was sighting on one of the turbofans. If he found his mark and destroyed the turbofan, the Mule would go into a sudden, terminal spin. Zoë would not be able to correct its violent gyrations. A crash would be as catastrophic as it was inevitable.

"Zoë," Mal warned, busy reloading.

"I know, sir," Zoë said, one eye on the rearview. "Believe me, I know."

"I'm out," Book said, nodding at the gun in his hands.

"It's all good news, isn't it?" Zoë bit her lip. "Okay. What would my husband do if he were here?"

"You mean apart from whine like a little schoolgirl?" said Mal.

"Yeah. Apart from that. He'd try something totally unexpected and more or less suicidal. Like a Crazy Ivan."

"Don't have time or room to turn."

"No, we do not."

Zoë, without another word, slammed the Mule into reverse. The turbofans revolved. Everyone was jolted forward, hard. Simon's hand slid and he almost lost the important seal he was making over Jayne's wound.

The Mule shot backwards, heading straight for the oncoming dune buggy. The buggy's driver hit the brakes, off-balancing the passenger just as he made his shot.

The bullet missed, whistling past Mal's ear.

The Mule and the dune buggy bore down on each other, the gap between them narrowing fast.

The driver, realizing the Flying Mule had no intention of stopping, braked and fumbled for reverse gear. He managed to find it and the dune buggy lurched backwards, fishtailing madly.

The Mule kept on coming, and the dune buggy driver, in his alarm, misgauged. A rear wheel collided with a roadside boulder. The back end of the vehicle bounced high, front fender grinding into the ground. For a split second the buggy teetered, looking as though it might come down backwards onto all four wheels, safely.

Then, instead, it tipped forwards, thudding onto its rollbars and trapping the two Scourers beneath it.

Seconds later, the Mule struck it a glancing blow. The dune buggy, by far the lighter of the two vehicles, flipped up and over, this time coming down on its side.

Zoë slowed the Mule and engaged forward thrust once more.

The dune buggy's passenger hung from his seat, limp like a broken marionette. The driver was struggling to get out. He slithered onto the road, where he knelt on all fours, dazed. He looked up to see the Mule coming for him and choked out a scream, but that was all he could do before Zoë mowed him down.

Improvements in the Situation, or Lack Thereof

Eighteen minutes later the Mule was back at *Serenity* and Jayne was on the med couch in the infirmary.

Simon, smeared all over with the other man's blood, set to work. He lengthened the gash made by Vandal's knife in Jayne's intercostal wall and used a retractor to separate the two adjacent ribs. Then he sewed up the puncture in the pleural membrane, after which he repaired his incision. A dermal mender would have neatened the end-result, but the infirmary had none. Besides, Jayne seemed proud of his battle scars. Even the diagonal slash left by River on his chest some months back was still visible.

It was an hour and a half of brow-sweat effort, requiring Simon's full concentration. Twice during the procedure Jayne's vitals crashed and Simon had to break off from the surgery in order to shock his patient back to life with the defibrillator paddles. Replacing the blood Jayne had lost used up all the packs of type O negative *Serenity* had on board.

At last Simon was able to stand back and pronounce himself done.

Mal had been stationed outside the infirmary throughout the entire operation, watching through the windows. Seeing Simon remove his surgical mask and gloves with an air of finality, he entered the room.

"He gonna live?" he asked.

"Maybe," said Simon. "Should do. He's got the constitution of an ox." *The brains of an ox too*, he nearly added. "If anyone can pull through from an injury like that, it's Jayne."

"But…?"

"There's no 'but.' We're just going to have to let him recover in his own time. I've induced an artificial coma, which'll help him heal. The rest is up to Jayne."

Mal clapped a hand on Simon's shoulder. "You did good, Doc. Thank you."

"Want me to take a look at those?" Simon indicated the bruises on Mal's face. The largest was the size of a golf ball and every shade of dusk.

"Huh? No. No need. Don't hardly feel 'em."

"Jayne got you good."

"So he did, and there'll be a reckonin', you can count on it. It don't bother me so much that he hit me. Bothers me that he was insubordinate."

"Brave, too," Simon pointed out.

"Foolhardy, more like. From what Zoë and Book tell me about the fight, he got overconfident. Made a mistake, and it cost him dear."

"He couldn't have known Vandal's knife could do that thing it did, spinning around and coming back."

"He *should* have known," Mal said. "It's a boomerblade and Jayne should have recognized it. Can't have lived this long doing what he does and never seen one before. He just wasn't payin' attention."

"Maybe he was distracted. He wasn't fighting for himself. He wasn't fighting for us or for Coogan's Bluff. He was fighting for family."

Mal snorted angrily. "*We're* his gorramn family. Not some woman he hasn't seen in nearly a decade and a half, and certainly not some girl he only just met. Jayne got careless, is all. And now we're a man down, we don't have a ship that can fly, and Elias Vandal's got the whole of Coogan's Bluff under his thumb. As usual, the Malcolm Reynolds luck is runnin' true to form. I'm looking forward to someone telling me this situation just got better, but I ain't holding my breath."

"The situation just got worse," said Temperance McCloud. "Much worse."

"I knew it," Mal seethed, wishing he wasn't half so gorramned prophetic.

Temperance had just ridden over to the crash site, along with Jane, and she had a tale to tell. She'd managed to make it out of Coogan's Bluff without getting caught, but only just. She and Mayor Gillis had taken advantage of the general disarray caused by the crew's departure and snuck out by means of a back route they both knew. They'd followed a gully which led to a culvert running under one of the main arterial roads. Beyond the culvert lay open country and the McCloud farm.

Gillis, however, balked at going further. "Nope," he announced. "Not for me. I'm staying."

"What?"

"Can't just up and run."

Temperance called him all kinds of names and urged him to rethink, but Gillis was adamant. His mind was made up.

"But," she argued, "this is your best chance of escaping. Most likely your one and only. What's gotten into you?"

"It's *my* town, Miz McCloud," Gillis said with a resigned shrug. "I'm Mayor. The chain of office comes with responsibilities. Folk look up to me. They expect me to set the tone. How can I abandon them in their hour of need? Wouldn't be proper. You go on home, good lady. You've Jane to get back to. You have a duty of care towards her, just like I have a duty of care towards my constituents."

Brooking no further argument, Gillis retraced his steps along the gully.

"There's guts inside that blubberous body," Temperance said to Mal and the other crewmembers gathered in the observation lounge. "Not just the entrail kind either. I'd never have thought Huck Gillis had it in him, but I guess I was mistaken."

"So the Mayor is back in the town," said Wash. "How is that so bad?"

"Bad for him," said Temperance. "And overall, things ain't looking any too rosy for Coogan's Bluff. After I went home to check in with Jane, I headed down the road a ways, taking a pair of binoculars for a look-see. To assess the extent of the problem, as it were. I lay myself flat on the brow of a hillock overlooking the town and scanned the scene. Sure enough, what had happened was what I feared was gonna happen."

"Which is?" said Zoë.

"Scourers have got the place completely surrounded. I mean *completely*. A ring of them. Every entry and exit point is now heavily guarded, and they're patrolling the perimeter. Four-man teams pulling sentry duty, marching back and forth. Ain't a jackrabbit could get in or out without them noticing—and shooting it."

"But what is this blockading in aid of?" said Book.

"So that they can do exactly what they did with Yinjing Butte," Temperance said grimly.

"Yinjing Butte?" said Wash.

"Neighboring town," said Zoë. "Caused the Scourers some headaches. They destroyed it."

"Didn't just destroy it," said Temperance. "'Destroy' makes it sound like the event occurred quick-smart, overnight. Weren't that way at all. The Scourers killed Yinjing Butte slow and direful. Took their time. First they encircled it, just as they've done at Coogan's

Bluff, cutting it off from the rest of the world. Then they blew up the wellheads. No water. Not for the townspeople, at any rate. Scourers had their own supply, jerry cans of the stuff they'd stolen from other towns, so they were okay. And pretty soon after the water ran out, so did the food. The townspeople were left to starve, but you can bet it was lack of water got them first. I can't even imagine what it must have been like. You've seen for yourselves how hot it can get on Thetis. Devilish hot. Ain't hard to picture those poor souls in Yinjing Butte, throats so dry they're cracking on the inside, gasping for water but there ain't a drop to drink. Licking out the last dribble of moisture in the cisterns. Probably fighting one another, *killing* one another over the dregs in the toilet bowl. Resorting to consuming their own urine, most like. Supposedly there was even cannibalism, drinkin' other people's blood."

She shuddered.

"I like to think that's just hearsay," she went on. "By most accounts, it took the last person ten days to die. Ten days of torment. The lucky ones were the ones the Scourers shot dead as they tried to get out. At least it was swift for them. There's many who killed theirselves in the end, rather'n face dying of dehydration. Shot their kin as a mercy before eating their own guns. Then, of course, there were the girls the Scourers took captive. They had their own special hell to endure."

"*Mó guǐ*," said Mal.

"Well, quite, Captain Reynolds. Monsters. The Scourers torched the place afterwards, for good measure. It went up like kindling, corpses and all. And now Vandal's gonna do to Coogan's Bluff exactly what he did to Yinjing Butte, and him and his cronies are gonna relish every minute of it."

"'Less we stop 'em."

"And how's that been working out for you? Not very well, on present evidence. Don't mean to sound ungracious, but you've nothin' to show for your efforts so far but a crippled ship and a man hovering at death's door. My advice would be to quit while the quittin's good. Take that spare shuttle of yours and vamoose. All of you. No one'd blame you. You did what you could and it weren't enough, and now's the time to cut your losses."

"Ain't gonna happen," said Mal.

"You keen to end your days on this here dirtball?"

"The captain," said Zoë, "is fond of hopeless causes. You could say he thrives on them."

"At least now I don't feel so bad about those Scourers River dealt with," said Wash. "Not that I was sympathetically inclined towards them in the first place. You know, on account of the whole 'let's dangle Wash from a rope by the neck' business."

"You referring to those four bodies I saw layin' outside with tarps over 'em?" said Temperance. She looked over at River, who was loitering in the doorway. "*She* did that? That slip of a thing?"

"My sister is… complicated," said Simon, with not a little pride.

Jane McCloud looked intrigued. "Badass, more like," she said. "Is it true, River? You took down four Scourers all by your ownsome?"

River smiled sheepishly. "Wash helped."

"I did?" said Wash.

"You were a diversion. Useful."

"Oh yeah. So I was. Hear that, Zoë? I did my bit. I was useful."

"My hero," said Zoë, batting her eyelashes.

"And don't you forget it."

"Still and all," said Temperance, "it doesn't change the fact that Coogan's Bluff is humped. Vandal's called in all the reinforcements he's got, judgin' by what I've seen. So there's even more of them now and even fewer of us. Might as well face it. This ain't a battle we can win."

"There's always a chance," said Mal. "There's some chink in

Vandal's armor. Got to be. Some flaw. Some way we can turn this thing around."

"I know Vandal. I mean, I know the sort of man he is. Mayn't surprise you to learn that back in the day, when Jayne and I were together, business partners as well as the other kind of partner, we dealt with more'n a few unsavory types. Not all of them were as bad as Elias Vandal but some were. Some were apex predators. Human sharks. Them, you don't mess with. You just get out of their way. In short, while I admire your optimism, I don't necessarily share it."

"I fought at Serenity Valley. It ain't about optimism. It's about doin' what's right even when everything's stacked against you."

So saying, Mal turned on his heel and walked out.

"Sir, where are you off to?" said Zoë.

Mal paused mid-stride. "Goin' to my bunk, to brood." He added, "In a manly way."

"Thank you for clarifying that."

"Might just come up with a plan while I'm about it."

"Can't come none too soon."

"In the meantime, Captain Reynolds," said Temperance, "may Jane and I stay here? On your ship? I don't reckon as our farm is the safest place to be right now. Scourers might stray out that direction. Might do so on purpose, they learn there's a girl Jane's age there."

"*Mi casa es su casa*," Mal said. "You're both of you under our protection." His eyes narrowed soberly. "For what that's worth. Even if the rest of the Scourers don't know we're here, they're bound to wonder what's become of the foursome Vandal sent out to look for the ship. That means sooner or later they're gonna go searchin' for 'em, and they're gonna find us."

Shortly after that, Temperance asked Simon's permission to visit Jayne in the infirmary. Simon accompanied her there and looked on as she gazed down fondly on Jayne's comatose form, stroking a hand through his thatch of close-cropped dark hair.

"You're gonna get well," she said, as though Jayne could hear her. "That's all there is to it. Don't make me have to cry over you. I ain't doin' that."

She looked as though she was close to it, though, wiping an eye with one finger.

Simon marveled that Jayne could arouse such affectionate feelings in someone as smart and level-headed as Temperance. For that matter, in *anyone*. The man was as callous as a wolverine and put nobody first but himself.

Then again, Jayne had been known to do good, usually in spite of his own intentions but sometimes by design.

What was certain was that he was more complex than he appeared. Though simple and predictable on the outside, Jayne Cobb had layers, like an onion. Gradually Simon was seeing them unpeeled.

Stanislaw L'Amour

Whiteplains Edge took its name from the salt flats it perched on the fringes of. Like a vast, arid white lake, the salt flats stretched away to the horizon, shimmering as blindingly as a magnesium flare in the noonday sun. The smell that rolled off them was like that of ocean brine but a hundred times more pungent, and if the wind blew the wrong way a pale haze of dust enveloped the town. Hence, when outdoors, most Whiteplainers went around with their mouths and noses masked and their eyes goggled.

Salt mining was the town's principal industry. Workers known as skimmers scraped up the stuff and crated it up to be shipped out to the Core planets, where Whiteplains salt was considered superior and something of a culinary delicacy. It was, it must be said, a niche market. Nobody got particularly rich off of it aside from a few entrepreneurial types who lived offworld and left the running of their empires to local middle managers and site overseers. On Thetis the average skimmer made minimum wage and had a prematurely wizened face, thanks to daily exposure to sun and abrasive salty wind. A thirty-five-year-old skimmer could easily be mistaken for someone twice that age.

The town boasted both an airport and a spaceport, and

consequently was not short on scrapyards. All of them were well supplied with reclaimed spare parts and, rather than being open-air affairs as scrapyards usually were, all of them were housed in huge, hangar-like structures in order to protect their contents from corrosion from the salt-laden winds.

Kaylee spent an enjoyable couple of hours roaming, inspecting, and selecting. She was in her element, surrounded by machinery. If time had not been of the essence, she could have lingered in the scrapyards all day.

Soon she had amassed every item on her shopping list. One dealer asked an astronomical price for a pair of selector cartridges. Kaylee adopted the tried-and-tested strategy of walking away, saying she would go somewhere else. He immediately dropped his offer by a third, and soon she had haggled him down to half. Another dealer attempted to pass off a grade-III burner plug for a grade-IV. Kaylee called him on it and told him that unless he threw in an adaptor unit for free, she wasn't interested. He did as asked.

All in all, a satisfactory afternoon's work. She even managed to come in under budget. Mal would be pleased to have a few extra credits in his pocket.

Kaylee ferried her purchases back to Inara's shuttle on a motorized trolley. Once she had loaded them aboard, she was all in favor of returning to Coogan's Bluff straight away. This seemed all the more urgent given the wave Inara had just received from Wash, in which he had relayed the news about the attack on him and River at *Serenity*, Jayne's life-threatening injury and the Scourers taking over the town.

Inara, however, pointed out that neither she nor Kaylee had eaten since breakfast. They deserved a decent meal. They also needed to consider that night was falling and they would be flying back mostly in the dark. Nighttime piloting was always more demanding than daytime piloting. Added to that, the nearer they got to Coogan's Bluff, the more alert they would have to be. With the town surrounded by Scourers, fully under their control, the odds of stumbling into a trap or ambush were high.

Kaylee assented.

It was to prove a fateful decision.

The best restaurant in Whiteplains Edge wasn't much to speak of, but it was at least relatively clean and some of the items on the menu, albeit not many, contained fresh, non-reconstituted ingredients.

As Kaylee and Inara were leaving, a drunk skimmer at a nearby table made some disparaging comment about Companions. He was speaking to the two men with him—also skimmers—but he obviously meant to be overheard.

Kaylee bristled. "That fella just called you a whore."

"Pay him no mind," said Inara. "Most people are respectful of Companions but there are a few who choose to sneer, usually so they can feel better about themselves."

"You should say something back. Set him straight. If you don't, I will."

"Leave it be, Kaylee. Just because he's ignorant and lacks class, it doesn't mean we should stoop to his level."

The skimmer himself, though, *wouldn't* leave it be.

"Guess the whore thinks she's too good to talk to the likes of us."

"Listen, mister—!" Kaylee began, but Inara restrained her.

"Don't engage with him. He only wants attention."

"Tell you what wants attention," the skimmer said to Inara. He pointed at his crotch. "Maybe you'll give it some. I've heard tell Companions can tie a knot in a cherry stalk with their tongues."

Inara smiled dazzlingly. "In your case, the dimensions sound accurate."

The skimmer took a moment to realize he had just been belittled.

Everyone else in the restaurant was listening in on the exchange and got the joke before he did. There was uproarious laughter. Even the skimmer's two friends joined in.

This, of course, made him mad.

"All right, bitch," he said, shunting back his chair. "Time to teach you a lesson. You ain't gonna be able to earn a living once I've finished with that pretty face of yours."

One of his friends pulled him back down into his chair. "Amos, don't. Feds already have their eye on you. Cause any trouble, you'll only end up getting arrested. Again. And this time your cousin the police chief mayn't be able to get you off."

Amos, fuming, relented.

As Inara and Kaylee went outside, Kaylee remarked, "That was a close one."

Inara grimaced. "I predict it isn't over. Let's hurry."

They picked up their pace, but sure enough, the restaurant door banged open behind them and Amos stumbled out.

"Hey, *whore!*" the skimmer called out. "What's the matter with you? You got a payin' customer here. I got money." He scattered a pocketful of coins on the ground. "Has to be at least ten minutes' worth there."

"Not even close," Inara said, reaching for her gold-braided clutch bag.

"I won't take long, I swear."

"I'm sure you won't."

Inara popped the clasp on the bag. Kaylee glimpsed a gun inside—a compact two-shot pistol, silver-plated, with a mother-of-pearl inlay on the grip. A typical, if upmarket, Saturday night special.

"C'mon." Amos staggered towards the two women. "You can't afford to be picky."

"I assure you I can."

Inara delved a hand into the bag. Any second now, Amos was

going to regret insulting and hounding her. Kaylee looked forward to seeing him get his comeuppance.

"Sir," said someone behind Amos.

Amos wheeled round.

"I invite you to leave these ladies alone. Otherwise it will not go well for you."

Standing haloed by the down-glow of a streetlight was one of the most beautiful men Kaylee had ever clapped eyes on. He was tall, broad-shouldered, slim-waisted, with a chiseled chin and swept-back collar-length hair. His outfit was immaculate, from the tailored double-breasted suit to the silk cravat to the patent leather shoes, the ensemble accessorized with diamond cufflinks and matching lapel pin. In a town like Whiteplains Edge, he stood out like a handsome, well-coiffed, expensively attired sore thumb.

Amos was unimpressed. "Who the ruttin' hell are you?"

"A man who came into town to sample the nightlife and has found it rather disagreeable. I may well also be the man who puts you on your backside if you don't apologize at once to Miss Serra and her friend."

Kaylee looked round at Inara. This walking pillar of gorgeousness knew her? Inara registered no surprise. She evidently knew him too, and was not displeased to see him.

"This ain't none of your beeswax, pal," Amos snarled. "Whyn't you take your fancy-ass suit and your hundred-credit haircut and scram? You're only gonna wind up getting a beatin' if you don't."

"Very well. I gave you fair warning."

It was over in a trice. Amos lay on the ground, out cold. The other man had barely seemed to move. Kaylee had had an impression of blurred activity, a flurry of blows too quick for the eye to process, the assault delivered with the economy and dexterity of an experienced martial artist. That was all.

Unflustered, not even out of breath, the man now bowed before her and Inara.

"I sincerely regret that that had to occur," he said. "But I cannot abide discourtesy, especially towards someone of such high standing as a Companion."

Inara shook her head, amused. "I had it under control," she said. "We weren't in any real danger."

"I am sure that's so. However, you can forgive a chap for surrendering to his chivalrous impulses, surely."

"In this instance I'm prepared to make an exception."

Inara proffered her hand, and the man took it and kissed it.

"Inara?" Kaylee nudged her. "Ain't you going to introduce us?"

The man turned to Kaylee, fixing her with a smile that made her tingle right down to her nethers.

"No, I am the one who is remiss, not Inara," he said. "The name is Stanislaw L'Amour. Whose acquaintance do I have the pleasure of making?"

"Kaywinnet Lee Frye," said Kaylee, holding out her hand as Inara had done. Her full name just sounded grander than the abbreviated version—and this Stanislaw L'Amour was someone she wanted to think highly of her.

L'Amour kissed her hand too. Kaylee felt herself blushing, and was embarrassed to have blushed, which only made her blush even more.

"I don't suppose the two of you would care to accompany me to my ship?" L'Amour said. "Inara, you and I haven't seen each other in some while. It would be good to catch up."

"We're in a rush but we can spare an hour," Inara said.

"Can we?" said Kaylee. She would have loved to spend time with this bewitching Adonis, but getting the engine parts back to *Serenity* as soon as possible surely took precedence over socializing.

"Trust me, Kaylee," said Inara. "We can. And we should."

The Condiment Trade

Stanislaw L'Amour owned a Seraphim, the latest model of Paradise-class private cruiser to roll off the production line at the Carshalton Spaceways plant on Greenleaf. In Kaylee's considered opinion the Seraphim wasn't a patch on Carshalton's all-time classic the Dreamcrest. It was underpowered for its weight and prone to stability issues in atmo, thanks to the overelaborate and entirely superfluous fin array at the aft. In the plus column, it was furnished inside with every luxury the mind could conceive, down to a lap pool and a sauna. Flight performance be gorramned. You wanted to travel the 'verse in style, you couldn't do much better than this.

While Kaylee and Inara wallowed on a couch so large and sumptuously upholstered it could have doubled as a king-size bed, L'Amour went off to the galley to fetch champagne. "I've given the staff the evening off," he said. "Anyway, it strikes me as rude not to serve drinks personally. A dereliction of one's obligations as host."

"Why are we doing this?" Kaylee asked Inara when they were alone.

"I've had an idea," came the reply. "I think Stanislaw may be able to help us out."

"How? He's just a blueblood."

"And a businessman. An immensely successful one."

"Legitimate?"

"Genuinely so. But still with considerable resources."

"I take it he's also a client of yours."

"Not exactly."

"Then what?" Kaylee glanced around, checking that L'Amour was out of earshot. She lowered her voice anyway. "I mean, my God, if I was a Companion, able to pick and choose who I, you know, rubbed bumpers with... Well, he'd be top of my list every time."

"He is rather exceptional, isn't he?"

"Yeah. Super-shiny, I'd say. There's got to be a drawback, though, surely. No one can be that perfect." Kaylee dropped her voice further. "Hung like a peanut, right?"

"A Companion never kisses and tells," Inara replied regally, but something about her manner made Kaylee suspect that the very opposite of her speculation was true.

"But he still ain't a client."

"He was. Once."

"So he could be again."

"No, 'once' as in 'one time only.' And you won't get any more out of me than that. Guild law forbids it."

"Oh, it's fine, Inara," said L'Amour, re-entering the lounge with three champagne flutes and a bottle of Xiangbinjiu premier cru. "I don't mind if you tell this charming girl about me. The truth, Kaywinnet Lee, is that when I engaged Inara's services, I was still figuring things out, sexuality-wise."

Kaylee liked the way her full name sounded coming from his lips and didn't ask him to use the abbreviated version.

"That was a few years back," L'Amour continued, "and, as it turned out, she helped me settle my orientation once and for all. I... found it difficult to summon up enthusiasm for the act. There Inara was, the most beautiful orchid in all the garden, and if I could not be stirred even by one such as her, then obviously my inclinations must lie in another direction, as I suspected. I said as much to her at the time."

"Yes," said Inara. "You actually did call me the most beautiful orchid in all the garden."

"And you still are." L'Amour began untwisting the wire around the champagne bottle's cork. He smiled at Kaylee. "Inara liberated me from uncertainty, and for that I am eternally grateful to her."

Which was lovely for him, Kaylee thought, but still a tragic loss to womankind.

"She and I have stayed friends ever since," L'Amour went on. "We meet up now and then, when our paths converge. I'd just never have expected to find you on a world like Thetis, Inara."

"I'd never have expected to find you here either," said Inara.

L'Amour popped the cork and began pouring. "Of late my business interests have been expanding and diversifying. I bought a controlling share in Whiteplains Salt Co. just last month, so now it appears I am in the condiment trade. Hence I am visiting Whiteplains Edge to see what's what. Some in my position don't care how their investments operate at ground level, so long as the money keeps flowing in. They neglect the nitty-gritty, often to their own detriment. I am not one of those."

He passed a filled flute to Kaylee and Inara each, and took one for himself.

"I'd like to propose a toast," he said. "To old friends." He nodded at Kaylee. "And new."

They clinked glasses and drank.

To Kaylee, the champagne was a taste of heaven.

Inara and Stanislaw engaged in small talk for a while—mutual acquaintances, Core planet politics—most of it sophisticated, gossipy, and a little over Kaylee's head. She devoted her attention to her champagne and the delicious tickle its effervescence made on her tongue.

Then Inara turned serious.

"Stanislaw, I have no right to ask this," she said.

"Of course you do. You can ask me anything, you know that."

Briefly she outlined the state of affairs at Coogan's Bluff and the *Serenity* crew's involvement in it.

"And what can I do to assist? Anything, darling Inara. Name it."

"You have private security, don't you?"

"When I need to. Only the very best. Not so much for personal protection. As you've seen, I can handle that myself. Sometimes, however, especially out on the Rim, there's a call for strong-arm tactics when industrial relations break down. Crowd control, union busting, and such. It's one of the downsides of doing interplanetary business."

"Then..."

L'Amour held up a hand. "Say no more. How many warm bodies do you require?"

"As many as possible. I can help out with the cost."

"Wouldn't hear of it! My goodness, what's the use in being a billionaire if you can't share it around amongst friends? Naturally it'll take time to organize all this. One can't just conjure up a battalion of security specialists out of nothing. I'll need to bribe certain Alliance officials to look the other way, too. Then there's the journey time to bear in mind."

"How long, do you reckon?"

"Two days to get them here, at best. More realistically, three. Will that do?"

"It will have to," Inara said. "Thank you, Stanislaw."

L'Amour waved a hand dismissively. "I owe you a debt, my dear. Perhaps not in the way most men do, but a debt nonetheless, and I am only too happy to repay it."

* * *

Through the dark, beneath a myriad of stars and a tiny, unsmiling moon, the shuttle whisked eastward, back towards Coogan's Bluff.

Inara was at the controls. Kaylee was curled up on the bed, fast asleep, with one of the day's smaller purchases—a burner plug—nestled against her chest. She looked like a child hugging a favorite teddy bear.

Inara didn't begrudge her the sleep. Kaylee had plenty to do tomorrow installing the burner plug and other new parts into *Serenity* and working on the repairs. She needed the rest.

As for herself, Inara was both pleased and grim. The trip to Whiteplains Edge had taken a surprising and positive turn. There was hope at last in a situation that had seemed entirely devoid of it.

Two days until reinforcements arrived. Three at the outside.

All Mal and the crew had to do—not to mention the people of Coogan's Bluff—was hold out until then.

A Man With the Heart
of a Mean Animal

Shem Bancroft lowered the 100x magnification binoculars and grinned a big, sloppy grin.

He had found the Firefly shortly after dawn. He had also found the posse of Scourers that had gone missing while searching for it yesterday. Who else could those tarpaulin-draped bodies lying in a row next to the spaceship belong to but the Hazzard siblings—Ellie-Mae, Frank, Rufus, and Isaac? Shem wasn't what you'd call well educated but even he could do the math. Four Scourers unaccounted for, four corpses. It was a no-brainer.

Nor was Shem's intellect any too taxed by the question of what had happened to them. The ship's crew had killed them, obviously. Somehow the people on board the Firefly had got the jump on the Hazzards and done them in. Vandal had strongly suspected that that was the case, when Ellie-Mae and her three brothers hadn't returned to the camp at Brimstone Gulch last night. Shem had just confirmed it.

It brought to ten the total number of Scourers left dead by these interlopers from offworld. Not forgetting Vandal getting shot in the shoulder, which unsettling event Shem had witnessed first-hand in the town square.

157

All of this told Shem two things. One: the people from the Firefly were more than they seemed; they were a force to be reckoned with. And two: they were going to get their due, and when it came, it would be hellish. Apocalyptic. Book of Revelation stuff. Vandal would see to that. He never did anything by halves.

These offworlders had gone and bought themselves a whole heaping helping of hurt.

As the sun rose higher, Shem continued his careful scrutiny of the ship. It was still too early to radio in a report to Vandal. Chances were his boss was still asleep, and Vandal never took kindly to being roused from his slumbers, whatever the reason.

Shem's vantage point was the only piece of cover for miles around: a small rise capped with a ghost tree. Everything else was bare, flat plain. The long-dead tree was just trunk and a few branches, polished smooth by wind and bleached bone-white by sun. It should have fallen over years ago but something—sheer cussedness, perhaps—kept it upright.

Half-hidden by the tree, he watched now as a handful of people emerged from the Firefly carrying tools. They began digging what Shem at first thought was a trench. The man called Reynolds broke the earth with a pickax while three others—the Shepherd, the woman who was Reynolds's second-in-command and the doctor fella—shoveled.

Soon the trench was a few feet deep, and then they lifted the Scourers' corpses into it. That was when Shem realized it was actually a grave.

He was puzzled. They were burying the dead? Even when the dead were not their own?

Sure enough, the four crewmembers heaped the excavated dirt onto the bodies and patted it down. Then, at an invitation from the

Shepherd, they stood around the grave, heads bowed. The Shepherd intoned words that Shem was too far away to hear but which could only have been funeral rites. Reynolds twitched impatiently throughout, like he didn't much care for the ceremony and was enduring it only to humor the holy man. When the gathering broke up, he was first back onto the ship.

Shem pondered what he had just seen. The Firefly's crew could simply have left the bodies to rot in the sun. Coyotes and other scavengers, lured by the smell, would have made short work of them. Instead, these people had done something decent, giving the Scourers a proper send-off. Admittedly, nobody wanted corpses festering right on their doorstep. It was unhygienic and impractical. The stench, the flies, the germs and so forth. But actually to bury them and pray over the grave, all Christian-like...

Conflicting thoughts clashed in Shem's none-too-agile brain. In the end he decided that it didn't matter. The folks from the Firefly were still the enemy. They were still the ones who had defied the Scourers and injured Vandal.

Shem knew where his loyalties lay.

His loyalties had lain with Elias Vandal for nigh on two years, during which time Shem had risen from being an itinerant troublemaker, layabout, and general ne'er-do-well to become one of the most feared people on Thetis. He had left behind the life of an insignificant petty crook and was now a man of status and substance—lieutenant to the leader of the Scourers, no less.

It had all started in Brownvale. To be precise, in the lockup at the Brownvale sheriff's office, where Shem was drying out after a night of drunken roistering that had gone sour. Shem had only the vaguest recollection of what he had done to deserve incarceration, but the state of his knuckles, all bruised and flecked with dried blood, was some clue.

Not many towns on Thetis even had a sheriff, and it was Shem's bad luck to wind up in one of them and, moreover, to fall foul of the law while there. It was also, in the event, a stroke of great good fortune and a turning point in his life, for his cellmate in the lockup was none other than Elias Vandal.

Shem's first impression of his cellmate was that here was someone to avoid. The scarring on the man's face was off-putting enough. More generally he exuded an aura of threat. Shem had grown up with a father who was quick with his fists and fond of dishing out discipline using belt, horsewhip, or any other suitable implement that came to hand. He knew what it was like to be around a man who loved cruelty, a man with the heart of a mean animal. Just as his father had been one, so was the fellow who lay on the adjacent wooden bunk. Even though he was presently fast asleep, Shem could just sense it. It was like an odor such people gave off, a scent you detected by instinct rather than with your nose.

Shem could not wait to be out of that cell.

Only trouble was, the sheriff didn't seem any too interested in giving him his liberty yet. Neither did the sheriff's deputy. Both men were at their desks in the main room a few yards down the corridor, drinking coffee and chatting. Shem, nursing a severe, cranium-cracking hangover, wished one or other of them would come back this way, keys jangling, and open the cell door before his cellmate woke up. The scarred man was restless and beginning to stir, liable to come to at any moment.

As the minutes ticked by, Shem grew increasingly anxious. He longed to shout to the sheriff and deputy, beg them to let him go free. At the same time he didn't want to disturb the guy next to him.

"What you in for?"

Shem nearly jumped out of his skin. Two eyes glinted across at him from the other bunk, one partially hidden by a fold of waxy skin.

"You talkin' to me?" Shem said warily.

"Ain't nobody else here I'd be talkin' to. I'll ask again. What you in for?"

"Uhmmm… Not sure. Musta tied one on last night. Mebbe got into a fight. You know how it is."

"I surely do."

The cellmate pushed himself up into a seated position. He was powerfully built. Shem was big and broad, no slouch in the brawn department. This other guy, however, had shoulders like a bull, forearms like hams, and several inches in height on him. His muscles didn't look the gym-won kind either, the balloon-like swellings you got from working out with weights. Rather, they were the coarse, sinewy variety you got from hard labor and a tough life.

"Well," he said to Shem. "You gonna ask me the same thing?"

"The same thing?"

"How come I'm here."

"Yeah. Sure. How come you're here?"

"Thereby hangs a tale," said the cellmate. "A tale that starts with someone mocking me for how I look and ends with me hammering that someone's face into the floor and stomping on the back of his neck till his spine shattered."

Shem gulped. The man spoke so matter-of-factly that Shem didn't doubt he was telling the truth.

"You killed a fella," he said. Statement not question.

The cellmate shrugged. "He weren't the first. Probably won't be the last. I'd've gotten away with it, too, if his girlfriend hadn't clouted me over the noggin from behind. Sneaky bitch up and hit me with a tire iron, six, maybe seven times, while I was busy stompin' on her man. Women. They ain't nothin' but trouble. Believe me, I know. Bane of my life."

The cellmate ran a hand over the ridged, rugged contours of the scarred side of his face.

"Anyways," he continued, "when I came to, I was handcuffed and staring down the barrel of old Sheriff Tooley's six-gun. Tooley's had me in this hole a week and he still ain't sure what to do with me. He's called the Feds. They ain't interested. Authorities at Whiteplains likewise. Meantime I'm stuck here, coolin' my heels. No company, other than the cockroaches, till you came along."

By that stage Shem had made a mental connection. A disfigured man, an unrepentant murderer—this could only be the dreaded Elias Vandal. My God, he was sharing a cell with the most wanted felon on Thetis! Elias Vandal, whose name was a byword for violence and mentioned only in whispers. Who for three years and more had roamed the planet, abusing and maiming and killing anyone who got in his way. A rogue and a savage who, it was rumored, had run with Reavers before fetching up here and who still clung to the Reaver philosophy of pain, rage, and nihilism.

Shem Bancroft had never been so scared in his life.

"What're you lookin' like that for?" Vandal demanded.

"Like what?"

"Like someone just took a leak on your boots."

"I ain't lookin' like that. Leastways not on purpose. No, see? I'm smilin'. Look at me smilin'. Nothing wrong here. No sirree."

"What's your name, boy?"

"Shem. Shem Bancroft."

"And I am...?"

Shem blinked. What to say? Should he admit to Elias Vandal that he had recognized him? Or should he play dumb?

Playing dumb came naturally to Shem. In fact he was an expert at it. So he opted for that.

"I don't know who you are."

"I ain't askin' if you know. I'm askin' you to ask. 'Cause of it's polite to do so, after another man asks who *you* are."

"Oh. Well, so, okay, and you are?"

"Elias Vandal."

Shem acted as if he hadn't heard the name before.

"You've heard the name before," said Vandal.

"No. Nuh-uh. Nope."

"I can tell. You got that kinda face, Shem, the kind that can't keep secrets. Everything you think, it's writ large, in ten-foot-high capitals. You're as easy to read as a picture book. I bet just about everybody wants to play poker with you."

Shem tried his darnedest to pretend that, right then, what he *wasn't* thinking was how badly he wanted to be elsewhere. If he hollered at the top of his lungs, would the sheriff get there in time before Elias Vandal's homicidal urges claimed yet another victim?

"Stay calm, brother," Vandal said. "You're as jumpy as a spooked cat."

"No. No, I ain't. I'm cool."

"It's all right. I don't intend on hurtin' you. Why would I? Got no reason to."

Did psychos *need* a reason to hurt someone? From what Shem knew about Vandal, you didn't have to do much to invoke his wrath. One story went that Vandal beat a man to death just for having the nerve not to step out of his path quick-smart enough. Another story went that he slit a woman's throat after she failed to keep herself from flinching when she saw his face. Sometimes stories like these were exaggerations, fables that grew in the telling, built around the tiniest kernels of truth. In the case of Elias Vandal, though, Shem was of the opinion that they were pure, 24-carat gospel.

"No," Vandal continued, "I reckon I need you, Shem."

"Need me? You?"

"Sure. I've been waiting all week for someone like you to happen along. Providence has brought you to me."

"It has?"

"You strike me as a fella as can take guidance. You've led kinda an aimless life, I think. Driftin' along day to day, getting into scrapes but not doing much with yourself aside from that. Not achievin' much at all."

This was a fairly accurate summation of Shem's twenty-odd years of existence so far. He had never held down a job longer than a month, and he had shown a knack for frittering away what little money he did earn, spending it on liquor and drugs mostly, sometimes gambling, occasionally women. A bit of pickpocketing, the occasional shakedown—that had kept him going during the lean times.

"You help me out today," Vandal said, "I can make something of you."

"Help you out how?" said Shem.

"Just follow my lead."

So saying, Vandal sprang across the cell and started strangling him.

Shem began screaming, screaming like he'd never screamed before, high-pitched, shrill, the sound of utter terror.

It didn't occur to him that if Vandal were strangling him properly, he wouldn't be able to breathe, let alone scream. He clawed at Vandal's hands, trying to break that remorseless, viselike grip, but mostly he just cried out in desperation, praying that Sheriff Tooley and his deputy could come and save him.

Come they did. Save him? Not so much.

For no sooner did the two law enforcers enter the cell, guns drawn, yelling angrily, than Vandal turned on them. He moved with feral speed, letting go of Shem and seizing the deputy's wrist. He swung the man's gun arm towards Sheriff Tooley and clamped his finger on the deputy's trigger finger. At point-blank range, the bullet tore a hole in Tooley's stomach, passing straight through his torso and leaving a bigger hole in his back.

As Tooley slumped to the floor, Vandal wrenched the deputy's arm upwards. The muzzle was suddenly beneath the man's chin. The deputy struggled but Vandal was stronger, far stronger than him. Abject fear etched his face. He knew what was coming and was powerless to prevent it.

His brains spattered the grimy ceiling.

Shem, seeing the sheriff and deputy die, was convinced he was next. His knees went weak. He felt like he was going to puke.

Vandal, for his part, belly-laughed as though he'd just pulled off some hilarious practical joke.

"Good work, Shem, my boy," he said, slapping Shem hard on the back—hard enough to leave him winded. "You did just great. That was some high-class actin'. I hadn't known better, I'd've sworn you was genuinely frit!"

"Yeah. No." Shem touched a hand to his tender-feeling throat. "Not frit at all. Not in the slightest."

"Come on, then." Vandal snatched up the sheriff's and deputy's guns, passing the latter to Shem. "Time we hightailed it outta this ruttin' dump."

Briefly, for the merest nanosecond, Shem considered shooting Vandal. The man's back was to him. He was an unmissable target. There might well be a bounty on his head, a sizeable one, and even if not, the kudos for being the man who shot Elias Vandal dead would be enormous. Shem would be famous all across the county. He'd never have to buy himself a drink again. The ladies would swoon when they heard who he was. He'd be a *bona fide* celebrity.

Vandal halted in the cell doorway. Without looking round, he said, "You'd best not be thinkin' what I think you're thinkin', Shem. And if you are, know this. Better men than you have tried. Better men than you have gone to meet their Maker believin' they had the drop on Elias Vandal."

Shem glanced down to see Sheriff Tooley's gun poking out

backwards from beside Vandal's waist. The barrel was level with Shem's groin.

"Now, you ain't that foolish, are you, boy?" Vandal said. "No, you ain't. You got a sagely head on them shoulders. You're gonna come with me and be my sidekick. Together we're gonna do great things. Unforgettable things. That's my promise to you, Shem Bancroft. I have plans for us, and you, my newfound friend, are going to just love them."

It wasn't fear that made Shem stick with Vandal. Fear was part of it, but largely it was hope. Even as a kid Shem had always reckoned he would never amount to anything. His daddy had predicted he'd be a waster and a loser all his life. Until Vandal happened along, Shem had been busy making that prediction a reality. Vandal, however, seemed to see something in him that his old man never had. Vandal felt Shem had *potential*, that was what it was. He gave Shem the sense that there was more he could do, more he could be.

The next twenty-four hours in Brownvale proved a baptism of fire for Shem, as he and Vandal went on a rampage that left the cash registers of every shop in town denuded of credits, several buildings gutted by fire, and ten men dead, two of them by Shem's hand, his first ever kills. It was as though Vandal was exacting vengeance on the place, getting payback for his imprisonment. He was a whirlwind of aggression, and Shem got exhilaratingly caught up in it.

Vandal saved his greatest ire for the woman who'd cold-cocked him and gotten him arrested. To this day Shem still shivered with horror whenever he remembered the long, slow torment Vandal inflicted on her, a death of unimaginable hideousness and squalor, the kind surely only a Reaver could have dreamed up. Vandal forced Shem to witness it—every sickening minute of it—and afterwards Shem knew there could be no going back now. He was implicated, committed, irrevocably, irredeemably. If he ever betrayed Vandal or tried to get away from him, a fate similar to the woman's would be his. They were bound to each other, he and this monster, in a knot of violence, devotion and complicity, henceforth until doomsday.

Over the next few months the carnage continued and others came into their orbit. Likeminded individuals, wild at heart, restless, nursing a grudge against life like a festering abscess. The duo of Vandal and Shem became a dozen, then a score. Before they knew it, they were a gang.

Vandal gave them a name: Scourers. It sounded somewhat like Reavers. It had a similar ring.

As the Scourers' numbers grew, so came the need for bigger and bigger paydays. The more of them there were, the smaller each's share of the loot became.

Vandal soon hit on a scheme to make them all some real money. Holding up hardware stores was okay. Waylaying trains and stagecoaches had an appeal. Simply robbing passers-by at gunpoint was not without its merits. That level of criminality was all well and fine. But Vandal had greater ambitions. He craved wealth, but also power. What interested him wasn't merely stealing from people. It was *controlling* them.

After all, that was what the Alliance did, wasn't it? It controlled. It ran every aspect of life in the civilized parts of the 'verse, from what you ate to what you bought, from the level of society in which you moved to the rules that governed your daily routine. The Alliance, with its troops and its law-enforcement operatives and its tame corporations and its bought-and-paid-for politicians, held everything tight in its tentacles. Even out on the Rim you couldn't escape it. There, its presence could be felt by its absence—by the lack of amenities, the lawlessness, the poverty, the poor healthcare. Those worlds and moons the Alliance could not encompass in its sphere of influence, it punished by denying them its benefits. *You want to live without us? Okay. Then we turn our back on you. We give you the cold shoulder.* That was the message. *You spurn us? Well, we spurn you harder.*

Vandal had a vision of creating an Alliance of his own, recasting it in his image. His Alliance would corner the market in Thetis's most precious resource, water. Monopolize that and you monopolized anyone who depended on it for their lives and livelihoods—which was everyone.

By then, Shem was starting to ask himself whether Vandal had really ever run with Reavers like he claimed. Whenever the subject arose, Vandal always deflected, muttering darkly about "stuff that ain't fit to share with others" and "sights like no man has seen nor wants to hear tell of" and leaving it at that. He gave the impression that being a Reaver was an experience you couldn't put into words— too big, too deep, too soul-searing. And maybe that was so. Or maybe, Shem thought, it was just a load of old baloney, Vandal making up his involvement with the Reavers so as to seem more fearsome.

Either way, he didn't dare call Vandal on it. And risk offending him and getting gutted with that boomerblade of his? No thank you. Besides, it didn't matter too much to Shem what Vandal had done in the past. Shem was part of something big now, that was what counted. Tied to Elias Vandal like all the other Scourers, their fates joined, come what may, for better or worse.

It started small-scale. The odd lone farmstead at first. Then a remote hamlet or two. Soon the Scourers had a swathe of properties whose owners paid for the right to extract water from under their feet, the water that had been and should be freely theirs. It was a stark but straightforward choice the Scourers presented them with: cough up the cash on a regular basis, or die. Sensibly, most folk plumped for option one.

The Scourers' ranks swelled. Vandal and Shem were the grain of sand around which a pearl of increasing size and luster formed.

In time there were enough of them—north of a hundred—that they could tackle entire towns. They were an avalanche that swept all before it. There was resistance, but always it was snuffed out. There were perks, too, like the girls they took captive. The vast majority of Scourers were male, and as males they had needs. Vandal made sure they were catered for. He had the same needs himself. Besides, kidnapping young womenfolk was another lever of control. It amplified the force field of terror that the Scourers projected. Not only did they commandeer your water, but your daughter, your sister, your niece, your cousin, your own flesh and blood was also at risk from them. Anything and everything was theirs for the taking.

That was power.

Shem stayed by the ghost tree for a further hour, making use of the scant shade it provided as Thetis's sun began its usual, relentlessly infernal brightening.

There was further activity at the Firefly. A blond guy and Reynolds's second-in-command started working on the ship's hull, panel-beating out the dings and dents and welding steel patches over the holes. Reynolds stepped out to talk with them for a while, and then the Shepherd appeared, obviously offering to help. He rolled up his sleeves and joined in with the repairs, exhibiting a degree of physical strength and capability the likes of which Shem had never seen in a man of the cloth. This was no lily-livered pulpit jockey. This was something else altogether.

Shortly after that, Shem made his most rewarding discovery yet about the Firefly's occupants.

Two girls came out of the ship. They were bringing refreshments to the trio working on the hull. The older of the pair was dark-haired and lissome, elf-like; the younger, only just in her teens, looked like a local, judging by her attire.

Shem adjusted the zoom on the binoculars, enlarging the image of the two girls and bringing them into focus. They were handing out lemonade in glasses beaded with condensation.

Overcome by a sudden thirst, Shem licked his lips. He had a canteen of water with him, but it was ambient-warm, no match for a tall, cool glass of lemonade. For a moment he yearned to be over there at the Firefly, enjoying the chilled, cloudy nectar with the rest of them. The lemonade was the powdered stuff, had to be, where would they have got fresh lemons from? Even so, he wished he was drinking some.

And it was at that same moment, just as he entertained this wish, that the dark-haired girl turned her head and stared in his direction.

She could not see him. The ghost tree was barely a dot on the horizon to her. No way did she know Shem was there.

Nevertheless she seemed to be looking straight at him. She was gazing into the dead center of the binoculars' field of view as though she could see Shem through the lenses as clearly as he could see her, for all that that was impossible.

It was an uncanny experience for Shem Bancroft. Gooseflesh prickled all over his skin.

He wanted to believe that he was imagining things, that it was sheer coincidence that the girl was looking his way.

But the expression on her face—curious, intrigued, penetrating—suggested otherwise. She could tell she was being observed from a distance. Somehow she sensed Shem's presence. There was no other way to explain it.

Then the other girl said something to her and, distracted, the dark-haired girl lost interest in Shem. Soon after that, the two girls headed back inside the Firefly with the empty lemonade glasses.

And not long after *that*, Shem decided it was time to beat a retreat. He snuck away across the plain, hunching down, keeping a low profile, until he reached the spot where he had left his horse, tethered to a stunted Joshua tree.

As he rode back to the Scourers' camp, Shem was feeling pretty pleased with himself. Not only could he tell Vandal exactly where the offworlders were laying low, he'd inform him that there were two nubile young lasses in their company. He could have delivered the news by radio but he preferred the idea of doing so in person, if only to see the smile it would bring to his boss's face. Even after all this time, Shem lived to make Elias Vandal happy. The happier Vandal was, the less Shem felt threatened by him. That was the unbalanced equation of their relationship.

He tried his best not to think about the way the dark-haired girl had stared directly at him.

Because that hadn't been creepy *one little bit*.

Clang Clang Clang

—*CLANG CLANG CLANG*—

C "Guess it was only a matter of time," Mal said. "One bunch of Scourers found us. Hardly surprising another has. Ain't as if you can miss a crashed spaceship sitting on a plain, 'specially if you already have half an idea that it's there."

—*CLANG CLANG CLANG*—

"You sure, though, River?" he went on. "Not to doubt you or nothin', but there ain't much around us 'cept open ground. If there was people out there reconnoitering, one or other of us'd have seen something, surely."

—*CLANG CLANG CLANG*—

"Not 'people,'" said River. "Person. Singular. Muddle-brain man. Not clever. Watching through binoculars beside the skeleton that was once a tree."

—*CLANG CLANG CLANG*—

"What tree?"

"That tree."

River pointed out of the cargo bay door to the rise on which the ghost tree stood. At this distance, the rise was a tiny swelling no bigger than a pimple. The tree was all but invisible, as thin as a bristle.

—CLANG CLANG CLANG—

"You must have sharp eyes, girl," said Mal.

"Sharp mind," River said, tapping her temple.

—CLANG CLANG CLANG—

"Question now is," Mal said, "how long until they— Oh, for the love of— KAYLEE!"

The clanging abruptly halted. Kaylee poked her head out from the engine room. She had a ball-peen hammer in her hand.

"Captain?" she said.

"Must you keep banging away like that?" Mal grumped. "It's gettin' so's a man can hardly hear himself think around here."

"Well now, there's problems with *Serenity*'s engine that can be mended with finesse and delicacy," Kaylee said, "and there's problems that require the application of brute force. Repeatedly." She brandished the hammer. "This happens to be one of those problems."

"Then will you, I don't know, maybe take it down a notch?"

"Sure thing!"

A moment later...

—CLANG CLANG CLANG—

Just as loud as before, if not louder.

Muttering under his breath, Mal took River by the elbow and led her outside to where Wash, Zoë and Book were working.

"Tell 'em what you just told me."

River did: the rise, the tree, the man.

"He was thinking about lemonade," she said. "Or I was. It's confusing. But I knew he was there."

"He'll have been using binoculars or a telescope or maybe a long-distance rifle scope," said Zoë. "Probably you caught sight of a flash of sunlight reflecting off the lens, River."

River shrugged. "Even if that was it, he was there, watching."

Not for the first time, Mal found himself pondering how he might use River's abilities—her superhuman *perceptiveness*—to his advantage on future jobs. All these months, they'd been putting up with the girl's weird, unpredictable behavior, as well as having to keep her hidden from the Alliance and deal with the likes of Jubal Early, the bounty hunter who had come after her hoping to claim the reward on her head. It was about time Mal got a bit of recompense for all that, so why not exploit her? Turn a liability into an asset?

Some day he would broach the subject with Simon—and for "broach the subject," read, "tell him how it was going to be."

Not today, though.

"This mean the Scourers'll be coming for us now?" said Wash. "Like, right here at the ship? Again?"

"Wouldn't bet against it," said Mal. "And more of them than last time, I'd say. A lot more. Maybe all of them."

"How soon?"

"Gorramned if I know."

"It'll be before Inara's gentleman friend comes through with his army of security specialists, that's for damn sure," said Zoë, adding, "If that miracle even happens."

"It'll happen," said Mal. "It better. But you're right. Vandal will be out for blood. He won't want to hang around. Ask me, this spot'll be crawling with Scourers by midday."

"We should make preparations to greet them," said Book.

"Just what I was thinking. You have any thoughts on what sort of preparations?"

"One or two," said Book with a sly twinkle in his eye.

"I reckoned you might." Mal gave him a look that said he might not know everything about Book's life before he left Southdown Abbey and joined the crew of *Serenity*, but he had an inkling it was not all catechisms and rosaries. Book was a pastor with a shady past.

"Don't forget, a shepherd isn't just someone who tends a flock," said Book. "A shepherd also has to know how to keep the wolves at bay. I'll need a few things from the ship, ordinary items, and someone to help me do some digging."

"More digging?"

"Yes. Only this time, it won't be bodies we'll be burying."

The Fatherly Thing

In the infirmary, Temperance looked on while Simon checked Jayne's wound and changed the dressing.

"How's he doing?" she asked.

"As well as can be expected," Simon replied. "There's no sign of infection, either external or internal. No visible inflammation around the wound, and he's not running a temperature. Prognosis is good. I'm cautiously optimistic he'll make a full recovery."

"When's he gonna wake up?"

"In his own time." Simon detached the bag of saline solution that was keeping Jayne hydrated through an IV line. It was near depleted. He hooked up a fresh one. "I've pulled him out of the artificial coma. He's sleeping naturally now. Rest really is the best medicine for him."

"Well, I for one appreciate your fine efforts, Doc."

"I'd do it for anybody. It's my job."

Temperance tilted her head to the side. "You're kind of an odd man out, y'know, if you don't mind my saying so. Amongst the rest of the folks on this ship, I mean. Them, I can sorta see how they all fit together, even the Companion and the Shepherd. But you? You're a piece from a whole 'nother jigsaw. Same goes for your sister. Neither of you seems to belong here."

177

"And yet we do." Simon gave a hesitant, lopsided smile. "It's hard to explain, Temperance. Mal and everyone else aboard *Serenity*, they've given River and me sanctuary. They've looked after us, in their way. Even Jayne. So I look after them back, by fixing them up when they get hurt—which happens with monotonous regularity. And somehow, as the weeks and months have passed, they've become…"

"Family?"

"Yes." Another hesitant smile. "Feels weird admitting it, but it's pointless denying it. The nine of us are a mismatched, highly dysfunctional family."

"No shame 'bout that at all," Temperance said. "Way I see it, there's two kinds of family. There's the one you're born into and there's the one you gather around you as time goes by. The first kind you've got no say about, and sometimes it ain't quite right for you. You try to be a part of it but you just can't. The second kind, though, you choose."

"Or else the choice gets thrust upon you."

"Either way, it's yours. It's a family you make an active decision to keep with. And it can be the right family for you even if it don't always seem to be. It's the family you need rather than the family you got given by accident of birth."

"Family seems important to you, Temperance. I mean Jane. Not *him* Jayne. Your daughter Jane."

"I'd do anything to protect that girl. I'd give my life for her."

"And you aren't the only one, it appears." Simon nodded towards Jayne on the med couch. "I've never before seen him act the way he did yesterday morning. He was like a man possessed. Punching out Mal, squaring up to Vandal, actively volunteering to put himself in the line of fire…"

"I know. I was there."

"Why did you never tell him?"

"Tell him what?"

"You know what. I hope I'm not speaking out of turn, but if it was me who'd unknowingly fathered a daughter, I'd appreciate being informed about it."

Temperance's mouth set in a hard line. "This really ain't your business, Doc. I'm grateful for what you've done here with Jayne, truly I am, but that don't mean you can go poking around in my affairs, offering me advice."

"I'm sorry." Simon had been bred to have good manners. He always apologized if he caused offense, whether or not he meant the apology sincerely and whether or not the offense was intentional. "You have to realize, though, that it was unfair of you. Think how Jayne's life could have turned out, had he known about Jane back then. He might have gone down a whole different path, perhaps a better one."

Her eyes flashed in anger. "Dr. Tam, I am telling you, butt out. Don't make me say it again. You know nothing about anything. I did what I did for a reason. Jayne's life, you say? Jayne's life would have been *over* if he'd found out I was pregnant."

"Over? That's fairly melodramatic. There might have been a tricky period of adjustment, certainly, but over?"

"You think it a figure of speech?" Temperance snorted. "It ain't. It's the literal truth."

"Jayne learning he was Jane's father would have literally killed him?" Simon laced the remark with as much incredulity as he dared.

"Look at him now. It ain't exactly done him any favors, has it? Doing the fatherly thing. And that's just as a for-instance. It's not even—"

"Momma?"

Jane McCloud was framed in the infirmary doorway.

"Honey," said Temperance, going pale. "How long have you been standing there?"

Jane's face suggested it was a while. Long enough. She looked distraught. Aghast.

"I just came to see where you were, to tell you something," she said. "River spotted a Scourer earlier. Captain Reynolds reckons they're going to attack us. But… Did I hear aright?"

"Now listen, Jane…"

"Did Simon just say that man is my father?"

"He did say that, honey."

"Is he the reason why I'm called Jane? Your so-called 'old friend' Jayne?"

"Well, yes he is, in a manner of speaking. But it's not that simple."

Jane's expression turned venomous. "Oh, isn't it, Mom? Seems pretty ruttin' simple to me."

"You mind your language, young lady. I appreciate you're upset. If you'll only hear me out…"

"It explains a lot," Jane said. "A hell of a lot. Why everyone on this ship keeps givin' me these funny looks. Why there's always this weird silence whenever somebody mentions Jayne's name around me. Like at the dinner table last night. Conversation turned to Jayne, and you coughed, as I recall, Simon, and then Wash changed the subject like he was leaping out of the way of a rattlesnake. River said something, too, only this morning. I don't always understand her. Talking to her sometimes, it's as though she's a radio and the signal keeps hopping, changing channels at random. But we were just hangin' out and she said, 'You don't know your daddy, do you, Jane?' And I said, 'No, never did.' And she said, 'No, you don't *know* him.' I kinda couldn't follow her meaning. I assumed it was just one of her turns of phrase, same as when she told me she can read cows' minds."

Simon offered no comment. From what he understood about the surgical alterations made to River's brain at the Academy, it didn't strike him as beyond the realms of possibility that she could form a telepathic connection with cattle. Those Frankenstein doctors had unlocked hidden compartments inside his little sister's mind, unleashing a whole host of latent talents. In the process, they had turned a sweet-natured girl with a genius-level intellect into a confused, deeply troubled creature, a borderline basket case with dangerous, deadly potential. Simon had yet to learn what the doctors had been hoping to accomplish. Unless it had been done merely for the sick pleasure of tampering. Because they could. Because they worked for the Alliance and the Alliance liked to play God with people's lives and was never held to account for it.

"He's it, ain't he?" Jane gesticulated at Jayne. "He's the one who knocked you up, Mom."

"Jane, child, now you just keep a civil tongue in your head," snapped Temperance.

"How else would you rather I put it? Left you in the family way. Put a bun in your oven. Got you up the duff. Made you preggers."

"That's enough!"

"And then either he bailed on you or you bailed on him. Don't know which it was. Don't much care. What I do care about is you've kept this thing a secret from me all my life. Every time I'd ask about my father—who he was, where he was, was he even alive—you'd tell me it doesn't matter. You'd say you and me, we had each other and that was all either of us needed. That one time I really pressed you—when was it, about a year ago?—you got all bent outta shape and you said my daddy was a bad man and we were better off havin' nothing to do with him. Only, he don't seem like that bad of a man after all, now I've met him. Given how he came runnin' straight to Thetis when you asked him to, and how he stood up to Elias Vandal. He seems kinda cool, actually. Know what that says to me?"

Jane did not give her mother a chance to answer.

"It says maybe *you're* the one who's the problem. Not him. *You're* the bad one. You're the bitch—"

"Jane!"

But Jane would not be stopped. "The bitch who lit out on a guy who's basically decent. The bitch who's lied about him ever since to make herself feel better about what she did. The bitch who claims she's my mom and she loves me but sure hasn't acted that way."

"Jane Mary McCloud, how dare you speak to me like that!"

Jane's eyes were brimming with tears. Her cheeks were burning red. Hatred emanated from her like a radioactive glow.

"How dare *you*, Mama! How dare *you*!"

And with that, the girl spun on her heel and raced off.

In the wake of her departure, an awkward silence fell over the infirmary.

Simon broke it by saying, "Shouldn't you go after her?"

Temperance shrugged, not so much in indifference as in resignation. "Wouldn't help. Jane ain't easy to reason with when she gets mad like that. I'll leave her to calm down, talk to her then. Right now, I'd only make things worse. She'd feel I was hounding her. She'd spit and claw at me like a cornered bobcat."

"But this isn't just teenage angst," Simon said. "Jane isn't blowing off steam. This is a genuine life crisis."

"And I will deal with it," Temperance said emphatically. "In my own time, in my own way. Meantime, I'd be obliged if you wouldn't tell me how to raise my child. You've already caused enough trouble as it is."

"What?" Simon said, cheeks crimsoning. "But I... That wasn't at all what I... I mean, I didn't..."

Normally so eloquent, Simon Tam could be easily left struggling for words when a conversation took an unexpected turn or he gave offense where none was intended or, as just now, both.

While he floundered, tongue-tied, Temperance exited the infirmary smartly, much as her daughter had done. Simon was left alone with his patient and a head full of consternation.

He'd caused trouble?

He wasn't the one who'd just had a blazing row with their daughter. He wasn't the one who'd kept the identity of her father a secret and spun a web of deceit to justify doing so. All he had done was inadvertently spill the beans when Jane happened to be within earshot. Which was unfortunate, yes, even mortifying. But trouble-causing? No. Looking at it another way, Simon felt he had in fact done Temperance and Jane a service. The truth about Jane's paternity had been festering too long between them. It was an undiagnosed condition and Simon had helped bring it to light. Now, thanks to him, they could begin the process of reconciling and healing.

This positive spin on his gaffe went some way towards mitigating his sense of embarrassment. But only a little.

On the med couch, Jayne groaned.

Simon was at his side in a trice.

Jayne's eyelids fluttered. He opened his eyes fully and fixed Simon with a bleary gaze.

"What the…? Doc?"

"Relax, Jayne. You're in the infirmary. Everything's fine."

"Two things… don't necessarily go together."

Jayne tried to rise, then hissed in agony.

"Gorramn it. That's sore."

"Of course it is. Just lie back down. If you try to move, you run the risk of undoing all my good work."

"Last thing I remember, Vandal was throwing his knife away. Then… That's it. Nothing."

"Well, the knife came back," Simon said, "and it hit you. Got you right in the lung. Mal says it's called a boomerblade."

"Aw crap. Yeah. Should've recognized it."

"Mal says you should have and all. Mal's pretty peeved at you, to be honest."

"Mal's a jerk. Did I hear people arguin' just now?"

"Temperance and Jane. The cat's well and truly out of the bag. About, you know, you and Jane."

"*Zāo gāo!* Jane knows?"

"Jane knows. Probably not the worst that could have happened. Everything's in the open now. No more lies and evasion. Healthier that way."

"Yeah. Huh. Healthier." Jayne scratched his head. "So. I miss anything else?"

"Good news or bad news?"

"Bad first. Always."

"The Scourers have found out where we are and are most likely on their way right now to end us."

"Okay. Well, that maybe ain't such a shocker. The good news?"

"Inara bumped into a billionaire friend in Whiteplains Edge. He's mustering an army of security specialists to come and end the Scourers."

"Hell yeah! Now that *is* good news."

"The only trouble is," said Simon, "we won't live to see them arrive if the Scourers attack us in numbers. Which they doubtless will."

"So we hold them off. We defend our position for as long as it takes."

"*We*, Jayne, won't be doing anything of the sort," Simon said sternly. "There is no way in hell you are getting up off that couch and picking up a gun."

"Try and stop me, asshole." Using an elbow, Jayne levered himself up into a sitting position.

"I don't have to." Simon backed away, giving Jayne space. "Go ahead. Stand up."

Jayne attempted to.

Five times.

Each time, he failed.

"Ribcage on fire?" Simon said. "Head spinning? Stomach churning?"

"Yeah," croaked Jayne, giving up and collapsing back onto the couch. His face had taken on a greasy gray pallor.

"You don't seem to realize how badly you've been injured,

Jayne. You are in no condition to be out of bed, let alone participate in combat."

"You can't be serious."

"Deadly serious. You overexert yourself, you could do yourself irreparable harm. You could even wind up dying. You're going to have to leave the defense of *Serenity* to the rest of us. This is one fight Jayne Cobb is sitting out."

"Oh man," Jayne sighed. "We are so damn screwed."

Preparations

Shepherd Book straightened up from his labors, kneading a fist into his aching back. He was not as young as he used to be. Maybe he wasn't giving Noah and Methuselah a run for their money just yet, but he was definitely getting there.

The sun was beating down like a blacksmith's mallet. Book's eyes stung with sweat, in spite of the bandanna wrapped around his head. His shoulders and arms felt leaden. His hands were caked in dust.

Still, the job was done. It had taken three hours, from gathering the necessary supplies aboard *Serenity* to mixing a certain concoction to completing the extensive spadework outdoors with Mal's assistance. Throughout, Book had been expecting the Scourers to show up at any moment, before he could get the job finished. However, it seemed someone up there was smiling on him. There had been enough time.

Now Mal came over, picking at a fresh blister on his palm. He, like Book, was soaked in sweat and covered in dust.

"If I never see a shovel again, it'll be too soon," he said. "Remind me, what did you call it? This type of contraption? Something French. Foie gras?"

"Fougasse," said Book.

"And they're gonna work?"

"They should."

"Should?"

"They will. My only real concern is the fuses. They're concealed well enough, but I don't know whether the layer of dirt we've scattered on top of them might not interfere with how they burn."

"You've done this before, yeah?"

"Not as such. I've constructed homemade fireworks before. This is something else altogether. The basic theory is the same. The order of magnitude is... somewhat greater."

Mal looked resigned. "Well, it'd be nice to test out at least one of them beforehand, but that might kinda give the game away. We'll just have to cross our fingers and hope for the best."

"Or, perhaps, have faith," said Book.

"The Good Lord hasn't given me much cause to believe in Him these past few years, Shepherd."

"That's okay, Mal." Book clasped Mal's shoulder and gave it a reassuring squeeze. "He'll keep giving you chances to. It's what He does."

Inside *Serenity*'s cargo bay, Zoë and Wash had assembled a five-foot-tall barricade out of crates and packing cases. It was akin to a wall a child might construct using building blocks, only on a much larger scale. There were narrow niches between the stacks through which guns could be fired, and one large gap for access that would later be filled in.

Zoë stood on the ramp and looked inward, hands on hips, surveying their handiwork.

"Ain't the best defilading position I ever saw," she said, "but it'll have to do."

"Defilading position," said Wash, popping up from behind one of the stacks. "Why, Mrs. Alleyne Washburne, I do so love it when you talk dirty."

"Assuming the Scourers don't run a flanking maneuver, we should be able to beat them off."

"Flanking maneuver. Beat them off. You're really making me hot, Zoë."

"They come at us in a rush, though, that's a whole different ballgame."

"No. Seriously. Getting all hot and bothered here."

"But we can still keep fighting a rearguard action, I reckon."

By now Zoë was doing it on purpose. Anything she said, her husband was just going to treat as saucy innuendo. Might as well play up to that.

"Of course," she added, "we can always keep grinding away at them. That way, we're apt to wear them down until they're begging for mercy."

"Our bunk," said Wash, jabbing a forthright forefinger at her. "Now. I am not kidding."

Zoë looked at him askance.

"Face it, Zoë, we might not get another chance. Ever." Wash was no longer messing around. "In which case, I would very much like to lie with my wife in a conjugal fashion one last time."

Zoë looked round. Mal and Book were still conferring outside. There was no obvious sign of the Scourers.

"All right," she said, striding aboard the ship. "But make it quick."

Wash frowned. "Don't I always?"

"Yes, but this time on purpose."

Inara was at the controls of her shuttle, running a pre-flight diagnostic. All systems were normal, green lights across the board, but it paid not to take chances. The last thing she wanted was a sudden malfunction simply because she'd neglected to double-check the battery-reserve levels or the fuel-cycle pressure.

There was a knock at the door.

"Come in."

Temperance McCloud entered.

"So this is what a Companion's boudoir looks like," Temperance said, glancing around at the swagged billows of silken wall hanging, the lush rugs, the low table with its hookah pipe, everything a symphony of golds and rich reds. "Pretty much how I expected."

"Temperance. To what do I owe the honor?"

"Your shuttle's our hole card," said Temperance. "That's the plan, ain't it? If everything goes to *gŏu shĭ*, this is how we're getting the hell outta Dodge. Thought I'd better make sure it's up to scratch."

"It is, I assure you," said Inara. "I have it serviced regularly."

"I'll just bet you do."

Inara arched an eyebrow. "Was that a sly dig at my profession?"

"No. Yeah. Yeah, it was. Sorry. Didn't mean nothin' by it. Kinda just slipped out. I'm on edge."

"We all are. There's a horde of bandits likely heading this way. We could be in very deep trouble."

"Yeah, there's that. Actually it's Jane that's worryin' me. I'm referring to my daughter, not Jayne the man."

"We keep having to make that distinction, don't we?" said Inara. "To avoid confusion."

"I'm beginning to regret choosing that name for my girl."

"Perhaps we could call them something else. Wash has suggested Jane without a 'y' and Jayne with a 'why oh why?' But that's Wash humor for you. What about your Jane, anyway? What's the problem? I did hear she now knows our Jayne's her father. Is that it?"

"Not many secrets on this boat."

"It's not a big boat. Close quarters. Everyone pretty quickly gets wind of what everyone else is up to. Even me, tucked away in my shuttle. For what it's worth, I don't judge you for what you did."

"I'm mightily relieved to hear you say that," Temperance said with just a soupçon of sarcasm.

"You seem to me a woman who gets her priorities straight. You made a decision based on your best interests and those of your unborn child. They outweighed Jayne Cobb's interests, and that was just how it had to be. Back then, I doubt Jayne was any more stable and dependable than he is now. I'm not sure he's ever been or ever will be father material."

"Yeah, about that." Temperance drew a deep breath, as though steeling herself. "I have a confession to make."

Inara had had her doubts about Temperance's claim that she was here because she wanted to look over the shuttle. She had had a sneaking feeling that this had been nothing more than a pretext.

"Confession," she said. "Isn't that more a Shepherd's province, rather than mine?"

"People tell Companions things too, don't they?"

"True. We are noted for our discretion. What is it you'd like to say?"

Temperance looked on the verge of replying.

Then she shook her head.

"Go on," said Inara. "Trust me, it'll go no further than the two of us."

"Nah. It's not that important. It can wait. Apologies for wasting your time, Inara."

"Temperance?"

But the woman had hurried out of the shuttle, back into the main body of *Serenity*. Inara went to follow her, but then baulked. No. It wasn't her place to play inquisitor. Whatever Temperance wanted to get off her chest, she could do it in her own good time, when she was ready. Right now she clearly wasn't.

Inara returned her attention to prepping the shuttle.

The Beginning of the End for Coogan's Bluff

For twenty-four hours, Mayor Huckleberry Gillis had lain low.

It was not easy.

After parting ways with Temperance McCloud and venturing back into Coogan's Bluff, Gillis had been faced with a conundrum. Where should he go? What should he do?

On the one hand, the town needed a figurehead, a focal point for its collective will. Someone it could get behind. It needed *him*. He could bring succor and balm, couldn't he? By his continued presence alone, he could remind people that order remained. The architecture of authority still stood. All was as it had been, even during this difficult period.

On the other hand, Coogan's Bluff was surrounded by Scourers and rapidly coming under their thumb. The bandits were rampaging up and down the streets, sending the townspeople scattering. Sporadic bursts of gunfire rent the air, often as not followed by screams.

On his way in, not far from the outskirts, Gillis came across a couple of dead bodies lying by the roadside. It was the Carter twins, Earl and Emery. A wagon burned nearby. It didn't take much to infer that Earl and Emery had been attempting to escape. They'd been caught, dragged from their vehicle and shot. Then the wagon had been torched.

From this chilling example, Gillis began to get a clear sense of how badly things were sliding out of control, and how little there was he could do to alter that.

He made it to his office and hid out there awhile. In time, the ruckus outside quietened down. By late afternoon an eerie stillness held sway over the town. Gillis, at that point, was very hungry and thirsty. He crept into the hotel that his office was adjoined to, via an interconnecting door. He was thinking the hotel's proprietor, Abner Marshfield, would have something in the kitchen he could eat, cold cuts or what-have-you. Even a protein bar would do. And of course there'd be milk in the refrigerator, maybe also a beer.

In the event, Abner was nowhere to be found. Instead, the hotel was crawling with Scourers. They had made it their base of operations.

What alerted Gillis to this fact was the sound of raucous voices echoing throughout the building. He was in the process of beating a hasty retreat when two Scourers rounded the corner ahead of him. Gillis ducked into a storage closet as nimbly as his corpulent frame would allow, praying the two men had not spotted him.

Ear pressed to the closet door, he listened, trembling, as they came closer. They were discussing Elias Vandal. Their leader was laid up back at camp, recovering from the bullet wound Captain Reynolds had given him. Vandal, it seemed, had ordered that nobody in Coogan's Bluff was to be shown any quarter. He wanted the entire town on lockdown. The Scourers had to stamp their mark on the place.

"By nightfall everybody's gotta be indoors," said one of the Scourers to the other. "We gotta have this place under curtfew."

"Curtfew?" said the second man.

"Yeah, curtfew."

"You mean curfew, right?"

"That's what I said. Curtfew."

"The word is curfew. There's no such thing as curtfew."

"Yeah, there is. When, like, you can't go outside or you'll get shot. That's curtfew."

The two men strode past the storage closet, deep in semantic debate, and once their voices and footfalls had faded, Gillis edged the door open and peeked out. The coast was clear. He scurried back to his office.

His office, however, was now the last place he should be. Right next to a building full of Scourers. At any time, one of them could come through the interconnecting door. Gillis locked it just in case, but if somebody happened to try the handle and couldn't open it, that might arouse curiosity. The Scourers might want to know what lay on the other side of the locked door and break it down to find out.

Gillis saw no alternative but to vacate the premises. The sun was going down. It wasn't long before the curtfew would come into effect.

Dammit, they'd got him doing it now.

He cracked open the office's other door, the one which gave onto a side alley separating the hotel and the general stores next to it. No Scourers in sight. He headed off down the alley at a fast waddle, then turned right onto an even narrower alley that ran a zigzagging course between various backyard fences. He had a vague idea of making for his house, a drafty, ramshackle cabin on the south side of town with a shingle roof that he'd never quite gotten around to mending and several missing window shutters. Suddenly, for all its failings, it seemed the most desirable place Gillis could imagine, as much fortress as sanctum. Hole up there, and he would be safe and sound, immune from the Scourers' depredations.

It was not to be. There were just too darned many of the bandits out and about. Gillis watched a group of them drive a man—Wallace Eames—back into his house by firing at his feet. Wally Eames danced clear of the volley of bullets, yelping in panic and protest. The front door slammed behind him, and the Scourers just fell about with ribald laughter, slapping one another on the back. Hil-*air*-ious!

He wasn't going to reach his own house. Gillis knew it. Not without encountering Scourers. Not without running the risk of being shot at, like Wally—or just plain shot.

Gillis wondered to himself, why didn't he simply go up to the next bunch of Scourers he came across and throw himself on their mercy? Explain who he was and where he was trying to get to? Beg them to allow him safe passage there? He was Mayor Huckleberry U. Gillis, after all. The name and title had some significance, did they not? Surely they carried some weight.

But without Vandal present to exercise his influence over them, the Scourers were a rambunctious, rabblesome lot: a body without a brain, operating solely on instinct and appetite. You could not trust them to behave in any way civilly. Common sense, common decency—these concepts were alien to them. As long as Elias Vandal was out of the picture, Gillis could not expect preferential treatment at their hands. He, the Mayor of Coogan's Bluff, was for the time being just as vulnerable, just as subject to the Scourers' whims, as any of his fellow townspeople.

He found refuge for the night in, of all places, a stable. He clambered up into the hayloft, built himself a bed out of straw, and settled down to sleep.

He did not think he actually would sleep, but the exertions of the day—the many stresses and strains—caught up with him. With the warm, somehow reassuring scent of straw in his nostrils, and to the accompaniment of the occasional soft snort and huff from the mare in her loose-box below, Gillis fell into a profound slumber.

From which he was rudely awoken, around midnight, by the sound of explosions.

What had disturbed him was a short sequence of muffled detonations, one *crump* after another, all within the interval of perhaps a half-minute. Gillis sat bolt upright, scraped straw from his face and hair, and blinked around him in the darkness. The mare stamped and whinnied in agitation.

There was a rectangular aperture cut into the outer wall of the hayloft for ventilation. Gillis peered out. He sort of already knew where the explosions had originated and what they signified.

As he'd suspected, the Scourers had blown up the town's wellheads. In four locations across Coogan's Bluff he could see the glow of flames and small plumes of smoke rising against the starry sky. Distant braying cheers told him that the Scourers were treating the demolition like a kind of party; they'd even coordinated the timings of the explosions close together, for maximum effect. They had also made sure to confiscate whatever stores of water they could find in the town beforehand and had smashed cisterns and other such large containers. They intended the punishment to be thorough and absolute.

Gillis had known the destruction of the wellheads was bound to happen. But knowing a thing and actually witnessing it were not one and the same. A kind of grim sorrow overcame him, like a dark cloud. Coogan's Bluff was going the way of Yinjing Butte. There was nothing that could change that now. The town's long, slow demise was unavoidable. The Scourers were going to teach its inhabitants the same lesson they had taught Yinjing Butte's, the lesson they were keen for everyone else in the county to sit up and heed.

Mess with the Scourers and expect the ultimate retaliation.

Mayor Gillis did not sleep much the rest of that night. Nor, he reckoned, did any of the other townsfolk.

Come first light, he was hungrier and thirstier than ever. A bucket of horse feed hanging outside the loose-box looked unbearably tempting. With great effort of will he passed it by and went in search of water. There was a standpipe a short way down the road. Gillis spun the faucet. A trickle came out but dried up before he thought to catch it in a cupped palm. The water seeped into the dirt, lost forever.

Dismayed but not disheartened, at least not wholly, Gillis knocked on the front door of a nearby house, home to elderly Jake Buchholz and his missus Sally. It was Sally who came to answer his knock. She was in her nightgown and she had a double-barreled shotgun in her hands.

"You going to invite me in," Gillis said, "or you going to blow my head off?"

"You ain't comin' in, Mayor," the old woman replied resolutely. "I'm sorry but that's just how it is."

"Now listen here, Sally. Not only is this most unfriendly of you, but I am a man in dire need. I ain't had a drop to drink nor a morsel to eat since yesterday morn. Can you not show me an ounce of charity?"

"Who's that at the door, Sal?" Jake Buchholz called down querulously from upstairs.

"It's the Mayor," Sally called back, not taking her eyes off Gillis. "He wants in and he wants victualing."

"Don't you dare let that man across our threshold," Jake warned. "It's him who's done this to us. Him who brought in them offworld folks, thinkin' they'd send the Scourers packing."

"You heard my husband, Mayor."

"Well now, Sally, strictly speaking it weren't me as did what Jake's saying. It was Temperance McCloud."

"But you knew she'd contacted them," said Sally. "Didn't you?"

"Now, there I must hold up my hand and say yes. Yes, I did. I hoped it might work. Granted, it was a Hail Mary, but at that stage things had reached such a crisis point, I was willing to take whatever I could get."

"Which makes you pretty much as guilty as Temperance. You sanctioned it. You gave her the go-ahead. And then there's that speech you made in the town square, all that dandy-soundin' guff about 'a loud, resounding no' and 'drawing a line in the sand.'"

The shotgun barrels bored into Gillis like two gimlet eyes.

"And look how well *that's* turned out," Sally went on. "There ain't no water coming through the pipes. Jake and I have got a bucketful that's liable to last us not much more'n a day or so. And we all know how it's gonna play out from here on in. We all know what's to become of this town. Yinjing Butte all over again."

She waved the shotgun at him with abundant menace and not a little anguish.

"Now git!"

Mayor Gillis opened his mouth in protest, then closed it again and trudged disconsolately away.

This was it. This was how it started. Neighbor against neighbor. Everyone protecting their own. Everyone jealously guarding their dwindling resources. Rats in a cage, growing increasingly frenzied and frantic, lashing out at one another, all teeth and talons. Soon it would degenerate into chaos. Mayhem. Suicide, murder, slaughter. And eventually, inevitably, mass death.

Coogan's Bluff was doomed. And there was nothing he could do but share in that dismal fate.

Sunk deep in these somber thoughts, Gillis scarcely heard the click of a gun being cocked behind him.

But he did hear the voice that drawled, "Now just where in hell do you think *you're* going, my tubby ol' pal?"

Confident and Captainy

"Shepherd, that look to you like a dust cloud on the horizon?" said Mal, squinting. "The sort of dust cloud you'd see if, say, there was a whole buttload of bandits headed towards us?"

Book shaded his eyes and stared in the same direction Mal was staring. "Looks exactly that way to me," he said.

"Too much to hope it might be a twister or a sandstorm or such?"

"Way too much to hope."

"Okay then."

Mal jogged up the cargo ramp and snatched the intercom handset off the wall.

"Everyone, pay attention. This is not a drill."

His voice was carried to every corner of the ship.

"We have bogies approaching from the north-west. Can't tell yet how many, but best guess? A lot. Now, we've prepared for this. Everybody knows what they should be doing. Take your positions. Await further instructions."

He released the thumb-button on the handset.

"That sound confident and captainy enough?"

"Admirably so," said Book.

"Good. Only, truth be told, I ain't feelin' any too confident and captainy right about now," Mal admitted. "I'm feelin' more like I did at Serenity Valley when word came through from Command that we were to lay down our weapons. That same kind of sickly sensation in the pit of my stomach."

"Mal, you're no longer fighting that war."

"So you say, Shepherd. But something tells me I am. Something tells me I'll *always* be fighting that war."

Zoë was perched on the edge of the bed, pulling her pants on. Wash, beside her, groped for her arm and stroked it.

"We can leave it another minute or two, can't we?" he said. "Stay here and snuggle?"

"You know as well as I do we can't. You heard Mal. You need to get up and get dressed too, honey. Duty calls."

"Duty can bite me."

Zoë whipped aside the bedcovers. "Out."

Wash fixed her with a serious look. "I love you, Zoë. You know that, don't you?"

"I love you too, Wash. But we're not doing this. We're not acting like this may be the last time we get to say that to each other. We've got plenty more time together. Years ahead of us." She slapped her husband's bare backside. "Now do as I tell you and move that peachy behind."

"Okay! Okay!" Wash scrambled out of bed and grabbed his shirt. "Jeez, woman. First you get me nekkid, then you want me clothed. Make up your mind, why don't you."

Seated cross-legged on the floor of her shuttle, Inara opened her eyes, emerging from a deep, cleansing meditation. By honing in on the movement of her breath, concentrating on each inhalation and exhalation to the exclusion of all else, she had managed to empty her mind. Her thoughts were now stilled, a swirling whirlpool transformed into a tranquil, unruffled pond. All seven of her chakras were in alignment, from muladhara up to sahasrara, and she seemed all the more fully present in her body, inhabiting every inch of it from marrow to skin.

She extinguished the joss-stick burning in front of her and, in a single, fluid movement, rose to her feet.

Ready for whatever might come.

Simon doffed his surgical apron.

"Goin' to shoot some people, Doc?" said Jayne.

"I'm going to help however I can. It isn't that difficult, aiming a gun and pulling the trigger. I've done it before."

"How about your, what is it? Your Hypocritical oath? 'First, do no harm' and all that."

"My *Hippocratic* oath and I are fine with killing in the name of self-defense," said Simon. "If it's a case of them or us, then for the time being I can forget I'm a doctor."

"Just remember. You draw a bead on a guy, you make damn well sure you don't hesitate. You put him down. Can't afford no pussyin' about in a situation like this."

"Thanks, Jayne. I'll take it under advisement."

"I'm in earnest," Jayne said. "You ain't got me on the front line, shoulderin' the burden. I'm a big gap to fill. So the rest of you gotta step up."

"I'll do my best."

"Sure as hell wish I was out there with you."

"Know what, Jayne?" Simon looked at him with genuine regret. "Today, of all days, I sure as hell wish that too."

* * *

River found Jane McCloud sunk in a chair in the rec lounge, sulking.

"Bad men on their way," she said.

"I'm aware."

"Mal told me to find you and tell you to go to Inara's shuttle. The plan is, Inara will fly everyone out if it all starts to get too crazy."

"So I'm supposed to just wait there and twiddle my thumbs?" said Jane. "Is that it? Like a good little girl? While everyone else gets to blow Scourers to kingdom come?"

River chortled merrily. "Who said that? I've told you to go to Inara's shuttle. I've done as Mal asked. Now come with me. I've got a better idea."

Jane rose. "You're disobeying your Captain?"

"I've played the tune," said River. "Now I'm adding a few trills and flourishes of my own. This way!"

She led Jane forward to the crew's bunks.

"Whose room is this?" Jane said as they shinned down the ladder into one of them.

"Jayne's."

Jane peered around, bemused. The room was untidy and stank of gun oil and male musk. It was more or less exactly how she would have expected Jayne Cobb's living quarters to be.

Then her eye fell on a yellow woolen hat that lay on the bed.

"What in heck is that thing?" she declared. "Looks like a giant piece of candy corn gone wrong."

"It's Jayne's."

"He wears it? Or is it for, you know, cleanin' toilets?"

"It's his Sunday best," River said. "He hates if anyone else puts it on."

Jane plucked the hat off the bed and lodged it on her head. She studied herself in the mirror above the washbasin.

"Looks ridiculous," she said. "I love it."

"You haven't seen anything yet." River drew back the strip of fabric on the wall to reveal Jayne's stash of weapons. "Jayne has guns."

"He has *all* the guns," Jane said approvingly. "I recognize some of these. Mom owns an over-and-under Carpenter and Liu double-aught gauge like that. And that one there's a nine-mil Sherrington semiauto. I fired one at a friend's house once. We were shooting gophers. See this?"

She pushed up the hat and tugged aside her bangs to expose a small triangular scar on one lobe of her forehead.

"That's from the front sight. I didn't realize how much of a kick a gun like that has. It bucked up in my hand, whacked me in the face. Hurt, bled bad, but didn't stop me from carryin' on. We bagged about a couple dozen critters that day."

A look of intrigue stole over her.

"Wait. Are you suggesting, River, that we take some of these here guns and use them?"

"No one has said we can't."

Jane thought for a moment. Then, grinning, she reached for the Sherrington.

"Mom is so going to kill me," she said, with glee.

On his way out of the infirmary, Simon met Kaylee. She was coming in the opposite direction with a bulky engine part in her arms, something that was all tubes and dangling wires, like a dead robot spider.

"Simon."

"Kaylee."

"Going down to man the barricade, huh?"

"Yeah. You?"

"Captain wants me repairing, come what may. 'The sooner

Serenity's flying, the better,' he says."

"He has a point."

"Ain't as if I'll have her airborne today," said Kaylee. "Nor even tomorrow. I can work every hour God sends and there'll still be more left to do. The job is as big as it is, and I can't go any faster than I already am. I'm sure Mal could do with an extra gun arm down in the cargo bay, but noooo, I'm stuck fixing stuff."

"Maybe he just wants you out of harm's way. Maybe you're too valuable to put in the line of fire."

"You think so?"

"If I were him, that's what I'd do. Keep you somewhere where you'll be safe."

Kaylee smiled sweetly but a touch uncertainly. "That's gallant of you. I mean, of Mal."

"Because, of course, we only have one mechanic," Simon said. "You can't be replaced like—well, like that engine part."

Kaylee glanced down at the object she was holding. "I'm an engine part?"

"A crucial one. A part we can't do without."

"Wow. Okay. Well, I'll take that as a compliment. But now this engine part had better go and stick the engine part she's carrying where it belongs. Simon?"

"Yes?"

"Please take care."

"You too, Kaylee."

They held each other's gaze for the space of several heartbeats.

Then, impulsively, Kaylee kissed him on the cheek and hurried off.

Simon watched her go.

Engine part?

He asked himself why he always got so obtuse in his speech when he was around Kaylee, especially when it was him and her alone together. Why he felt he wasn't ever saying what he was hoping to say. Something about her simplicity and directness brought out an unwanted evasiveness in him. Her brand of plain speaking wasn't what a sophisticate like him was accustomed to. It caught him on the hop, every time.

One of these days, he told himself, he would figure out how to respond to Kaylee in kind. He would tell her what was in his heart.

One of these days.

Inara joined Zoë and Wash at the barricade. Temperance McCloud was with them there already, slotting rimfire .308 shells into the breech of a bolt-action rifle.

One glance at Zoë and Wash, and Inara could tell they had just recently made love. She wouldn't have been much of a Companion if she couldn't identify the signs. The flushed cheeks. The satisfied glow. The warmth in the eyes. Unmistakable. *Good for them.*

Zoë passed her a pistol. Inara ejected the clip, worked the action, and inspected the sights for straightness. Everything seemed in good order. She slotted the clip back into position and chambered a round.

Simon arrived a few moments later. Zoë gave him a gun too. He held it gingerly, like it might bite.

Meanwhile, out on the cargo ramp, Mal and Book stood side by side, watching the Scourers draw closer, closer, ever closer.

Unleashing Hell

The Scourers rolled across the plain towards the Firefly like a swarm of ants making for the carcass of some larger insect, eager to dismantle it and haul its component parts back to their nest.

Riding at the head of the throng was Shem Bancroft. He had explicit instructions from Vandal. He was to make Malcolm Reynolds an offer. One final offer. One last chance. If Reynolds turned it down, then the next step was very simple.

Unleash hell.

On arriving at the spaceship, the Scourers encircled it, charging round and round, firing their weapons into the air, whooping and hollering, a human vortex. They did this for several minutes until Shem decided that was enough terrorizing and intimidating to be getting on with. The offworlders ought to be, if not quaking in their boots, at least softened up a little. Tenderized like hammered meat.

He drew his horse to a halt in front of the cargo ramp, where Reynolds and the Shepherd were waiting. The other Scourers fell in behind him. The dust cloud they'd raised drifted in front of the sun, dimming its light to a sulfur-yellow haze.

To Shem, neither of the men on the ramp seemed any that impressed by the Scourers' show of strength. Deep down, though, they were fretting, Shem reckoned. They must be. They knew they didn't stand a chance against such overwhelming odds. They were as good as dead—unless they seized the olive branch he was about to extend to them.

"Reynolds!" he called out.

"That's me. Who in heck are you?"

"They call me Shem. I'm Elias Vandal's second-in-command."

"Mr. Vandal not able to make it? He got a prior engagement?"

"He sent me as his proxy," said Shem. "I'm authorized to speak for him."

"Well, first off, tell him I said hi. How's his shoulder? They get the bullet out?"

"They did, and I'll be frank with you, Reynolds, Vandal ain't at all happy 'bout you shootin' him. Not one bit. Least of all like that, from a distance. 'A snake's trick,' he called it. But still and all, he's prepared to let bygones be bygones."

"He is, is he?"

"Sure. Elias Vandal is not an unreasonable man. He don't always hold a grudge. He 'specially don't if a person who done him wrong is prepared to make amends."

"Interesting," said Reynolds. "And how might I go about doing that?"

Shem couldn't tell if the fella was just snarking or if he was truly willing to consider some form of reparation. Most probably, if his performance in town yesterday was anything to go by, he was snarking. But, regardless, Shem went ahead with the offer Vandal had told him to make.

"There's two young women aboard that there ship of yours," he said.

"Is that a fact?"

"It is indeed. Pretty things, both of 'em. You hand them over to us, right now, no quibblin', and we promise to leave you alone. You don't, and… I guess I don't have to paint a picture."

"Hmmm." Reynolds stroked his chin. "What do you say, Shepherd? Shem here is askin' us to give up two young women in return for not attacking us. That sound like a fair trade to you?"

"On the face of it, yes," the Shepherd replied. "Two lives in exchange for the lives of the rest of us? Can't argue with arithmetic like that."

"Ain't even their *lives* we're talkin' about," said Shem. "I want to make that plain. We just get the use of 'em for a spell. We'll send 'em back to you when we're done, and there's an end of it."

"And who's to say we let you take receipt of these two girls and you don't then just attack us anyway?" said Reynolds. "Seems you're askin' us to take an awful lot on trust."

"I'm a man of my word. So's Vandal."

"That is reassuring," said Reynolds. "Ain't that reassuring, Shepherd Book?"

"Positively heartwarming, Mal."

"Shem, I'm gonna have to think about it."

The huge smile that was plastered over Reynolds's face turned abruptly into a scowl brimming with spite and disgust.

"I've thought about it, Shem, and know what? You can take your offer and shove it up your ass. You *tā mā de hún dàn*! No way in hell are you gonna drag anyone from this ship back to your camp as 'entertainment' for you and those scumbag sons-of-bitches you call friends. That just ain't gonna happen. Instead, I'm going to make *you* an offer. I'm going to give you to the count of five. If, by five, you and all these other inbreds aren't turning tail and making for the hills, you're gonna regret the day your momma and her brother ever got together and decided to conceive."

Shem struggled to decode that remark about his mother. She didn't even have a brother. She was one of three sisters.

Then the penny dropped, and Shem was, to put it mildly, incensed.

By that point, however, Reynolds had already started counting. "Three. Four."

Shem was flabbergasted. This guy actually expected the Scourers to do as he said and leave? *He* was threatening *them*? With what? Shem had spied the arrangement of crates just inside the ship's cargo bay, and the crewmembers lurking behind them, toting guns. Did Reynolds seriously believe the handful of them were going to deter fifty-odd heavily armed Scourers? Not in a million years!

"Five."

Reynolds ambled down the ramp. There was something in his hand. A cigarette lighter?

"Can't say I didn't warn you," he said, kneeling at the foot of the ramp.

The lighter clicked. A flame flared.

Reynolds touched the flame to the ground, and all at once there was a sizzling sound. Several sizzling sounds coming from separate sources.

Reynolds hotfooted it back up the ramp, even as Shem looked blankly around, trying hard to figure out what was going on.

That sizzling. It sure sounded like ignited fuses.

He couldn't see any fuses. But he could smell burning, which suggested maybe there *were* fuses somewhere.

And Shem decided that if there were fuses, there must by definition be explosives. And that was not a good thing.

He was about to yell a command to the Scourers to get out of there, now!

But too late.

Hell was unleashed that morning, in that spot.

But it was not the Scourers who did the unleashing.

Landmines of an Improvised and Somewhat Homespun Nature

The fuses were made of braided cotton thread soaked in alcohol. The explosive material was a mixture of surgical spirit and hydrogen peroxide, distilled and dried to a granular white powder.

The things called fougasses were small shafts sunk into the earth, packed with plenty of the white powder and topped with loose rocks. They were effectively landmines, if of an improvised and somewhat homespun nature.

They worked nonetheless.

Positioned around *Serenity*, the fougasses erupted one after another in swift succession. There were a dozen of them in all. The majority—eight—were concentrated to the rear of the ship, right beneath the Scourers' feet.

These ones caused the most damage, sending rock fragments hurtling in all directions at speed, like stone shrapnel. Anyone within a fifteen-foot radius was either blown to bits or badly shredded.

The remaining four fougasses were located on either side of the ship. They inflicted lesser injuries, and one failed to detonate at all, owing to a faulty fuse that had petered out halfway to its destination. Still, they added to the general distress of the Scourers and their mounts. Horses reared. Riders were thrown. Other horses galloped around in blind panic, oblivious to every attempt to curb them.

Chaos reigned, not helped by the blizzard of bullets which began to pour from the rear of the Firefly, strafing the Scourers. Bandits, horsed and unhorsed alike, scattered this way and that to escape the fusillade. Bodies fell, some never to rise again.

For a full two minutes the Scourers were in absolute disarray. The patch of ground where they had previously been gathered in massed ranks was now a shambles, riddled with craters and strewn with corpses and body parts, both human and equine. Screams of pain mingled with cries of consternation and the horses' shrieks. None of the Scourers still alive and intact even thought to return fire. They were too busy trying to rein in their runaway mounts, or seeking cover.

Among the wounded was none other than Shem Bancroft. He had been caught sidelong by the blast from one of the fougasses. His horse had collapsed under him, all but disemboweled by flying rock debris, and Shem now lay sprawled beside it. He himself had been hit in the head. The entire left side of his face had gone numb and he could feel hot blood oozing down his neck. His probing fingers found a stippling of tiny shards embedded in the skin of his cheek and temple, like sharp Braille dots.

Shem's ears were ringing and he felt a sense of weird dislocation, as though he was floating, physically not fully present. The carnage around him seemed unreal. A nightmare. Everything had gone haywire. The Scourers were being decimated by the offworlders. This wasn't right. This wasn't how it had been supposed to go. Shem had let Vandal down badly. Vandal was going to be mad.

A cocktail of violent emotions—outrage, guilt and fear—brought Shem to his senses. His thoughts cleared. He remembered he had a mission to fulfill.

Propping himself up on one elbow, he drew his gun and began firing back at the offworlders.

"What're y'all doin'?" he yelled at the still-stricken Scourers. "Runnin' around like headless chickens. Shoot 'em! Shoot those motherhumpers!"

Gradually, one by one, the Scourers got the message. They broke off from whatever else they were doing and followed his example. Some threw themselves prone on the ground in order to present as low-profile a target as possible before opening up with their sidearms. Some crouched behind fallen horses and fired over the top of them. Meanwhile, the riders whose steeds were hysterical with fright managed to get them back under control and joined the fray, guns blazing.

The rout had become a fightback. Rallied by Shem, the Scourers were on the offensive once more.

Bullets pounded into the crates. Ricochets whined across the cargo bay. The din of the crew's own gunfire echoed in that confined space. It all amounted to one long percussive cascade of noise.

Mal fired and fired and fired, pausing only to reload. Beside him, Zoë, Wash, Inara, Temperance, Book, and Simon did the same, emptying their weapons through the niches in the barricade. Zoë, Wash, Inara, and Temperance were shooting to kill. Simon was trying to, if with somewhat less success than those four. Shepherd Book, for his part, was going for wounding shots only. His aim was good enough that he could pull off this feat with aplomb; so was his understanding of anatomy. When he went for a Scourer's thigh, he missed the femoral artery. When he got a Scourer in the shoulder, it was a clean through-and-through hit, usually avoiding the bone. He disabled without causing fatalities or even lasting damage.

Serenity herself was taking hits. Not all of the Scourers' rounds struck the barricade, or for that matter the cargo bay's interior. The Scourers' strategy, if it can be called that, seemed to favor volume over accuracy. The route to victory lay, apparently, in the sheer quantity of bullets they were expending rather than the precision placement of shots. This wasn't so much a surgical strike as carpet-bombing.

The ship's hull could handle small-arms fire. The multilayered composite-alloy tiles which covered it had ablative properties to dissipate high-heat radiation, for instance during atmospheric re-entry, and the tensile strength to repel kinetic impactors such as micrometeoroids and other minor space detritus. Bullets—even armor-piercing rounds—could not penetrate and scarcely left a scratch.

Mal was not so confident that his ship could maintain integrity against a rocket-propelled grenade, however. And he knew the barricade definitely could not.

So when he saw one of the Scourers adopt a kneeling position with an RPG launcher lodged on his shoulder, he let the man know in no uncertain terms what he thought about *that*.

He fired his Liberty Hammer not at the Scourer himself but at the launcher. Bullseye! The weapon exploded in a gratifying fireball, obliterating its wielder from the waist up. The Scourer's lower half remained kneeling for several seconds, smoke rising from the charred, truncated ruin that had been his midriff, before it toppled over sideways.

Nonetheless, the barricade was slowly succumbing to the Scourers' withering onslaught. The crates and packing cases were being eaten away, affording scanter and scanter protection to the people behind them. It was only a matter of time before a bullet got through a crate whittled down to nothingness.

"Fall back!" Mal shouted. "We can't hold position any longer. Fall back!"

Book, Inara, Temperance, and Simon complied straight away, Simon making no secret of his relief. Zoë and Wash continued to lay down fire while Mal scurried over on all fours to the door-closing switch. He thumped it with his fist, and the ramp began to rise.

Scourer bullets pinged and rattled futilely against the underside of the ramp as it settled snugly into place. Little by little the salvoes subsided. The Scourers had grasped that they were just wasting their ammo. They weren't able to get at the people inside the ship that way anymore.

But it wouldn't be long, Mal thought, before they tried another approach. The Scourers were not going to leave *Serenity* alone. They had taken significant casualties—he reckoned their numbers were at least halved—but this would only make them all the more determined.

It wasn't merely about taking River and Jane captive now, or about disposing of the inconveniences that were Mal and the rest of the crew.

It was about a thirst for blood. It was about revenge.

Serenity Under Siege

Shem Bancroft was in considerable pain. The numbness had faded and now the left side of his face felt as though it was on fire. It hurt to talk. It hurt to turn his head. It hurt to *blink*.

For that, if for no other reason, the offworlders were going to pay.

Malcolm Reynolds and his crew had taken refuge inside the ship, the cowards. Not that Shem wouldn't have done the same in their shoes. The Firefly was now their castle, with the drawbridge pulled up. It was a wise tactic. But still a gutless one too, he felt. Retreating, not facing down their enemy.

Besides, castles weren't impregnable. They could always be besieged, couldn't they?

He asked himself what Elias Vandal would do in this situation. Vandal would get aboard that spacecraft by hook or by crook, that was what he would do. As an ex-Reaver—a *supposed* ex-Reaver, Shem corrected himself, because all said and done, Vandal's story simply didn't stack up—Vandal would stop at nothing until the two girls were in the Scourers' possession. He would use brute force to get what he wanted.

Shem thought he himself could be a mite subtler. He began studying the ship for weak points. From what he knew of the layout of

219

a Firefly, there was at least one EVA hatch high up. A hatch could be pried open, cut open using a blowtorch, even blown up with dynamite. The viewing ports on the bridge might also be vulnerable to forced entry. Diamond-coated quartz glass was marginally more fragile than hull tiles. A well-placed RPG or two might crack a pane so extensively that it could then be smashed in with a few energetic kicks.

Getting people up there onto the ship's structure was difficult but far from impossible. The Scourers had ropes. They could improvise grappling hooks out of stirrups and spurs.

Although the pain from his face wasn't easing off—if anything it was becoming worse—Shem felt a sharp sense of satisfaction.

He knew he wasn't bright, not in a book-learning way.

But at times he could be pretty gorramn cunning.

Jayne had listened to the cacophony of explosions and gunfire with a mounting sense of frustration. It was hard to lie there on the med couch while a pitched battle was raging around him. It was an agony almost worse than the pain coming from his chest. He needed to be involved. Not because he was some macho bonehead who relished shooting people. Okay, maybe a little bit that. But mostly because he was the best on the ship at that sort of thing, better even than Mal and Zoë. It was his element. Fish swam in water, birds flew in the air, and Jayne Cobb did gunfighting. He lived and breathed it. Some might even say he got off on it. That girl from Nandi's bordello, for one. Helen, wasn't that her name?

Added to which, *Serenity* was his home, and a man defended his home, did he not? It was one of the fundamentals of masculinity. If somebody should come to your house with ill intent, you put the *qiáng bào hóu zi de* bastard down. It was the right and proper thing to do and you didn't feel one tiny morsel of regret about it.

Defending *Serenity* was all the more important to Jayne now, given that there was family aboard. His own daughter. His own flesh and blood.

Jayne was still acclimating to the idea that he was a father. It was a hell of a shock to the system. All these years spent free and footloose, his only family ties being his mother and Matty. Now, all of a sudden, he had offspring, and the many obligations that came with that.

He didn't know quite how he felt towards Jane McCloud as a person. She seemed like a decent kid. From the brief interactions he had had with her, she struck him as smart, tough, and feisty.

Towards her as a daughter, however, he felt strange, powerful emotions, deep-seated urges he was unaccustomed to. Principally, a need to protect her, to keep her safe at all costs. Like when he'd decided, against all good sense, to take Mal's place in the duel with Elias Vandal. One moment he'd been looking forward with some curiosity to seeing how the fight between Mal and Vandal would pan out and wondering idly if he mightn't find somebody he could wager on the outcome with. Next, in the wake of Mal's series of increasingly unsubtle digs about fatherhood and the dawning realization that Jane must be his daughter, Jayne had been engulfed by this surging tide of *certainty*. It had come out of nowhere, blindsiding him. He had known there was nothing he would not do, no place he would not go, no depths he would not stoop to, in order to ensure Jane's well-being. He still felt it, perhaps even more overwhelmingly than before.

What that meant, right now, was that he could not stay in the infirmary anymore. That was no longer an option. To hell with Simon Tam and his medical opinion. What did that stuck-up little snotnose punk know anyway?

First things first. He had to get the intravenous drip out of his arm.

Jayne simply yanked hard on the tube until the needle sprang free.

That was kind of unpleasant, especially as blood started dribbling from the vein the drip had been plugged into. Unpleasant but bearable.

Then came climbing off the med couch.

Awful wasn't the word for it.

Downright abominable, more like.

Jayne tried to move himself tentatively, an inch at a time. No sooner had he got one leg off the side of the couch, however, than his entire body seized up, locking rigid in a paroxysm of pain. He couldn't continue, but neither could he go back. He was stuck, leg dangling helplessly. Anything he did just increased the hurting.

In the end, there was only one course of action open to him.

Gritting his teeth, Jayne forced himself to roll off the med couch.

He hit the floor on his uninjured side.

That was about the only positive thing to be said for the experience. In every other respect it was misery. The pain was atrocious. He just wanted to stay on the floor, curled up, and bawl like a baby.

Instead, somehow, he made himself get up onto all fours. Then, with a great deal of hissing, growling, and whimpering, he pulled himself to his feet, using the med couch for support.

Panting hard, slick all over with perspiration, Jayne stood awhile and waited for the pain to go away. He nearly puked. He nearly passed out. Only by dint of a huge effort of will did he do neither.

Gradually the pain started to relent. It seemed to have no intention of going away completely. That would have been too convenient, too obliging of it. But it was at least dialing itself down a fraction, as if out of respect for his sheer point-blank refusal to be beaten by it.

"Okay now. Okay. Okay. Got this far. That's the worst over. Gonna be a cakewalk from now on."

So saying, Jayne directed his gaze towards his T-shirt, the one he'd been wearing during the fight with Vandal. It was sitting on a work surface, bundled up, spattered with bloodstains, partly ripped. Jayne was naked from the waist up save for the bandaging around his ribs. He couldn't go around like that, bare-chested. Not with

Jane on the ship. A man had to be fully dressed in his daughter's company. Propriety and so forth.

He managed to put the T-shirt on, but only just. It was touch and go. Lifting his arms above his head, poking them through the sleeves, tugging the T-shirt down around his torso—this sequence of simple, everyday actions was now a torturous ordeal that left him breathless and nauseated.

"Hah!" Jayne exclaimed, T-shirt finally in place. "Weren't so bad. I got this. I got this."

Next up: finding weapons.

He took three steps towards the infirmary door.

He had no recollection of taking a fourth. All he knew was that he was flat on the floor again, face down, and a small volcano was erupting within him, molten lava flooding his chest cavity. Every breath he took, the volcano spewed out more.

Well now. Seemed this whole getting-up-and-joining-in-the-fight business was going to be a damn sight more of a challenge than he'd thought.

But that wouldn't stop him.

Proving Simon Tam wrong was an incentive.

Proving himself a worthy father to Jane was even more of one.

A half-dozen Scourers were selected to climb up onto the Firefly and break in.

Selected or, more accurately, dragooned. Shem didn't give them much choice in the matter: do as he said or they'd answer to Vandal. That was the ultimate sanction where Shem was concerned: invoking their leader's name. It was like divine authority, and you just didn't argue with it, not if you had any brains. In the past, more than one Scourer had learned to their cost what happened when you disobeyed Elias Vandal or earned his displeasure. During the final, dreadful minutes of their lives they had surely regretted the error and wished they could atone. But it was hard to recant your sins when your tongue had been cut off, your eyes had been gouged out, and your skin was being flayed off you in strips with a knife.

At Shem's command, one of the Scourers fashioned a lasso and snared the loop around the static discharge spike just to the rear of the Firefly's bridge module. Another snagged a makeshift grappling hook over one of the spaceship's wings.

The Scourers began shimmying up the ropes onto the vessel.

Meanwhile, another Scourer with an RPG launcher lined up the bridge viewing ports in his crosshairs.

From the bridge, with Wash beside him, Mal had been watching the Scourer activity around the ship. He'd anticipated that there would be an attempt to board *Serenity*. What he hadn't counted on was how quickly the bandits would get their act together and how reckless and brazen they were being about the assault.

As if they didn't think *Serenity*'s crew would be lying in wait at every potential point of ingress, ready to repel them.

Mal spoke into a comms handset. "Zoë? You in position at the EVA hatch yet?"

"Just got here, sir," Zoë replied. "And there's a teensy problem."

Mal suppressed a groan. "Care to elucidate?"

"The hatch is open."

"So close it."

"Yes, sir, but who opened it? And why? Must've been one of us. Hate to say it but do you think we have a traitor on board? Someone working hand-in-hand with the Scourers? Someone wanting to help them by leaving a door open for them?"

"Impossible. Can't be that. Only candidates are the McClouds, and Temperance has been fighting alongside us, while Jane

McCloud's got no reason to side with the Scourers and every reason not to. This is something else."

"I'll find out what's going on."

"Do that, Zoë. And hurry. We don't got much longer before the ship's crawling with Scourers."

Sitting Ducks Shooting at Sitting Ducks

Zoë scaled the ladder to the hatch, her Mare's Leg poised. She nudged the hatch open and peered out.

"*Wǒ de mā hé tā de fēng kuáng de wài sheng*," she breathed. *Holy mother of God and all her wacky nephews.*

Lying on the apex of *Serenity*'s observation dome were River and Jane. Neither was looking Zoë's way. Both had guns, and Jane, for some reason, was wearing Jayne's repulsive hat.

The two girls had been keeping an eye on the Scourers who were busy climbing onto the ship.

Now they were getting ready to start shooting at them.

In theory, taking potshots at the Scourers from the observation dome wasn't a bad plan. It was high ground. The Scourers were sitting ducks.

In practice, however, it was madness. The observation dome was also *exposed* ground. It made River and Jane sitting ducks themselves.

Zoë knew that as soon as they opened fire, they would draw attention to their position. The Scourers surrounding the ship would spot them immediately and start shooting back.

She hissed out a warning—shouting might have alerted the Scourers—but neither River nor Jane heard. Jane was sighting down a pistol, aiming at a Scourer on *Serenity*'s port wing.

Zoë scrambled out of the hatchway and crawled up the slope of the observation dome on her hands and knees. The gradient was too steep, and the hull tiles too slippery, for normal walking.

Jane loosed off a shot. She clipped the Scourer's arm. He staggered backwards and tumbled off the wing.

Jane whooped and high-fived River.

Then it was River's turn. Of all the weapons she could have gotten ahold of, she was using Jayne's very own Vera. She handled the ungainly rifle like a pro. One eye to the scope. Finger curled round the trigger. Body relaxed. Breath coming easy and slow.

Zoë would have been impressed if she hadn't been so desperately trying to reach the two girls.

River squeezed the trigger. The report from Vera was ear-splitting.

A Scourer's head vanished in a red mist.

That was the moment, just as Zoë finally drew level with River and Jane, that return fire came their way. The Scourers had pinpointed the whereabouts of the two snipers. Unable to get a clear view of them, they didn't realize that these were the two young women Shem was keen to capture alive. All they saw was a threat to be neutralized.

Bullets assailed the girls' position from both sides of the ship, an upward-angled crossfire.

Zoë grabbed Jane by the arm.

"Back to the hatch! Stay low!"

Jane looked startled by the sudden counterattack. It simply had not occurred to her that the Scourers might retaliate.

Zoë shoved her towards the hatch.

"You too, River," she said.

"I can take out more of them," River protested.

"You can also get your gorramn head blown off. Move!"

Jane was now at the hatchway. River slithered down the dome after her, still clutching Vera. Zoë, meanwhile, laid down suppressing fire to the right and left with her Mare's Leg.

When both girls were safely back inside *Serenity*, Zoë thrust herself backwards. She kept blasting away with the Mare's Leg even as she slid feet-first down the dome towards the hatch. A Scourer bullet passed over her head so close that it ruffled her hair.

She fell through the hatchway, landing on the floor below in a less-than-graceful manner. Then she darted up the ladder, slammed the hatch shut and locked it.

She rounded on River and Jane.

"What in the name of God were you up to?" she barked. "Were you trying to get yourselves killed?"

"It seemed like a good idea," said Jane.

"River, I'd have expected better from you."

"Two more Scourers downed," River said simply. "Twenty-three to go."

"Even so," said Zoë. "We have the situation under control. Last thing we need is the two of you getting all gun-happy on us and acting like idiots. You have no idea how much danger you were in up there."

"I do," said River. "It was quite a bit."

"You call *this* 'under control,' Zoë?" said Jane with a sneer. She gesticulated wildly around her. "Your ship is about three minutes away from being invaded. The Scourers are gonna break in, and then you'll be fightin' 'em in the corridors and cabins, door to door, and you'll keep retreating and they'll just keep on coming until all of us are dead."

"We're a great deal more combat-savvy than you give us credit for, Jane."

"You and Mal maybe. You're both war vets. But the rest of the crew are civilians. So are me and my mom. We're lookin' at a massacre here. You can't blame me and River for getting proactive. Doing something beats just sittin' on our asses waiting to die."

Zoë saw the look flashing in Jane's blue eyes. She knew that look. That particular brand of petulant defiance. She'd seen it numerous times in another pair of blue eyes, those of Jane's father. There was a heck of a lot of Jayne Cobb in Jane McCloud. Perhaps more than was good for her.

"'Sides," Jane added, "you can't tell me what to do. You're not my mother."

"Yes, but *I* am," said a voice from behind Zoë.

Temperance. She had appeared at the entrance to the short passageway that led to the EVA hatch.

"And I am sorely disappointed in you, young lady," Temperance went on. "Zoë just risked her neck to save you. Least you can do is show some contrition."

"Butt out, Mom. This ain't your business. Anyway, how do you know what Zoë and me have been sayin' to each other?"

"Ain't as if you've been quiet with your arguin'. Your voices are carrying clean halfway across the ship. I thought I raised you better than to pull off the kinda damn-fool stunt you just did."

"Miz McCloud…" River began.

Temperance held up a shushing index finger. "Not now, River. This is somethin' Jane and I need to sort out."

"Why?" Jane snapped. "Why bother to sort out *anything*? We're all about to die, Momma. Don't you get it? That's best-case scenario. Worst-case, I end up a rut-doll for the Scourers. I'm well aware that's what'll happen if they get their paws on me. Girl my age, I'm prime meat for them. Honestly? If I'd gotten myself killed topside just now, I'd have been doing myself a favor."

"Don't you talk like that, girl," said Temperance.

"You know I'm right. Most we can hope for in the circumstances, any of us, is a quick death."

"Not gonna happen," said Zoë. "Not on my watch."

"Zoë?" said Mal over her comms handset. "How's it going back over that-a-way? Heard shooting. Sounded like your gun, among others. Everyone okay?"

"All fine, sir," Zoë replied. "We had us a hairy moment or two, but everyone's intact and accounted for."

"The hatch?"

"Shut tight."

"You discover why it was open?"

Zoë eyed River and Jane. "Nothing to worry yourself about. Just a… minor mishap. Settled now."

"Nice to know," said Mal. "For what it's worth, I think we can expect some loud knockin' at the front door any moment now."

Taking Hits

Mal looked out of the viewing ports once more.

The Scourer with the RPG launcher—which, to Mal's relief, appeared to be the only other RPG launcher the Scourers owned—had been having some trouble with the weapon. It seemed that the warhead end of the grenade had not been aligning correctly with the trigger mechanism. He'd had to slide the projectile out of the launcher and readjust the assembly of the booster and the sustainer motor, screwing the one more firmly into the other.

Now it was all fixed and ready for action. The inevitable had merely been delayed. He hoisted the launcher back onto his shoulder.

"Think *Serenity* can take the hit?" Wash said.

"You tell me. You're the pilot."

"She can take it. I'm sure she can. Nothing's built as solid as a Series-Three Firefly."

But even as he said this, Wash was backing away from the viewing ports.

The RPG launcher briefly sprouted a fiery tail.

There was a *bang*. A fluting *poont* sound.

Next instant, an enormous explosion shook the bridge. Flame filled the viewing ports from end to end.

Then there were billows of smoke, and when those cleared, Mal and Wash were delighted to note that the glass was unbroken and more or less unblemished. Black scorch marks here and there, but not a crack to be seen.

"Ha!" Wash exclaimed, jumping up and down. "Didn't even scratch the paintjob. Take that, bozo!"

"He's gonna try again," Mal remarked.

The Scourer was already reloading.

"Times like these," Mal sighed, "I really wish this ship had cannons."

Jayne was leaning against the frame of the infirmary door when the first RPG struck. The impact reverberated throughout *Serenity*, making her groan like a cracked, tuneless gong. Jayne was jolted and nearly fell over. Gripping the door frame, he shoved himself off and staggered towards the cargo bay.

When a second RPG struck, he had nothing to hold onto. His knees buckled. He collapsed to the floor.

That was where Simon found him, lying in a crumpled heap, mewling like a kitten.

Simon picked him up and coaxed him back to the med couch, meanwhile giving a lecture about healing and the care of injuries that Jayne barely even heard.

There were now a dozen Scourers on the ship, and more coming. Two had made it as far as the EVA hatch. One had begun working a crowbar under the hatch's rim.

Two more were attempting to break into the spare shuttle, taking it in turns to batter the external door with a sledgehammer. Another Scourer was prowling purposefully around Inara's shuttle with an ax.

A third rocket-propelled grenade finally marred one of the

viewing ports. A few cobweb-thin fractures appeared in the glass.

At this and every other potential ingress point one of the crew lay in wait, poised to start shooting the moment a Scourer got through.

It seemed only a matter of time before *Serenity*'s integrity was compromised, and then, sure as night follows day, a close-range indoor firefight would ensue.

Mal, still on the bridge, squared his jaw. Escaping in Inara's shuttle remained their last resort if *Serenity* fell to the Scourers. He hated the idea of abandoning his ship, but if the bandits overran her, there'd be no alternative.

He would make them pay dearly for their success, though. He'd be shooting the bastards right up until the shuttle took off.

This thought, and the meager consolation it provided, sat uppermost in Mal's mind as he watched the Scourer with the RPG launcher take aim for a fourth time. Mal was feeling the impacts of the grenades as though they were punches to his own face. He took the assault on *Serenity* that personally.

He braced himself for the next blow.

It did not come.

The Scourer lowered the launcher. He was looking round, puzzled. It was as though someone had told him to hold fire.

A moment later, a small personal transport hovercraft hauled into view. Aboard it were a driver and three others. One of the three was some random Scourer. The other two were Elias Vandal and Mayor Gillis.

Gillis sat slumped, disconsolate. The Scourer had a gun to the Mayor's head.

Vandal, by contrast, stood erect and was looking very pleased with himself.

Bad Blood

The hovercraft drew to a halt a short distance in front of *Serenity*. Its rubber skirts sagged outward as they deflated.

Vandal picked up a loudhailer.

"Reynolds, I know you can hear me in there. Look who I came across, wanderin' around Coogan's Bluff like a little lost sheep. Pal of yours. Say howdy to Mr. Reynolds, Mayor Gillis."

Gillis lofted a hand dejectedly.

"Now," Vandal continued, "the Mayor and I, we've arrived at an understanding. He says he doesn't wanna die—and who can blame him for that?—and I've promised him he won't, not today. But on one condition. Want me to tell you what the condition is?"

Vandal cupped a hand behind an ear.

"Can't hear you, Reynolds. You got an external speaker on that boat. Now'd be the time to use it. Reynolds? Come on. You really want this nice, harmless fella's death on your conscience?"

Mal picked up the intercom handset and flicked the feed switch from INTERIOR to EXTERIOR.

"All right, Vandal," he said. His amplified voice resounded outside the ship. "So you have a hostage. Big deal. Ain't as if the Mayor and I are best buddies. Gotta be honest with you, I've found

237

him something of a pain in the ass this past couple days. Don't rightly care what you do with him. Kill him, don't kill him—don't make no nevermind with me."

"Oh, I think that's very much a lie, Reynolds," said Vandal. "I don't think you could abide my man spattering the Mayor's brains all over the ground, not when you could've done something to prevent it. This is one of those situations where you can bluff all you want but we both know you've got a busted flush and I'm holdin' aces. Time to fold."

"You ain't yet said what you're after in exchange for Gillis's life."

"Haven't I? How remiss of me. Just surrender. That's it. I want you to come on out of that ship, you and your crew, every last one of you, with your hands in the air and not a firearm in sight. Sound reasonable?"

"You must know I'm gonna say no."

"And *you* must know that weren't the answer I was looking for."

Vandal gestured, and the Scourer ground the muzzle of his gun into Gillis's skull. Gillis cringed and bared his teeth in terror.

"I'll give you one last chance," Vandal said.

"How's that shoulder of yours?" Mal said. "Betcha it's givin' you grief."

"Don't make me do this, Reynolds. It's gonna be a scene that replays in your mind's eye from now on, whenever you try to go to sleep. It's gonna keep you awake long past midnight, every night. For months to come, maybe years, you'll be hearing the gunshot and seeing the mess it made, over and over again."

Vandal wasn't far wrong there. Mal had witnessed many deaths in his lifetime, caused a fair few of them himself. Not all stuck with him, but some did. Some he couldn't forget, no matter how he tried. The ones that weren't justified. The ones where innocents suffered. The ones he could have prevented.

A light flashed on the piloting console. The screen showing a side-elevation schematic of *Serenity* indicated that the cargo ramp was in operation.

"Who in hell…?" Mal breathed.

He dropped the intercom handset and sprinted out of the bridge. He hurtled down the steps into the cargo bay.

The ramp was lowering, almost fully open. Mal glimpsed someone striding down it as it completed its descent.

Temperance McCloud.

He called out her name, and she must have heard, but she kept on going without so much as a twitch of the head. She appeared to be unarmed.

Gorramn her! What was she playing at? Was she going to surrender to Vandal unilaterally? This was crazy! This was not part of any plan!

He hurried after her.

Temperance moved fast, however. She knew Mal was in pursuit and she clearly had no wish to be diverted from the path she was on.

He caught up with her just as she was presenting herself in front of Vandal's hovercraft.

"Well, well, well," Vandal said to Temperance. "What have we here? You don't look like one of Reynolds's people. You look local. Oh, and here comes Reynolds himself. Rushin' to join you like a gallant knight. So I guess the decision's been made for you, huh, Reynolds? Got no choice now. The die is cast, yadda yadda."

Scourers, led by Shem Bancroft, swarmed in to surround Mal and Temperance. A dozen cocked guns were pointed at them.

"Hey, Shem," Vandal said.

"Boss."

"Your face. What happened?"

"*They* happened," Shem said, sweeping an arm angrily at Mal, Temperance and *Serenity*.

"All messed up down one side," said Vandal. "You ain't careful, you'll end up lookin' like me."

239

"Worse people to look like."

"Spoken like a true sycophant."

"Thanks, Vandal." Shem, it appeared, did not know what *sycophant* meant. Or if he did, he knew better than to answer back when his leader insulted him.

Vandal turned to Mal again. "I presume the rest of your crew'll be comin' out shortly. This little standoff is over. Somebody's won, and it ain't you."

"Elias," Temperance said. "I'm surprised at you."

"Huh? Surprised at what, lady? And why're you calling me Elias? Don't nobody get to do that. Not without my say-so."

"It's the hat. Got to be. Maybe if I take it off…"

She removed her broad-brimmed headgear.

The effect on Vandal was instantaneous and remarkable.

His jaw dropped. His eyes grew large as saucers. He lost a considerable amount of his puff and swagger.

"No," he said, aghast. "It can't… You can't be…"

"But I am," said Temperance. "You didn't recognize me in town yesterday. I don't think you even noticed me. But I recognized you. I don't forget a face—even one that's changed so much."

"I don't forget a face neither," Vandal snarled. "Least of all yours, Temperance Jones."

Mal stared at Temperance. Then at Vandal. Then at Temperance again.

"You… know him?" he said to her.

"From a long time ago," she replied. "Thetis is the last place I'd have expected him to turn up."

"And you didn't realize it was the same person, this old acquaintance of yours, who's head of the gang that's been tearing up the place? Not until you saw him yesterday?"

"Back when I knew him, he went by a slightly different name, like I did. Elias was his first name but his surname wasn't Vandal. I never saw a picture of Elias Vandal, only ever heard about him. Had no reason to put two and two together until he was right there before me, in the flesh. Should've made the connection before then, maybe, but didn't. Same goes for him, it'd seem."

"And when were you plannin' on telling us about this?"

"I'm telling you now, ain't I, Captain Reynolds?"

"Could've been sooner. Sooner might've been helpful."

"It wasn't necessary before. Now it is."

Vandal was recovering from his astonishment. "You got a heck of a nerve, Temperance Jones, showing yourself," he said. "After all that happened. You can't think I'd be any too pleased to see you."

"On the contrary. I'm countin' on you being none too pleased. That way, you'll listen when I tell you to take me prisoner. Not anyone else from the ship. Just me. Because of the bad blood between us."

"Bad blood?" Vandal gave a hoarse, cracked laugh. "Too damn right there's bad blood. You want to know what this woman did to me, Reynolds?"

"Sniggered when you dropped your pants in front of her?"

"Ha ha, very funny. Nope. You are looking at the person I hate most in the entire 'verse."

Vandal indicated the ruined side of his face.

"Temperance gave me this, and as you can imagine, that ain't endeared her to me. No way, no how. Although in a sense I should be grateful to her. She made me the man I am. I should be grateful in another sense, too, because the bitch has just offered herself up to me on a plate, and boy, am I gonna take advantage of that."

Vandal ordered some of the Scourers to keep their guns trained on Mal. The rest he told to pat Temperance down for weapons, then bring her to him. They marched her over to the hovercraft and made her get aboard. Mal, encircled by firearms, could do nothing to intervene.

"I got me *two* captives now, Reynolds," Vandal gloated, nodding at Temperance and Mayor Gillis. "You could call them my insurance policy. You come after me, and a terrible badness will occur to one or other of them, and it will be on your head."

Temperance fixed Mal's gaze with her own. "Listen to him, Captain Reynolds. You do as he says. Whatever else happens now, I want you to promise me something. You'll look after everyone on your ship. *Everyone.*"

Mal understood what she meant. Temperance was not going to admit in Vandal's hearing that there was somebody closely related to her aboard *Serenity*. That would undoubtedly put Jane in jeopardy. Nonetheless she was asking Mal—telling him—to take care of her daughter.

"I will do exactly that," he said with a nod. "Rely on it."

"And you," Temperance said to Vandal. "You've just got a bonus you weren't expecting. Me. I know it's made your day."

"It most assuredly has," Vandal said.

"So then, in return, you leave these people be. You let them go on their way. That's only fair. They don't bother you no more, and you and your Scourers don't bother them none either. How's that sound?"

"It sounds like a bargain you ain't in any position to make, Temperance Jones."

"Ain't Jones these days. It's McCloud."

"Whatever. Look around you. See these dead bodies? And these here Scourers all torn up and bloodied and sorry-looking? You're askin' the fella whose people have just taken a severe pounding to have pity on the folks responsible. That ain't likely."

"You can be lenient," Temperance insisted. "You can afford to be. Remember who I am. The woman who disfigured you. For your information, I'm also the woman who invited Captain Reynolds and his crew to Thetis. *I'm* to blame for everything that's happened since. *I'm* the one responsible for all the misery in your life. And I'm yours to deal with however you see fit. Reynolds and the rest, they're insignificant by comparison. They're nothing."

Vandal rubbed a knuckle against his scrubby chin. Slowly he came to a decision.

"Okay. I reckon I can see my way to acceptin' that. Reynolds? Here's your one-time-only offer. Get your ship mended and get off this planet. You ain't never gonna receive a kindness like this from me again, and it's only because, like Temperance says, having her in my clutches has made my gorramn day. So long! We won't be seein' one another again."

The hovercraft's skirts inflated with an enormous roar of blasting air. Its fans spun to a blur, and shortly it was scudding off across the plain, bearing Vandal and his two hostages away.

The remaining Scourers dispersed, keeping their guns trained on Mal until the last possible moment. Shem Bancroft gave him an ironic salute.

Soon Mal was looking at the Scourers' retreating backs and a whole lot of kicked-up dust. And all he could do was grind his teeth in frustration.

"I've Had Enough. This Ends Now."

"I've had enough," Mal said. "This ends now."

He was in the cargo bay, addressing the full complement of his crew, minus Jayne, plus Jane.

"Ain't nothing else for it. We're going to do as Vandal says. Fix *Serenity* and leave. Find another job, keep flying. We're done here. We've tried. We've tried our damnedest. We've taken a licking and we're still standing, and that's a thing for to congratulate ourselves over—but there ain't no point in carryin' on anymore. Inara's friend's security guys, when they come, will do what we can't and liberate Coogan's Bluff. They're two days out, max. The townsfolk can surely hang on for two more days."

"You're giving up, Captain?" said Kaylee.

"No, I ain't," Mal replied firmly. "I'm acknowledging the futility of what we're doing. This is beating your head against a brick wall. Only a fool keeps that up and thinks it's smart, and Ma Reynolds didn't raise any fools. I'm considering not just myself in all this. I'm considering you people too. You're my foremost concern. I can't ask you to push on when it's quite plainly hopeless."

"Don't we have some say in the matter?" said Book.

245

"Yeah," said Kaylee. "Aren't you going to ask us how *we* feel about it?"

"In a word, no," Mal said. "In case you've made the mistake of thinking this ship's a democracy, let me remind you it ain't. There's a clear chain of command and I'm at the top of it."

"Maybe we should take a vote on that."

"And maybe you weren't paying attention, Kaylee, when I said what I said just a second ago about a democracy. You don't have to be okay with my decision. Truth be known, I'm none too proud of it myself. But it's what's sensible and practical, and in my mind that makes it right."

"And my mom?" said Jane. She sounded small and sad. "What about her, Mr. Reynolds? You're just going to let Vandal have his way with her?"

"Yeah," said Kaylee. "Come on, Mal. You told us he called Temperance the person he hates most in the entire 'verse. The man's a beast." She shuddered. "I can't even begin to imagine what he's going to do to her. We may not be able to help all of the people in Coogan's Bluff but we can surely help *one* of them."

"Two of them," said Book, "counting Mayor Gillis."

"If I'd been there when Vandal got ahold of Mom," Jane said accusingly, "I'd've gotten involved. I'd've fought tooth and nail to prevent him."

"But you *weren't* there, Jane," Mal said. "You didn't have about a million Scourers aiming guns at your head. And if you had been there, right now you'd be sitting alongside your mother in that hovercraft, 'cause Vandal would have figured out you were her daughter and he'd have nabbed you too. Didn't I make it clear? She knew what she was about when she stepped out of the ship. She's bought us all our lives. Maybe at the expense of her own, I don't know. But you need to remember that and you need to accept it."

If looks were javelins, Mal would have been speared through the heart by the one Jane directed at him then.

"Listen to me, girl," he said. "Your mother, as they were taking her away, told me to look after everyone on this ship. Meaning you, Jane, specifically. Temperance McCloud has done something brave— possibly the bravest thing I've seen someone do—and the best and only way to honor her sacrifice is to honor the conditions it came with. If I were her and I gave instructions like they were my last will and testament and then they were disobeyed, I'd be more'n a mite pissed."

"And Gillis?" said Book. "I don't mean to harp on about him, Mal, but he didn't surrender to Vandal the way Temperance did. Vandal forced him to be a bargaining chip at the point of a gun."

"Everybody, you nagged at me to come to Thetis. You insisted. You used every form of persuasion at your disposal." Mal shot a glance at Inara, who parried it with an unrepentant look of her own. "And I caved, and here we now are, and see what good it's done us. I shouldn't have listened to you. It went against my better judgment, not to mention my gut instinct. For that reason, I'm not gonna listen to you now. This is over. Kaylee? Wash? Why are you still standing there? There's a ship's gotta be made shipshape again. Get to it. The rest of you, pitch in where you can or stay out of the way, whichever's more useful."

Mal exited the cargo bay to a resounding silence.

The crew, generally, were not happy about the choice he'd made. That was obvious. Even Zoë, who knew how to take orders. She didn't have to say anything. She had a certain expression she would adopt to let Mal know she wasn't going to object but she was still disgruntled. It had been there on her face the whole time he'd been talking.

Well, that was just tough titty. Mal himself wasn't happy about the choice he'd made either.

But he'd made it, and that was that. End of story.

* * *

Some while later, Jane McCloud crept into the infirmary.

Jayne, on the med couch, did not know what to do with his face. Should he look pleased to see her? Wary? Anxious? He felt all of those things and more besides.

How did you act around a daughter you'd only just met and never known you had?

"Umm, so, hey," he said. "How're you doing?"

"Not great." Jane seemed as antsy in Jayne's company as he was in hers. "You?"

"Same. You have my hat on."

Jane touched her head. She looked like she'd forgotten the hat was there. "Oh yeah. You mind?"

"Anyone else, I might. You, I can't really, can I?"

"Want it back?"

"Not right now. Got no use for it while I'm stuck lying here."

Jane shuffled her feet. "You heard, I guess. 'Bout my mom and everything. What she's gone and done."

"Yeah. The Doc told me. Temperance—your mother—she's got some balls, I'll say that for her. I'm sorry, that sounds disrespectful. But you know what I mean."

"I know what you mean. She is one ballsy woman. Always has been. I guess Simon must have also told you that it turns out she and Vandal used to know each other."

"That," Jayne said, "I'm havin' a little trouble adjusting to."

"Me also. I always thought she had some kind of past, mainly because she hardly ever speaks about it. I just didn't think someone like *him* would be a part of it."

"She's surely full of surprises," Jayne said. "But seeing as I'm a part of her past too, maybe it isn't such a stretch."

"You're not like him. You're nothing like him."

Jayne had a feeling he was more like Elias Vandal than even he dared to admit.

He said, "So, uh… What're you gonna do now?"

"Huh?"

"With your mom bein'… well, bein' at Vandal's mercy and all."

"Do? Ain't much I *can* do, is there?" Sullen resentment bristled in Jane's voice like a porcupine's quills. "Your captain's mind's made up. He's callin' it quits. Don't matter what I feel or anyone else feels. Mom's on her own now."

"Mal's kinda headstrong," Jayne said. "But maybe he has a point. You've got to know when to keep on plugging away and when you're defeated."

"You saying that just to back him up or because you think it's true?"

Jayne frowned. "Actually, I'm not sure."

"You're my father," Jane said.

"So it transpires."

"Kind of weird."

"Am I?"

"No, it feels kind of weird. Meetin' my daddy after all this time. Must feel weird for you too, meetin' your daughter."

"Can't say it doesn't."

"We have some catching up to do."

"Thirteen years' worth."

Neither of them, however, could think how to go about that. They just looked at each other awkwardly.

"Here's the thing," Jane said eventually. "I'm going after Mom to rescue her. I'm gonna sneak into the Scourers' camp and break her out."

Jayne shook his head. "I don't think that's a good idea."

"I don't care what you think."

"I'm just sayin' you're liable to get yourself—"

"I'm not interested in what you have to say, Jayne," said Jane. "I'm not seeking your approval or your opinion or any of that. I certainly don't want any paternal advice from you. You're not qualified, is what it is."

Jayne was somewhat relieved. He himself didn't think he was qualified. To be all father-like to your child, you had to at least have spent time with that child, didn't you? Years, not just a couple days.

"Then why are you telling me?" he said.

"Because I realize I can't go it alone," Jane said. "My mother was someone to you, wasn't she? Someone special."

"You could say that."

"And Vandal, he's going to kill her. Kill her slow. Slow and awful."

Jane's voice was close to cracking. She took a breath, mastered herself.

"If you could," she said, "you'd make sure he didn't. You know you would."

Jayne hesitated, then nodded.

"So I'm asking you, Jayne. I'm begging you. Come with me. Help me out."

Jayne nearly said, *Have you seen me? Can't you tell the state I'm in? I can barely gorramn walk. I'm about as much use right now as a fart in a garbage chute.*

But Jane McCloud was his daughter. His *daughter*. She was looking to him for help. Imploring him to save her mother's life. She was even wearing the hat his own mother had knitted. Like it belonged on her. Like she was meant to have it. A family heirloom or some such.

What choice did he have?

"Okay," Jayne said. "Okay, dammit. You and me, Jane, let's get your mom back. It's high time I got up off my butt and did something anyway. Man can only be benched for so long."

Analgesics and Amens

Simon dropped by to check on Jayne last thing before he turned in for the night.

"Got all you need? Comfortable?"

"Managing. Well, kinda. It's just… the pain, Doc. It's pretty bad."

Jayne grimaced and did a bit of eye-rolling, to get the point across. It was theatrics, but not entirely. "Not sure I can make it through the whole night without something to help," he said.

Simon fetched a bottle of pills out from a drawer. "Got some analgesics here."

Jayne was alarmed. "Anal what now? Don't want me none of them suppositories. Nothing's going up *my* butt."

"Sometimes, Jayne, I can't tell whether you're joking or you genuinely mean the things you say. Analgesics. It's another word for painkillers. Take one at a time—one only—as and when the pain flares up. That should see you right."

"Gotcha. Thanks, Doc."

"Goodnight, Jayne. Sleep well."

"'Night."

When Simon had gone, Jayne popped three of the pills, dry-swallowing them. He took a fourth, for good measure. If one was

251

effective, four would be four times as effective, right?

Then it was just a case of waiting until Jane appeared.

She came shortly after eleven o'clock. By that time *Serenity* was completely quiet. The crew were tucked up in their bunks, most likely asleep.

By that time, too, Jayne was pain-free and in an exceedingly good mood. He felt as though he could dance a jig. Everything in the infirmary was dazzlingly bright and fascinating. The world was, in every sense, shiny.

"You're pretty," he told Jane. "Pretty as your mom was when I first met her."

"Uh, thanks?" said Jane.

"Not that Temp ain't pretty now, but there's pretty when you're young and then there's pretty when you're older, which ain't *pretty* pretty but still's pretty. If you see what I mean."

"Not sure as I do." A small vertical crease formed between Jane's eyebrows. "Are you feeling okay, Jayne?"

"Okay? Fine. Dandy. Never better."

"Right. Only you're acting a bit... off."

"Eager, is all. Eager to get going." Jayne brisked his palms together. "We're gonna get you your mother back, Jane. That's a good thing."

They retrieved weapons from Jayne's bunk. They were as stealthy as could be, but even so Jayne kept putting a finger to his lips and going "Sshhh" so that Jane wouldn't forget.

Toting Vera and a bunch of other guns besides, they headed down to the cargo bay. Jayne lowered the ramp using the emergency backup manual crank. "Hydraulics make too much noise," he said. "Slower this way but quieter."

Then they took the Mule bike, its trailer now laden with guns, and rolled it by hand down the ramp and out into the night air. They were pushing it away from the ship when a figure stepped out of the darkness into a shaft of moonlight to confront them.

"Going somewhere?"

"Shepherd?" said Jayne.

Shepherd Book cast a speculative eye over the two of them. "Looks like you're taking a little trip. Wouldn't be to the Scourers' camp by any chance?"

"Nope," said Jayne. "Absolutely not. That'd be crazy. Why would you even say that?"

"Just a hunch," said Book.

"Were you lying in wait out here to catch us? Did Mal put you up to this?"

"Mal thought somebody ought to be on lookout, in case Vandal sent some of his Scourers to mount a sneak attack. I volunteered. Vandal's not the kind of man you can trust to keep his word. I'd say his mind was changeable, to put it mildly. Of course, Mal didn't reckon on anybody *leaving* the ship."

"You'd best get out of our way, Shepherd."

"Come now, Jayne. There's no call for threats. What makes you think I'm going to stop you?"

"I just assumed."

"And assumption is the mother of all foul-ups," Book said. Gently, almost lovingly, he patted the corrugated faring over one of the Mule bike's front wheels. "You and Jane, you're embarking on a rescue mission, in deliberate contravention of Mal's orders. One can regard that as either mutinous or noble. Me, I err on the side of noble. Why do you think I volunteered for watch duty? It wasn't because I enjoy missing a night's sleep. It was because I had a feeling someone might try something like this. And by 'someone' I mean you, Jane, although somehow it doesn't surprise me that you, Jayne, are with her."

"So… You're sayin' you're gonna let us pass?" said Jane.

"I'm getting on in years, my dear. These eyes of mine aren't so good, especially in the dark. Likewise my ears. Could be I was looking the other way and you snuck by me, and I didn't hear a damn thing."

Book sauntered away, hands behind his back.

"Go with God," he said softly.

"Amen," Jayne said reflexively, as he and Jane started pushing the Mule bike again. Such a funny word, amen. Jayne wasn't even sure what it meant. You just used it at the end of prayers and such, didn't you? Amen. Didn't even think about it. You learned it in Sunday school and it stuck with you, like a habit. Even if you weren't particularly religious anymore, still it was part of your vocabulary.

"Stop saying that," said Jane.

"Saying what?"

"You keep saying 'amen,' over and over."

"Do I?"

"Yeah. Sort of muttering it."

"I wasn't aware."

"Are you sure you're all right, Jayne? Seriously, you're acting so goofy. I know I don't know you that well, but your behavior ain't what I'd call normal. If there's something you need to tell me, you'd better tell me now. I mean, if you're having second thoughts..."

"I'm not having second thoughts."

"Can I trust you to be on top of your game?"

"I'm on top of my game. I told you, I ain't felt better. Not in a long while. The Doc gave me these pills."

"What pills?"

"Painkillers. Amnesiacs or somethin'. They've done wonders."

"Let me look at your eyes."

"What for?"

Jane studied his eyes. "Your pupils are majorly dilated."

"Sure they are. It's dark, in case you hadn't noticed. Night vision."

"I think you're high," Jane said. "For heaven's sake, Jayne, you've taken too many of them, haven't you?"

"I've taken enough so's I can do what I need to do. Got a hole in my damn side, girl. Hole in my lung, too. No way I'd be walkin' and talkin' now without pharmaceutical assistance. And maybe I am a little bit squiffy, yes."

"Little bit? You're outta your gourd."

"But," Jayne went on, "it's that or I'd be a screaming basket case, no help to anyone. Without those pills I wouldn't be able to push this machine, for starters. Only have to try and I'd be lying on the ground like a deathly sick dog, pleadin' to be put down. So, you want me with you or not? 'Cause if you do, this is how it has to be."

Jane weighed it up, shrugged. "As if I have a choice."

"Attagirl."

Jayne reached out to pat her head, like fathers did with their children.

"Nope." Jane swatted his hand aside. "You don't get to do that."

"Aww."

A short while later, Jane said, "We have to be far enough away from the ship that we can fire up the motor on this thing now." She was panting hard from the exertion.

Jayne glanced back. *Serenity*, her hull glinting in the moonlight, was so small he could obscure her from sight by raising one thumb.

"You're right."

He made to sit behind the bike's controls, but Jane shunted him to one side.

"No, you don't," she said. "You're riding shotgun. *I'm* driving."

Brimstone Gulch

Two hours' journey across the undulating plain saw Jayne and Jane nearing a ridge of low hills. By then the moon had set, but the stars were so plentiful that even with the loss of the moon's silvery glow the headlights on the Mule bike weren't required.

The terrain became rugged, its ups and downs steeper and more frequent. Jayne began to feel pain in his side again, little electric shocks as the bike went jarringly over rocks and crevices. He chugged down another of the pills, and soon his body was sunbeams and rainbows once more. He studied the girl he was with as she guided the vehicle on its way by means of deft twists of the throttle and flicks of the handlebars. She was confident. She had spunk. What's more, his hat looked good on her—better, even, than it looked on him.

Yeah, he could see himself growing to like this kid a lot. He could even see himself staying on Thetis after all this Scourer business was over, helping to raise Jane, shepherd her through to womanhood. Perhaps he and Temperance could give it another shot. He could handle the life of a homesteader, couldn't he? Wasn't as if jaunting around the 'verse in *Serenity* was such a barrel of laughs. They just seemed to get themselves into one scrape after another, almost on a weekly basis. Might be it was time he tried something else, something different. Gave himself the chance to take things easy. He reckoned he deserved it.

Or was that just the medication talking?

Eventually the going got so rough that even the Mule bike began to struggle, tires slipping on the gravelly, rock-strewn slopes, unable to get a good grip.

Jayne tapped Jane on the shoulder. "How much further?"

"They're holed up in Brimstone Gulch. That's about another three or four miles on."

"We should stop and go the rest of the way on foot. Engine sound's gonna carry, even more so at night than during the day. Don't want the Scourers to know we're coming, and, you keep having to rev her like you are, they're gonna know."

Jane shut off the motor and the bike coasted to a halt. The chirruping of cicadas filled Jayne's ears, sweet music after the bike's burring rumble.

They loaded themselves up with as much ordnance as they could carry and began the final leg of the trek to the Scourers' camp, Jane leading the way. She was more surefooted than he. Several times Jayne stumbled. It wasn't so much that he was clumsy, more that his gaze kept straying up to the stars rather than fixing on where he was treading. Their glittering brilliance was just so irresistibly alluring. It was odd how, when you were travelling among them in a spaceship, you didn't really pay them any mind. You even kind of took them for granted, those steady points of light outside the portholes. But when you were on-planet, all at once they gained a fascination and a luster like they were thousands of diamonds spread out for you to admire. Jayne wasn't normally a man prone to contemplation, but he wondered why that phenomenon was. Perhaps it was the same way that the sea looked exciting and mysterious from the shore but when you were out in a boat, water all around you, it became just sea.

"There," Jane said.

Jayne wasn't sure how long they had been walking. It certainly didn't feel as though they had gone three or four miles. It seemed a shorter distance than that. Or longer. He couldn't say. But they had arrived at the edge of a sandstone cliff, and below them lay a ravine. The base of the ravine was dotted with tents—dozens of them, maybe as many as a hundred—and intermittently between them the embers of campfires glowed. Here and there, horses stood at tether, heads drooping.

Jayne invited Jane to hunker down so that they wouldn't stand out, silhouetted against the stars. He scanned the scene, taking stock. He soon found what he was looking for. A couple of the tents were larger than the rest. One in particular looked like the kind of tent a boss man would have for himself. The clincher was the horse tied up outside. Jayne recognized it. The black stallion on which Vandal had ridden into Coogan's Bluff. There wasn't another horse like it in the camp.

"He'll be in there," he said to Jane, singling out the tent for her attention. "Vandal. And if he's there, that'll be where your mom is too. Maybe Gillis as well. So that's where we hit."

"Okay. So, just to be clear, we're gonna sneak into the camp, get to that tent, get Mom, get out."

"That's the general idea." Jayne, recalling how the Scourers had a penchant for doing unspeakable things to young girls, paused to consider whether he ought to let Jane accompany him into the camp. What if they got caught? Wouldn't that just be handing her over to the exact same fate her mother had saved her from? But he knew Jane wasn't going to stay behind willingly, and he couldn't force her to. They had come this far already. They were committed to seeing things through to the end, together. "What's important is we don't shoot unless we have to. I'm not seeing any perimeter guards. My guess is the camp's mostly empty. The majority of the Scourers are over in town, enforcing the lockdown there. As long as we don't raise a ruckus, odds are good we'll infil and exfil with no trouble."

"What about Vandal himself?"

"You leave him to me. Bastard took me down last time by being guileful and underhand. I'm gonna return the favor. If I end up cutting his throat while he's asleep, he's only got hisself to blame."

They set off along the cliff edge until they came to a section that had crumbled away, creating a spill of scree that descended into the ravine at a shallow gradient. As they picked their way down, Jane heard Jayne humming a tune.

"What's that song?" she whispered.

"What?"

"The song you're humming."

"I was humming? Oh yeah, so I was. It's called 'Hero of Canton.' You want to know what it's about?"

"No," said Jane. "I want to not hear you humming. Aren't we supposed to be being all surreptitious-like?"

"You have a point. Schtum from here on. Mum's the bloomin' word, mate."

"Was that… an attempt at some sort of accent?"

"No?"

But it had been. He'd been trying to speak like the black marketeer Badger. For some unknown reason.

Careful, Jayne. Maybe you are *in danger of losing it. Focus.*

A prickle of adrenaline started in his gut as they reached the edge of the camp. That was good. The adrenaline sharpened him, helping to disperse some of the waftiness the painkillers had brought to his thought processes, like sunlight burning off mist.

As they ventured into the camp, Jayne took point, treading slowly, toe-to-heel, with Vera held at port arms. Jane followed in his shadow. A horse snorted as they passed. Jayne patted its mane reassuringly. More than once they stole by a tent whose occupant was snoring so loudly, it drowned out any sound they made. So loudly, in fact, that they could have been a marching band and nobody would have noticed.

Soon they were nearing the large tent. This had been easy. Jayne was just beginning to think it had been a mite *too* easy when, as if to prove his point, the flap of the tent started to open.

Jayne held up a fist, then jabbed a finger downward.

Jane, though unfamiliar with military hand signals, got the gist.

They both sank into a crouch, sidling behind one of the normal-size tents. Jayne leveled Vera, resting the elbow of his supporting arm on one thigh. A Callahan full-bore auto-lock's armor-piercing 12-gauge rounds would make a mess of a human target at any distance but, from barely ten yards away, as here, it'd be more like butchery than assassination. The report, too, would wake up everybody in the camp, sure as a thunderclap. He would fire only as a last resort.

Pushing the tent flap aside, a man stepped out into the open.

Jayne relaxed, letting out the breath he had been holding.

It was Mayor Gillis.

He lowered Vera.

"Hsst! Gillis. Mayor Gillis."

Gillis blinked owlishly around him.

"Hey! Over here."

Gillis still seemed unable to ascertain where the voice hissing to him was coming from.

Jayne gesticulated urgently.

"Right here. At your ten o'clock. No, your *other* ten o'clock."

Gillis finally zeroed in to him. His look of surprise rapidly segued into a look of concern. He bustled over, casting nervous glances in all directions.

"What in tarnation are you two doing here?" he said.

"What's it look like?" said Jayne. "We've come to rescue you."

"You and Mom," said Jane.

"Well… I mean… Hell, that's awfully good of you."

"Damn right it is," said Jayne. "How come you were able to just wander out of that tent? I thought you'd have been tied up or something. Did you manage to work yourself free from the ropes?"

"No. Nothing like that. I was stepping out to take a leak, as it happens."

"So, not tied up. How come?"

Gillis gave a hapless shrug. "Elias Vandal tells me to stay put, I stay put. You don't need ropes to restrain someone you know is too scared to defy you. Look at me. I look like the resisting type to you?"

"No."

"Exactly. If Vandal came back and found me gone, he wouldn't rest till he'd gotten ahold of me again. He'd hunt me down like a dog. And he wouldn't treat me at all nice once he caught me."

"Don't seem as if he's treated you too harshly so far," Jayne observed. "I don't see a mark on you."

"That's because he has Temperance to occupy him."

"Where is she?" Jane said. "Is she here?"

The Mayor of Coogan's Bluff shook his head. "Afraid not. She's over in town."

"From the sound of it, Vandal ain't here neither," Jayne said. "I see his horse but not him. He over in town too?"

"That he is," said Gillis. "Didn't ride there. Went by vehicle. He's… Well, Jane, there's no easy way of saying this. He's torturing your mother."

Jane paled. Her lips compressed together.

"Okay," said Jayne. "Then that's where we're headed next. Town." He shouldered Vera by the strap. "Come on. No shilly-shallyin'."

He moved off. Jane fell in step behind him.

Gillis did not.

Jayne stopped and turned. "Gillis. What's keepin' you?"

"Like I said, Mr. Cobb. I leave here, Vandal's going to hunt me down and make me suffer."

"You think he's not gonna make you suffer anyway? Why in hell else is he holding you prisoner? Temperance is the main course. He's just saving you for dessert."

"No, really, I can't…"

Jayne strode over, putting his face right up close to Gillis's. "Now you listen here, pal. Jane and I ain't risked our asses walking into this camp, only to go away empty-handed. You are gonna come with us even if I have to knock you out and carry you over my shoulder."

"When you put it like that…"

They had gone no more than twenty paces when Gillis said, "I really do have to pee."

"You can hold it till we're clear of here," Jayne said.

"I can't. My bladder isn't the strongest. When I've got to go, I've got to go. It'll only take a moment."

Jayne grunted in exasperation. "Quickly, then."

Gillis waddled off behind a tent for privacy. While he fumbled with his fly, Jayne kept watch. They had wasted time already. Too much time. The longer they lingered, the more chance there was of getting caught.

"Hurry it up, Gillis," he growled.

"I'm nervous. Hard to get started when I'm nervous."

"How's about I aim this gun at you? Vera's frightened the piss out of more than a few folk in the past."

"It's coming. Slowly, but it's coming."

There was, at last, a trickling sound, a feeble stream of liquid spattering onto the ground in fits and starts. Shortly, it trailed off.

"There. Done."

"Thank God. On we go."

They were almost out of the camp when Gillis tripped over a

guyrope and fell. The guyrope twanged, and he landed face first in the dirt with a mighty *thump*.

The noise was surely enough to awaken somebody.

And it did. From an adjacent tent, a muffled voice uttered a curse. Jayne saw the tent flap stir. The occupant was coming out to see what the matter was.

Jayne darted over to the tent's entrance. As soon as the inquisitive Scourer's head emerged, he grabbed it with both hands and gave it a violent twist. There was the *crick-crack* of neck bones parting. Jayne carefully lowered the man's lifeless body back inside the tent and closed the flap.

"Do something that ass-achingly dumb again," he said to Gillis, "and so help me, I'll snap your neck too."

Gillis gulped.

They got out of the camp without further incident.

Magic Hat

The sky was brightening in the east but the sun had not yet broken the horizon when Jayne, Jane, and Mayor Gillis reached the outskirts of Coogan's Bluff. They had driven most of the way on the Mule bike but had ditched the vehicle a couple of miles outside town and continued onward on foot.

During this latter part of the journey Gillis had begun bitching and moaning. Among his many gripes was that they were walking towards certain doom. There were more Scourers in the town than at the camp. Talk about out of the frying pan into the fire. They had left behind a place where the prospect of getting killed was relatively low, in order to head to a place where the prospect of getting killed was practically a dead cert. What kind of lunatic did that?

Jayne chose to ignore him, although the temptation to shut him up with a smack in the mouth was strong. He decided to down a couple more of the painkillers. It had been a goodly while since his last dose and not only would more painkillers ease the steadily growing ache in his side, they would help make Gillis's complaining more bearable.

To his great disappointment, Jayne discovered that the bottle was empty save for two pills. Without realizing it, he had guzzled practically the entire supply. Gorramn Simon Tam. Somehow this was his fault. Simon should've given him more of the painkillers to start with. Must've underestimated how many a man of Jayne's size, with Jayne's injuries, might need. Call himself a doctor? Jayne dry-swallowed one. He was in for a rough ride ahead.

As Coogan's Bluff came into view, Jayne asked the Mayor the best way to get into the town undetected.

"There ain't one," came the reply. "The Scourers have got every access point sealed up tight as a bung in a bottle."

"What about the route my mom took to get out?" said Jane. "Worked for her. Would've worked for you too if you hadn't turned back."

"They've got to have plugged that hole by now."

"Maybe so, maybe not. It's worth a try."

"You know where it is, Jane?" said Jayne.

"Of course. Culvert round the north side of town. Part of a gully that acts as a storm drain when it rains. Which it hardly ever does. Ground's so hard, the rain doesn't soak in, so it needs a runoff."

"Then we use that," Jayne said. "Ain't never gonna be a better time for it than now, either. This hour of dawn, people who've been on sentry duty all night are getting tired. They ain't concentratin'. And the light's gray. Makes everything kinda murky and you can see less well than you can even in darkness."

Soon they had entered the gully by the outfall end and were creeping along it. The gully was shallow and flat-bottomed to start with but its sides steepened and grew sheerer the closer they got to town.

As they neared the culvert, Jayne spied two Scourers stationed on the roadway crossing above. He signaled to Jane and Gillis to stay put and carried on alone on all fours. Crawling made his injured flank scream in protest but he ignored it.

One of the Scourers broke out a pack of cigarettes. Jayne grinned to himself. *Amateurs*. The moment you fired up a match or a cigarette lighter in this gloom was the moment your eyesight lost its adaptation to the dimness. You'd be technically blind for several seconds, and wouldn't see an enemy coming until too late.

So it proved. The Scourers lodged cigarettes between their lips, lit them—and it was the last smoke either would ever have. Jayne knifed one of them from behind, then wrestled the other to the ground with a hand clamped over his mouth and skewered him in the gut. The Scourer died with incredulity on his face, berating himself for being such an idiot.

Jayne checked around. No other Scourers to raise the alarm. He dragged the two bodies down into the culvert, then gave Jane and Gillis the all-clear. He popped the very last of the painkillers and tossed the empty bottle aside. He chose to pay no heed to the fact that the dressing over his wound was now damp. He knew what that signified. Thanks to the exertion of killing the two Scourers he had reopened the Doc's incision and it was seeping blood. But so what? The blood would congeal and form a scab. That was how it worked.

The three of them continued along the gully. Jayne was about to ask Gillis where he thought Vandal would be holding Temperance. Then, as if in answer to his unvoiced question, he heard a scream of anguish.

"That's her," said Jane in a chilled whisper. "That's Mom. I know it."

"Me too," said Jayne.

"Oh my God. What's he doing to her?"

"No idea, but her voice came from over there."

"Town square," said Gillis. "Vandal's got her on display. Of course he has. He's making an example of her. He's teaching her a lesson and teaching the whole town one at the same time."

Grim-faced, Jayne picked up speed.

They clambered out of the gully where it ran closest to the town square and loped between buildings until they came to a fence through which they had a more or less unimpeded view of the square.

Jayne cursed under his breath.

The Scourers had built a platform three feet high. On the platform was a box-like structure, a crude wooden cage made of planks. Temperance was inside the cage, standing on tiptoe, her hands fastened behind her back.

The reason she was having to stand on tiptoe was a kind of collar which formed the topmost surface of the cage. It encircled Temperance's neck with a ring of spikes—nine-inch nails—pointing inwards and upwards at such a height and at such an angle that if she sank down onto her heels, the nails dug into her flesh. Her shirt-collar was sodden with blood from several scrapes and gouges in her neck. Jayne had no way of knowing how long she had been made to stand like that but she was plainly exhausted. The effort of remaining on tiptoe was almost too much for her. Her legs wobbled like jelly and kept threatening to give way beneath her. If her legs went altogether, the nails would impale the soft underside of her chin agonizingly— perhaps fatally.

Elias Vandal and a dozen of his Scourers were lounging around the platform, drinking beers and generally enjoying the spectacle. Vandal himself sat in a lawn chair, for all the world as though it was a lazy Saturday afternoon and he had nothing better to do than watch a woman in torment.

Jayne was inclined to put a bullet in him there and then. But that would have the other Scourers returning fire in an instant, and amid all the excitement one of them might think to shoot Temperance.

His other thought was simply to shoot Temperance himself. Put her out of her misery and deprive Vandal of his sick, humiliating sport. But then, too, he would alert the Scourers to his presence—and the presence of Jane and Gillis—and the three of them were unlikely to get out of there alive.

No, he had to be smarter. He had to figure out some strategy that would end up with everyone saved who should be saved and everyone dead who should be dead.

Temperance lost her balance and several of the nails raked her throat, provoking another cry of distress from her. She just about managed to get herself back up onto tiptoe again. The Scourers all roared with laughter, Vandal loudest of all.

"How's it feel, Temperance?" he bellowed. "Huh? Gotta feel pretty bad. Feet aching. Calves cramping up. All those cuts in your neck. But not as bad as it felt havin' my face pressed into a gas burner flame. Let me tell you, bitch, that gorramn *hurt*."

"And you deserved it," Temperance said, choking the words out. "You surely couldn't have thought I'd let you off scot-free. Not after what you'd just done."

"What *I'd* done? Best I recall, we did it together. I mean, you weren't exactly resisting. Seemed to me like you were into it."

"Just goes to show how much you know, asshole."

Jayne sensed Jane stiffening beside him. He was worried she was going to do something rash. He placed a hand on her shoulder, both to calm her and to restrain her.

Think, you moron, he said to himself. *It's all down to you. You have to turn this around somehow.*

It was then that he realized that Mayor Gillis was no longer with them. While he and Jane had been focused on Temperance's plight to the exclusion of all else, the Mayor had slipped off somewhere. Probably back to the gully to get his sorry ass out of town. Gorramn chickenshit. If Jayne ever saw him again, he'd have a thing or two to say to him. Man might not be fighting material, probably couldn't even handle a gun, but you did not just light out on your allies. 'Specially not at the crucial moment.

Well, never mind Gillis for now. Temperance was what mattered.

Jayne studied the lay of the land. An idea began to form in his head. It wasn't much but it was better than nothing.

"Jane. This here is Vera." He proffered her the gun.

"We've met."

"I want you to take her and I want you to get up on that roof there. See the one? On top of that bar."

"Billy Kurosawa's place."

"Yeah. There's crates out back. See 'em? You can pile them up so's to make steps. Roof's nice and flat. You lay yourself on it and you'll have clear range of view across the whole of the square."

"Okay. Sure. Then what?"

"Then you wait for me to do my thing. You're there to give me cover. When the trouble starts—and it will—you set to shooting. I warn you, Vera has a kick on her. You're gonna have to show her who's boss, otherwise she'll get away from you and you won't hit squat. Also, you're gonna have to shoot to kill. No half measures. You're taking out Scourers and you ain't thinking twice about it. Can you do that?"

Jane's face betrayed not a shadow of a doubt. "No problem."

"For what it's worth, you should know that that hat you're wearing, it's my lucky charm. I ain't never missed a shot when I've got it on."

"You don't have to baby me, Jayne."

"I ain't. It's the God's honest truth. That hat is like magic. It makes you, like, a Zen master of sniperdom."

"Well, I guess it's got to be good for something," Jane said, "seeing how butt-ugly it is."

"Do not mock the hat."

"Ain't mocking. Just stating a fact. Smells funny, too. But I like it anyway. A thing don't have to be beautiful to get the job done."

Jayne half-smiled. "Truer words were never spoken. Listen, girl. There's a chance this could all go belly-up. If it looks to you like I'm a goner, not a hope in hell of making it out alive, you just skedaddle. You don't stay and do anything brave. You run like a rabbit till you're back at *Serenity*. Promise?"

"Nuh-uh."

"Promise or nothing's gonna happen and your mom dies."

She saw how deadly serious he was.

"All right, all right."

"'I promise.' Let me hear you say it."

"I promise."

"Good," said Jayne. He began divesting himself of every item of weaponry he had on him, including his knife.

"What are you doing?"

"Getting naked. My equivalent of naked. Got to make the Scourers think I don't mean them no harm. Else I can't get up close and personal with them. One last thing."

Jane looked at him expectantly, warily.

"I ain't much good with words," he said, "nor with any of that 'expressing yourself' malarkey."

"I noticed."

"But I just want to say, if I had a daughter…"

"You do have a daughter."

"Yeah, but a daughter I knowed I had, if that makes sense."

"I think I follow."

"Then I couldn't imagine her turning out better than you have. And I'm thinking, Jane, maybe if we get the chance, we should get to know each other some more."

"I'd like that," Jane said. "Now are we gonna kill us some scumbags and rescue Mom, or what?"

Jayne's heart nearly burst with paternal pride.

The Dumbest, Insanest, Reckless-est Plan Ever

His heart was pounding as he strode towards the square, making the throbbing of his wound that much more acute. This was without a doubt the dumbest, insanest, reckless-est plan he had ever come up with, in a life marked by no lack of such plans. It was like Daniel entering the lions' den. Except Daniel had had the Lord's grace for protection, whereas Jayne Cobb was relying on a slip of a thirteen-year-old girl with a gun that weighed not much less than she did.

Still, Jane McCloud had half his genes. That counted for something. And the other half were Temperance's, which also counted for something.

He was almost at the square when a figure detached itself from the shadows of a front porch to his left. He saw the gun before he saw the man holding it, a Scourer.

A second figure came at him from the right, also with a gun leveled. Perfect pincer movement.

"Best stop right there, big fella," the second Scourer said.

Jayne was irked. This wasn't quite how he'd foreseen things panning out. He'd hoped to walk into the square unmolested. That would at least have looked cool and given the Scourers pause for thought. If nothing else they'd have realized he had a big swinging pair of cods on him.

This way, being taken prisoner, wasn't nearly so impressive. But it would have to do.

"Okay, you got me," he said. "I'm not packing. Feel free to check. I want to talk with Vandal."

"Hands behind your head."

Jayne complied.

"Lace your fingers together."

Again Jayne complied.

Hands frisked him roughly all over.

"You weren't lying," one of the Scourers said.

"I'm good that way," Jayne replied.

There was a blinding flash of light in his brain. A sudden sharp pain at the back of his head. Jayne reeled.

"Shut your mouth," the Scourer said. "Any further smart remarks, keep them to yourself. 'Less you want me to hit you again."

"No." Jayne tasted blood. The blow to his head had made him bite his tongue. He could feel a gun-butt-shaped bruise on the back of his skull starting to swell.

"It's Vandal you want to see, huh?"

"Yep."

"Ain't you the fella he had that fight with?" the Scourer went on. He was a big, shambling lummox of a man with a collage of sticking plasters over one side of his meaty face. He'd been cut up bad, and Jayne reckoned the Shepherd's homespun munitions might well be responsible. "We all thought you were dead."

"Takes more'n a punctured lung to kill me."

"And now you're back for a second helping."

"What can I say? I'm greedy. So, are we gonna stand here yakkin' or are you gonna take me to your leader?"

He anticipated another blow, but none came.

Instead, he took a hit of a different kind.

An emotional gut punch.

Because a third man appeared, moving cautiously into Jayne's line of sight.

Jayne shook his head in disbelief. "Oh, you have got to be *yòng yòu shī yòu ruǎn de yáng jībā dǎ wǒ* joking…"

"Hello again, Mr. Cobb," said Mayor Gillis. "I would have said 'long time no see,' but it isn't, is it?"

Jayne looked from Gillis to the two Scourers and back again, just to make sure that what he thought was going on *was* going on. The Scourers bore no apparent hostility towards Gillis. They weren't regarding him as an opponent or a victim. They were treating him much as though he were one of their own.

"You're with them, ain't you?" Jayne said. "You're on their side."

Gillis at least had the decency to look sheepish.

"Guilty as charged, Mr. Cobb," he said. "Guilty as charged."

Typical Political Type

"How long?" Jayne said. "How long have you been cozying up to these bastards? From when Vandal took you captive? Is that it? You were only pretending to be his hostage, weren't you? Vandal made you an offer you couldn't refuse. You play along so that he could use you as leverage against us, and in return you get to live."

Gillis shook his head. "It's been a mite longer than that. The Scourers and I, we've had what you might call an arrangement since... Since when, Shem?"

The Scourer who had hit Jayne, the one with the sticking plasters, said, "It's been a month or thereabouts."

"Four or five weeks," said the other Scourer.

"That's kinda the same, Grady," said Shem.

"Just trying to be a little more exact."

"There ain't no need."

"You see, Mr. Cobb, I'm a pragmatic man," said Gillis. "Know what that means?"

"Means you're a lyin', cheatin' *hún dàn*. Lower than a snake's vest buttons. Typical political type."

"It means I know which side my bread's buttered on. And when it became clear that Coogan's Bluff was the next town the Scourers had in their sights, I said to myself, 'Huckleberry Ulysses Gillis,' I said, 'you can either stand up to these guys or you can come to some sort of accommodation with them. One way's liable to get you dead, and probably a lot of other folk. The other way's going to ensure you survive and maybe everybody else in town too.' Now, it wasn't as if I was going to be able to convince people to roll over and give in to the Scourers without a fight, necessarily. That was what I wanted, the path of least resistance. But I knew there might be some holdouts, and I could have predicted that Temperance McCloud would be one of them, ornery coot that she is. More to the point, it was important to me that I got on the Scourers' good side from the off. That meant putting myself out there as a go-between, a friendly, agreeable face. Somebody they could do business with."

"Handing them the town on a plate, in other words."

"Giving them viable options," said Gillis. "Providing them with an insider in Coogan's Bluff, someone who could keep them apprised of the situation here so as they'd have some idea what to expect."

"So this was all about making life simple for the Scourers."

"Making the transition as easy as possible, yes. For the Scourers *and* for the majority of the people in this town. In order to avoid another Yinjing Butte."

"But also making sure you had immunity, if things went south."

Gillis half shrugged, half nodded. "Should the Scourers indeed end up inflicting a holocaust on us for whatever reason, like at Yinjing Butte, I wanted a get-out. So one fine evening, shortly after the Scourers had set up camp in Brimstone Gulch, I headed off there. I have to say, it was no mean feat, walking into their midst. I was pretty goshdarned scared. Wasn't I, Shem?"

"You looked nervous as a raccoon at a coonskin hat convention," said Shem.

"I asked to be taken to see Elias Vandal, and I put my case to him, and there was a moment—just a moment—when I thought I'd completely misread what sort of a man he was. He started toying with that knife of his and looking at me all leery, like I was a dog with rabies, and I thought to myself, 'This is it, Huck Gillis. You have well and truly screwed the pooch. Goodbye, cruel world.' You were there, Shem. Didn't Vandal look like he was about to kill me?"

"Cut a few bits off you at the very least."

"But then all of a sudden he smiled and I knew I was in the clear. 'You ain't come to me with much, Mayor,' he said, 'and for that I admire you. It don't look it but there's some backbone there. Aren't many men who'd up-front sell out their own hometown, all in aid of coverin' their own ass.' Which wasn't what I'd done, of course."

"Seems to me it was exactly what you done," said Jayne.

"Well, be that as it may, I had certainly smoothed the way for the Scourers to seize Coogan's Bluff. Who's to say it wouldn't have saved a life or two in the process? And everything looked to be going swimmingly, until Temperance got it into her head to call you offworlders in. She didn't consult me beforehand. Just presented it to me as a done deal. 'Cause that's how she is."

"That is how she is."

"I didn't know whether there'd be any response to her plea or not. Doubted there would be. I told Vandal about it anyway. Mentioned Temperance by name, only of course I didn't know that he and she were hitherto acquainted. He didn't make the connection himself, not then, not until he came face to face with her at your ship. If he *had* realized that the Temperance McCloud I mentioned was the same Temperance he used to know by another name, you can bet he'd have gone round to her place faster'n a greased polecat. Anyways, he found out about her soon enough. The truth came out, and now he's making her pay for what she did to him back when."

Jayne had to restrain himself. Right then he wanted little more than to throttle the life out of the mayor of Coogan's Bluff. But the likely outcome of that was him getting shot dead by the Scourers, which wouldn't help Temperance none. He bit back his anger, stowing it deep down inside him where it might come in handy later.

"Then Vandal and I," Gillis went on, "we staged a little performance. Had us a face-off in front of witnesses at Billy's Bar. Twofold purpose. One: so as there'd be no question that I wasn't colluding with him. Two: to give folk an idea of what to expect if they, maybe inspired by some outside influence, were to challenge him."

"Yeah, that was some acting," Shem chuckled. "You looked about ready to brown your undies!"

"Well," said a somewhat-flustered Gillis, "Vandal was very convincing. I wouldn't have put it past him to take authenticity too far and actually kill me."

"Instead of which, some cranky old-timer got acquainted with the business end of a boomerblade," said Grady.

"It must have worked, at any rate," said Gillis, "because after that there was even less appetite in town for opposing the Scourers. Meanwhile Vandal had put his people on alert, telling them to be on the lookout for a spaceship full of new arrivals. They had a heat-seeking missile all lined up to blow you out of the sky."

"Which they nearly did," said Jayne. "And now I see why you didn't escape from town along with Temperance, right after Vandal and I fought. You weren't goin' back to lend your people support or anything. You were goin' back because you knew you'd be safe from the Scourers but you still had to be *seen* to be behaving like good ol' reliable Mayor Gillis, the townsfolk's friend, so's no one'd suspect."

"And I continued to do so until the time arrived when I couldn't."

"Namely when Jane and I rescued you from the camp. Only we weren't rescuin' you, were we? We were just pulling you out of the comfy little nest you'd made for yourself with the Scourers. Explains a lot. The reason, for instance, why you stopped for a piss, and why you tripped over that rope. Sabotage tactics. You were *trying* to get us caught."

"And nearly succeeded," said Gillis. "The time for dissembling is past, however. You've forced my hand. I'm with the Scourers formally. I suppose you could say I *am* one. And as such, it is my right and duty to deliver you to Vandal, with the assistance of these gentlemen. Where's Jane, by the way?"

"She ain't around," said Jayne. "Just after you ducked out on us, I decided to send her back. It's too dangerous for a girl her age."

"Don't kid a kidder, Mr. Cobb."

"Who's kidding, Gillis? You can go and look. Where we were hiding earlier, behind that fence, you won't find nothing but a pile of guns. Jane's gone."

Gillis turned to Shem. "I don't believe him. I reckon someone should check."

Shem sent Grady off, Gillis having furnished him with directions. Jayne waited patiently.

Grady returned with the news that, yes, it was just as Jayne had said. There were only guns. No sign of any girl.

"Well then," Gillis said. "Seems you weren't lying after all, Mr. Cobb."

"Damn straight. But I'll tell you something, Gillis, and this ain't no lie. I am going to beat the living crap out of you, and I will keep on at it until you stop breathing. But not right now."

"Why not? Because of these guns pointing at you?"

"Nah. Because I got other, more important business to attend to."

Jayne set off, barging past Gillis hard enough to knock him off-balance. Shem and Grady hastened after him, anxious to keep him in easy range of their weapons. Gillis, bemused, followed.

A Second Bite of the Cherry

Jayne strutted into the town square as if he owned it. The two Scourers with him, and Gillis, they were just his retinue. Hangers-on. He was the star of the show.

He strode straight up to Vandal, but a half-dozen guns were drawn on him before he could got close, adding to the two that were already aimed at him.

"That's far enough, pal," Shem warned. "Stop there."

Jayne halted.

"Vandal," Jayne said.

"You," said Vandal. "Man with a girl's name. What is it? Jayne. Thought you must be dead, Jayne."

"Seems a load of people thought that."

"What do you want? You here for a rematch?"

"Guess I am," said Jayne.

"You're clearly a glutton for punishment. What makes you think you'll do any better this time around?"

Jayne twisted his head from side to side as though working out a kink in his neck. "You got lucky last time. I figure it can't happen twice in a row."

"Well, fun as it might be to beat your sorry ass into the ground again," Vandal said, "I ain't interested."

"But this time it's different. I'm not askin' for you to give up Coogan's Bluff this time. I'm askin' for you to let Temperance go. We fight, I win, you cut her loose."

"Still no dice. Watching that woman suffer, it's the most pleasure I've had in years. I ain't giving her up for no one."

"Jayne?" said Temperance hoarsely. "Don't do this. It ain't worth it. *I* ain't worth it."

"I'm gettin' you out of that contraption, Temp, by hook or by crook."

Vandal eyed Jayne with curiosity. "Now don't tell me. You and her, you have somethin' going on. Sure looks like it."

"She's a friend."

"No, she ain't. The way you just spoke, callin' her 'Temp'… You're more than friends. Or at least, you used to be. Yeah, now some things are startin' to make sense. That's why she called you in, along with your buddies. You, of all people. And that's why you put yourself on the line the other day, punching Reynolds out and taking his place. You and Temperance used to have a thing goin' on. Once upon a time the pair of you knocked boots. And then when her town was in trouble, when she needed help, she clicked her fingers and you came running. Oh, Jayne. You are a classic patsy. You thought maybe Temperance loved you, and maybe she might love you again if you scurried to her side like a faithful hound. Hah! Temperance Jones never loved anyone, and Temperance McCloud, or whatever she's callin' herself now, surely ain't no different. Look at this face of mine. You think a woman would do that to a man if she was capable of love?"

"I think she'd do that to a man she despised," Jayne said. "Her being capable of love's not the issue. Temperance injured you like that, you must have had it coming."

"I did not. I had just finished conducting a very satisfactory transaction with her when she turned vicious on me, for no reason, and scorched half my face off."

"Weren't no damn transaction," Temperance spat out.

"Sure as hell was," Vandal said. "You were buying me off, woman. You mightn't have been using money to do it, you might have been using your body, but same difference."

Jayne swung round to stare at Temperance. "You slept with this guy?"

"Just the one time. Not willingly. It was… complicated."

"How complicated? Try me."

"I can make it simple for you," said Vandal. "See, what happened was Temperance stiffed some fella. Cain Stephenson was his name."

Jayne turned back to Vandal, blinking slowly.

"Gave him the raw end of a deal on a couple Earth-That-Was jazz long-players," Vandal continued. "This was some time ago, on Bellerophon. Now, to a certain extent it was Stephenson's own fault. He was a rich asshole who didn't know enough about old-timey music to distinguish between a good jazz record and a bad one, and if somebody took advantage of his ignorance, then more fool him. But he was pissed all the same when someone pointed out to him that Temperance had screwed him over, so he contacted me. Back then, I was in the restitutions trade. That was my living. Anyone did you wrong on a deal, I'd make things right again, for a small consideration. We're talking about the kind of deals that happen on the sly, the kind you don't want the Feds or the courts involved in."

"I know the kind," said Jayne. He might have sounded calm but his thoughts were in turmoil. Revelation was piling on revelation. First, Temperance's prior acquaintance with Vandal. Then Gillis's complicity with the Scourers. Now this: the fallout from the con they pulled on Cain Stephenson, an epilogue which Jayne had had no inkling about.

"I'll just bet you do. So I called Temperance on Stephenson's behalf and I told her we wanted recompense. I didn't have to threaten her none. She knew the score. We arranged a meet, and Temperance, well… she was sweet as can be. All sugar and spice. I said to her that I'd hate to have to cause her any distress. I'd heard, too, that she had some fella she worked with, a colleague who was more than just a colleague, accordin' to rumor. It'd be a shame if harm came to him, I said. Know what she said to me in answer? 'Then maybe you and me, we can reach some sort of arrangement.' It was pretty obvious what she was offering. In those days, before all this—" Vandal pointed to his face "—I wasn't unhandsome. I had my fair share of admirers among the ladies. And Temperance Jones was an attractive proposition, as you yourself would have to admit, Jayne, no?"

"Yeah," Jayne said stiffly. "She was."

"I was still intendin' to get the money off her she needed to pay back to Stephenson, but I thought to myself there was nothing wrong with havin' me a little jollification while I was about it. Anyways, one thing led to another and we ended up at my apartment, and we shared a beer or two, and it was going well. Clothes came off. She seduced me."

"Ain't how it went down," Temperance interjected.

"It's exactly how it went down," Vandal snapped. "And after we were done, Temperance offered to make coffee. She turned the cooker on, and then she said could I come and help her in the kitchen? She couldn't find any mugs. So I went to the kitchen, all obliging, and what did the *jiàn huò* do? I bent to open a cupboard and she clobbered me with something hard, maybe a saucepan, maybe a rolling pin, I don't know. Then, while I was dazed and reelin', she shoved my face into the burner. Left me screamin' on the floor and vamoosed."

"Couldn't have happened to a nicer guy," Jayne said.

"I know you're being sarcastic but I had the same exact thought. Not right then but later, as I lay in a hospital bed, face all bandaged up. What'd I done? All's I'd done was show a woman a good time. That ain't no crime. I got to tell you, I was hurt. Not just physically. I was *offended*. And when I'd recovered and been discharged by the doctors, I went looking for Temperance in order to get her to explain herself to me."

"And not looking to get your own back on her or anythin'."

"Obviously that as well. But she was nowhere to be found. She'd up and quit the planet. The guy she worked with, whoever he was, he'd gone too. Neither of 'em had left a trail I could follow. After that, I went into a kind of downward spiral. It weren't pretty. Burned a few bridges. Lost a lot of friends. I ended up out on the Rim, smugglin' military-grade weapons, but my face made it difficult to turn a profit doing that kind of work. I was too recognizable, too distinctive—not anonymous enough. Alliance were all over me. So I drifted out further."

"And that's when you fell in with a pack of Reavers."

"Yeah. Yeah. That's right. With them I fit in. I was one of their kind. But it didn't last, so I came back. Thetis was the first place I made planetfall, and here I've been ever since. And that is my tale."

"Didn't ask for it."

"Got it all the same. Now you know why I am giving Temperance the full works and why I'm not gonna hand her over to you or anyone, not ever, not for any reason. By sheer happenstance I managed to wind up on the very world where she's been hiding out. Fate has reunited us, after all this time. It's the kind of second bite of the cherry a man can usually only dream of getting."

"And you don't mind these here Scourers of yours hearing about how a woman got one over on you?"

Vandal made an expansive gesture. "We're among friends," he said, beaming. "And they're seeing justice bein' served. Where's the shame in that?"

"Mr. Vandal?" Mayor Gillis said. "Just for the record, I'm the one who brought Mr. Cobb to you. I set this whole thing up. Shem and Grady did their bit. I got them to apprehend him, but it was all my idea. I'm the instigator."

"You're just a piece of A-grade slime, ain't you, Gillis?" Jayne said.

"I want it recognized, is all," Gillis said. "How loyal I am."

"Duly noted," said Vandal. "The question remains, though, what am I going to do about you?"

"You talkin' to me or Gillis?" said Jayne.

"Maybe I should just have someone shoot you in the head."

"Oh, hey now, wait."

"No," said Vandal. "Not you, Jayne." He nodded at Gillis. "You."

"Oh, hey now, wait," said Gillis. "There's no call for that. Here I am, just brought you a gift. What kind of way to repay me is that? I nearly brought you another gift as well."

"Really?"

"Oh no, you don't, Gillis," Jayne warned. "Don't you dare."

"Yeah," said Gillis. "Temperance McCloud's daughter."

"*Cháng shé*," Jayne snarled. *Blabbermouth.*

"Huh. Temperance has a daughter," said Vandal, mildly intrigued.

"You didn't know?" said Gillis.

"You never said. No one said."

"Well, she does, and she's a spirited gal. The daughter, I mean."

"And where is she now, this daughter of Temperance's?"

"Have to say, I'm not sure. She came into town with us, but Jayne here sent her back."

"Maybe we should concentrate on the matter at hand," said Jayne. "Namely me."

"Or maybe we should talk a bit more about Temperance's daughter," said Vandal. "How old is she?"

"Thirteen, I think," said Gillis.

"Old enough. Hmmm. That's certainly good to know, Mr. Mayor. Mighty kind of you to volunteer such information."

"Think nothing of it."

Vandal's expression curdled. "Would have been a damn sight better if you'd told me sooner, though."

"I didn't think it was relevant."

"Up to me to decide what's relevant or not. You've been negligent, my man. I truly dislike negligence. Shem? Would you do the honors?"

Shem redirected his gun from Jayne to Gillis.

"No. No," said a panicking Gillis. "There's no need."

"There's every need," said Vandal. "Face it, you're no use to me anymore. You never were much. And you can't think you'll be able to go back to being mayor of this town after all this. Pretty soon there ain't gonna *be* a town to be mayor of. Did you think you were going to run with us from now on? You were going to become a Scourer?"

"Yes. Yes! I *am* a Scourer. I definitely am."

"You ain't. You just ain't the type. No, Mayor Gillis—or should I say *former* Mayor Gillis?—you really have nothing left to offer. To anyone. What this is, my friend, the thing Shem is about to do, it's a mercy killing."

Gillis sank to his knees and raised clasped hands, like a parishioner praying in church. "Mr. Vandal. Don't. Please don't. I can be a Scourer. I *can*. I can be the best damn Scourer there's been."

"Have some dignity, man," Jayne said out of the side of his mouth.

"I implore you, Mr. Vandal. Think it over. Spare my life and I'll work harder for you, I'll be more obedient to you than anyone ever. I'll be as cruel as you could want. You'll see."

Vandal shrugged indifferently.

He waggled a finger.

And Shem pulled the trigger.

Scarcely had Gillis's body fallen to the ground than Vandal was rising from his lawn chair. He took a few steps towards the platform.

"Well, well, well, Temperance," he said. "You sneaky cooze. A daughter. You kept *that* from me, didn't you?"

"You… You leave her alone, Elias Vandal," Temperance said. More and more she was having difficulty keeping her head clear of the nails. It was as though the cage was a pool and she was slowly drowning, in danger of going under for good.

"Leave her alone? I don't think so. I think I'm going to find this daughter of yours, and when I do, I'm going to treat her nice. I'm going to treat her reeeal nice."

"Damn you, you son of a bitch. Touch one hair on her head and I'll…"

"You'll what?" Vandal scoffed. "You'll come back from the grave and haunt me? Because that's about the only gorramn option you got, Temperance. I give it another ten minutes—fifteen, tops— before those legs of yours won't hold you up no more. Then you're gonna hang there by your neck, stuck on them nails, losin' blood, findin' it harder and harder to breathe, until finally your heart gives out or you suffocate. I've seen it before. Ain't nothing gonna change what's in store for you. Might as well accept that. Just know that your barely teenage daughter is going to be mine for a long, long while, maybe years. I'm going to look after her, make sure she lives life to the full, until such time as she's no longer at her best. Until the bloom is off the flower, as it were. Then I'll let my men have her, what's left of her, to do with as they please."

From Temperance came a guttural howl of anguish like a sound a wild animal might make. She writhed, straining at the ropes that bound her wrists. Madness was in her eyes. Had she been at liberty to do so, she would have torn Vandal apart with her bare hands.

It was then, while all eyes were on Temperance in her paroxysm of desperate, futile fury, that Jayne made his move.

The Longest of Long Shots

Jayne dove at Vandal. He had one chance to pull this off. If he didn't get it right, all was lost.

He got a hand around the haft of Vandal's boomerblade. He wrenched the knife out of its sheath. Vandal was caught off-guard. But he was fast. Appallingly fast. Almost by reflex he grabbed hold of Jayne's wrist. There followed a struggle for possession of the boomerblade, Jayne battling to break Vandal's grip, Vandal wrenching Jayne's wrist around in order to force the knife out of his hand.

It might have been an even contest if Jayne were in full-fighting fettle and not still recovering from a major surgical procedure. He nevertheless matched Vandal effort for effort. Vandal was not going to relinquish the boomerblade easily.

Then the Scourers' leader punched him in the ribs with his free hand, right on his wound.

Agony lanced through Jayne's torso. Excruciating. His vision blurred. The world seemed made of rubber. Everything wobbled like in a heat haze.

Vandal drew back a fist to punch him again. Jayne doubted he could take another blow like that and still retain his hold on the knife, let alone stay conscious.

Come on, Jane, he thought. *What are you waiting for, girl? An engraved invitation?*

As if on cue, a gunshot resounded across the town square. Someone yelped in pain.

Three more gunshots blurted out in quick succession. Each was the glorious, throaty *boom* of a Callahan full-bore auto-lock spitting out a heavy-caliber round at a velocity of a thousand yards per second.

For a moment, Vandal was startled. He froze.

Jayne seized his opportunity and twisted out of the other man's grasp.

He lunged at Vandal with the boomerblade, but it was an ungainly, cumbersome thrust. His whole chest felt on fire. Nothing in his body was working quite right. Vandal sidestepped out of the way, then made a grab for him.

At that very instant a bullet struck the ground just by Vandal's boots. Instinctively he sprang backwards.

Jayne had a few seconds' respite during which he was able to see that the Scourers were in pandemonium. They were scurrying this way and that to find cover. Two lay on the ground, not moving.

As Jane continued to strafe the square with bullets, Jayne lurched away from Vandal, making a beeline for the platform. The Scourers' leader gave chase, but Jane was now focusing her attention solely on him. Vandal dodged right and left to evade her shots but was driven back, fetching up on the verandah of the town grocery store. From there, sheltering behind one of the posts that held up the store's awning, he returned fire.

Jayne, meanwhile, clambered onto the platform and staggered over to the cage. He studied its construction, quickly establishing that the nail-fringed "collar" consisted of two sections held together by a peg. He hammered the peg out with the boomerblade's pommel and pulled the sections apart. Temperance immediately sagged down with a gasp of relief.

The cage itself was not the sturdiest thing ever made and Jayne was able to break it to pieces with a few hefty kicks. He pulled Temperance to him. She could hardly stand.

Yet she still had the strength to say, "You gorramn moron. Who do you think you are, coming here like this? Like someone with a death wish? Gonna get your stupid self killed."

"You're welcome," Jayne replied. "And now, if you don't mind, we need to make tracks. Jane's about to run dry and she won't be able to keep the Scourers off our backs while she's reloadin'."

"Jane? That's my Jane up there shooting everybody? You brought my *daughter* in on this ridiculous raid of yours? Of all the dumb, irresponsible—!"

"It was her idea, mostly."

"She's a child. You're an adult, or supposed to be. So help me, Jayne Cobb, if we get out of this alive, I'm going to *murder* you."

"I'd rather that than listen to any more of your nagging, woman," Jayne growled. "Now let's haul ass."

He helped Temperance off the platform. Her legs were as weak as a newborn foal's and she could walk only if she clung onto him at the same time.

A Scourer spotted them and turned her gun on them. Jayne prepared to hurl the boomerblade at the woman, not sure he could throw it before she pulled the trigger. Then her chest burst open. Gory chunks of gristle and bone peppered the ground behind her. She crumpled like tissue paper.

"Nice shootin', girl," Jayne murmured.

He scooped up the Scourer's gun—a Murphy-Elam Model 76 double-action revolver with swing-out cylinder and laser sight on the accessory rail—and used it to kill a Scourer who was pinned down behind an empty oil drum. The man, busy trying to draw a bead on the sniper on the roof of Billy's Bar, had failed to register another threat nearer by.

Then, in fulfillment of Jayne's prediction, Vera's clip emptied.

The sudden lull in the sniper fire gave Vandal an opening. He rallied his Scourers.

"Whoever that is, they're out!" he yelled. "Rush them! Now!"

The Scourers moved hesitantly out from their positions, making for Billy's Bar. Vandal laid down covering fire. The angle was such that he was unlikely to hit Jane, but Jayne could picture her cowering behind the roof's low parapet, swapping out the spent clip on Vera for a full one while rounds thudded into the brickwork beside her, sprinkling her with masonry fragments. He could imagine the stark terror she was feeling, her awareness of the imminence of death.

He was coldly enraged.

He stooped to pick up the gun dropped by the Scourer beside the oil drum. He intended to go on the attack with both this weapon and the Murphy-Elam, one in each hand blazing away. Temperance, however, put paid to that idea by snatching the second gun from him. Propping herself against the oil drum, she began shooting at the Scourers. They instantly scattered, then retaliated by shooting back at this new, unexpected source of gunfire.

Jayne joined Temperance behind the oil drum, and together they blasted at Vandal and the Scourers across the square.

By now the Scourers' numbers were significantly depleted. Jayne counted six, no, seven of them remaining, plus Vandal. Once Jane got back into action with Vera, the scales would be tipped further in the good guys' favor. There was, he thought, a very faint hope that he, Temperance and Jane might even win the gunfight.

That hope was dashed by the arrival of additional Scourers from the town's periphery. They had heard shooting and could not help but come to investigate. All at once there were ten more bandits in the square, then twenty more.

Jayne grabbed bullets from the dead Scourer's bandolier and hurriedly snugged them into the cylinder of the Murphy-Elam.

Jane, at the same time, resumed firing.

But there seemed to be Scourers everywhere. The oil drum rang like a bell as round after round pounded into it. It seemed meager protection indeed. The air was thick with gunsmoke. The stench of cordite burned Jayne's nostrils, and gunshot tinnitus howled in his ears. There was nothing else he could do but just keep shooting, shooting, shooting. This was it. This was his last stand. Gone was any chance of him making it out of the square with Temperance, the two of them rendezvousing with Jane, the three of them fleeing Coogan's Bluff together. Honestly, it had always been touch-and-go whether his plan would work. The longest of long shots. A pigs-might-fly scenario. But he had tried. He had had to. He had done his best, given it his all. Nobody could ever say he hadn't.

Amid all the cacophony and chaos, Jayne felt weirdly tranquil. It was almost as if this was foreordained. This was how he was always meant to die, with bullets whizzing all around him while he defended himself against insurmountable odds. A man couldn't really ask for a better way to go than that—except maybe passing away peacefully in his own bed at a ripe old age, which, now that Jayne thought about it, was the way he would have much preferred.

Then gunfire was augmented by gunfire. The smoke began swirling in violent vortices. There was the thunder of jet engines.

A shuttle loomed above the town square, slowing to a hover. In its open doorway stood Mal, legs apart to brace himself. He rained down bullets from above onto the Scourers. He was yelling something but Jayne had no idea what. There was too much other noise drowning out his voice.

One thing was for certain: Jayne had never been happier in his entire gorramn life to see Malcolm Reynolds.

Serenity Valley All Over Again

Half an hour earlier, Mal had been woken by a furious knocking on the door of his bunk.

"Mal! Mal!"

It was Simon Tam.

"Jayne's missing."

"You mean the Jane we all like?" said Mal. "Or the male one?"

"He's not in the infirmary," Simon said. "I've looked all over the ship. There's not hide nor hair of him."

"Maybe he's outside, stretching his legs."

"He shouldn't be, not in the condition he's in. But also, the Mule bike's gone."

Mal swung himself out of bed, swearing.

Ten minutes later Mal had established that not only was Jayne absent but Jane McCloud as well. It wasn't hard to put two and two together. The pair of them had taken the Mule bike and headed off on a rescue mission to get Temperance back. That was the only possible explanation.

Shepherd Book was eating breakfast in the dining area.

"Shepherd," said Mal, "you were on lookout all night."

"And I have the bags under my eyes to prove it."

297

"Are you telling me that Jayne and Jane somehow got past you without you noticing?"

"I couldn't tell you any such thing."

"So you knew they went," Mal said. "You let them."

"Mal, I was not going to stand in their way. It wasn't my place to."

"You're condoning what they've done?"

"My conscience is good with it," said Book. "If I have sinned, it was a sin of omission only. I feel they are about the Lord's work."

"The Lord's work, huh?"

"God invites us to show mercy and turn the other cheek, but He also wishes us to do what's right, no matter what the consequences. A girl wishes to save her mother from a cruel end, and a man wishes to help out a woman he once loved. Who am I to dissuade them from that?"

"It's funny." Mal's lip curled bitterly. "Plenty of folk seem able to square things with their conscience by citing the Lord as justification. Historically there's been a lot of evil done because somebody reckoned God would be okay with it."

"A lot of good, too. But what we would do well to remember, Mal, above all else, is that God is always watching."

"And what's that supposed to mean?"

"It means I had a feeling someone might pull a stunt like Jayne and Jane did," said Book, "so I took the precaution of putting a tracer beacon in my pocket before I went out on watch. I also took the precaution of secreting said tracer beacon under one of the Mule bike's wheel arches. A little sleight of hand, a little misdirection— neither of them had a clue. We couldn't have any of our people going up against the Scourers *totally alone*, could we? I mean, what if they got into difficulties?"

Mal stared hard at the other man. Then he grabbed Book's head with both hands and planted a big smacker of a kiss on his brow.

"Shepherd, I apologize for what I said just now about God. I misjudged Him."

"Well," said Book with a smile, "He certainly moves in a mysterious way, His wonders to perform."

With Wash at the controls and Mal and Zoë as passengers, *Serenity*'s shuttle homed in on the signal from the tracer beacon. Keen-eyed Wash was the first to spot the Mule bike. It was parked up in a hilly region a couple of miles north of Coogan's Bluff, its grubby yellow paintwork camouflaging it well against the ocher-colored landscape.

There was no sign of Jayne and Jane in the immediate vicinity. Logic dictated they had ditched the bike and continued on foot either towards the Scourers' camp or towards the town.

"But which?" said Zoë.

"My guess would be the camp," said Mal, "but since we don't know exactly where that is, we're better off trying Coogan's Bluff. We could spend hours looking for the camp, and time may be of the essence."

"Also, there's Scourers in the town," Zoë pointed out. "If Jayne and Jane aren't there, we can always persuade one of them to tell us how to get to the camp."

"You mean beat the location out of 'em?"

"Thought never crossed my mind, sir."

"Well, it's a judgment call," Mal said, "and I'm not happy making it, but it's what I'm gonna go with. Coogan's Bluff, Wash."

Wash turned the shuttle around.

In the event, Mal's judgment call was a good one. As the shuttle soared across the rooftops of Coogan's Bluff, the sound of gunfire became audible—a series of faint, crackling pops. The town square was the nucleus of an intense shootout.

Mal opened the shuttle door as Wash brought the craft in to

hover above the square. He quickly identified Jayne and Temperance down there amid the gunsmoke. The Scourers were giving them hell, and Jayne and Temperance were returning the compliment. He also spied Jane lying prone on a roof with a rifle—Vera, no less. She was taking potshots at the Scourers from on high, but she too, like her mother and father, was under heavy fire. Not only that but a handful of the bandits were gathering around the building she was on. Jane appeared to have no idea they were there.

As he opened fire on the Scourers himself, Mal shouted to her, "Jane! Watch your six! You've got company!"

She didn't—couldn't—hear.

"Zoë? We need to get down there and help Jane out."

Zoë relayed the command to Wash.

"Where am I supposed to land?" Wash said. "There's no open space big enough to put this thing down in except the square, and in case it's escaped your notice, crossfire? Guns everywhere? Bullets flying?"

"Rope," said Zoë. "There's rope stowed in a locker somewhere on this craft, right?"

"Rope?" said Wash. "Oh no. No, you don't. That is a bad idea, Zoë. I'm nixing that idea. Hear me? The husbandly foot is being put down. Not gonna happen."

Zoë affixed one end of a length of sturdy rope to a bulkhead fitting, then paid the rest of the rope out of the doorway.

"Bring us low, Wash. Low as you can."

"Still registering a formal objection," Wash said as he descended to an altitude of thirty feet, directly overhead of Billy's Bar. "I want it on record that I wholeheartedly disapprove."

"You can take it up with management at our next AGM," said Zoë. "Mal? Cover me."

Mal's Liberty Hammer boomed repeatedly as Zoë coiled the rope around one leg and rappelled down, braking her descent with a gloved hand. She pendulumed violently to and fro in the downdraft from the shuttle's jet engines but made it to the rooftop unscathed. Immediately her feet touched the roof she fell into a defensive crouch, while the shuttle ascended again with a roar.

"Zoë!" Jane cried. "Thank God. This is getting scary."

"You don't know the half of it."

Across the roof, at the back of the building, a head popped up. A Scourer.

Zoë shot him dead.

"Wow, I thought River was badass," said Jane, "but her badassery's got nothing on yours."

"There's more where he came from," Zoë said. "We need to get off of here."

"Now you mention it, that's not a bad idea."

"But Scourers have got the place surrounded. We can't jump off the front, the back or the sides. We'll get mown down." Zoë looked at her feet. "What is this roof made of anyway?"

"Tarpaper? Plywood?" said Jane. "I don't know, but not much."

"Perfect. Jane? Shield your face, honey."

Zoë shielded her own face and aimed the Mare's Leg at the roof right in front of her. The first shot made a ragged hole the size of a saucer. Two more followed, creating a triangle of saucer-sized holes. She stamped on the section of roof between them and it fell away.

The result was an aperture large enough for a person to slide through.

"Jane, you first."

Jane didn't hesitate. She shoulder-slung Vera, then slithered into the aperture, hung by her fingertips onto its splintered edge, and dropped to the floor of the bar below.

Zoë, in the meantime, accounted for two more Scourers who'd

had the temerity to show their faces over the edge of the roof.

"You coming?" Jane called up.

"You bet."

Zoë landed catlike on the floor of the bar, scene of the unseemly brawl three days earlier between the townspeople and her, Mal, and Jayne. Several bullet holes now starred its windows, and stray rounds had shattered bottles behind the counter.

"Quick," she said. "Get behind there."

She and Jane huddled in the lee of the counter. Zoë slotted cartridges into the breech of her Mare's Leg.

"How do you manage it?" Jane said.

"Manage what?"

"To look so calm in the middle of a gorramn gunfight."

"Don't be fooled. What you see, this..." Zoë circled a finger at her impassive face. "That ain't calm. Only looks like it. That's sheer terror."

"But you must be used to being shot at."

"Nobody ever gets used to being shot at, Jane, and anybody who says otherwise is a liar. I've found a way of coping, is all. There's this voice inside me tells me what to do next in order to get through a situation like this. Tells me when to stay quiet, when to move, when to reload, when to get down. I've learned to listen to it. Used to sound like my own voice, once. Now it sounds like Wash's."

"Your husband's?"

"He's always there." Zoë tapped her temple. "And here." She tapped her sternum. "He may not come across as any great shakes in the manliness department, but what he's got is worth way more than muscles and chest hair and a bulge in the front of the pants. He is my lodestar; my anchor."

"That's amazing."

"Ain't it? I knew he was the one for me the first time I laid eyes on him. No, actually, the second time. After he'd shaved off that sorry excuse of a mustache of his. I honestly don't know what I'd do without him, and I hope I never have to find out. And on that note…"

There were Scourers outside the front door of the bar, and noises coming from somewhere out back that sounded very much like someone smashing a window.

"How's about you let loose with Vera there a little more, huh?"

Jane grinned grimly. "Don't have to ask me twice."

She swung Vera up over the countertop and fired a volley of shots at the front door, sending the Scourers outside scuttling away. Meanwhile Zoë crawled on all fours towards a doorway that led to a backroom, where the sounds of breaking glass were coming from. She caught sight of a Scourer squirming in through a small quarterlight window above a sturdy, barred door. His head and shoulders were showing. He looked round and saw Zoë and her Mare's Leg. His face was a rictus of dismay.

"Oh shi—"

Zoë's gun bellowed, and that was an end of him.

The shuttle was taking hits, and Scourer bullets were coming perilously close to Mal in his vantage point just inside the doorway. His luck was holding so far, but it wouldn't last forever. So many rounds were coming his way that sooner or later one of them was going to find a home somewhere in his body, by the law of averages alone.

The gunfight in the town square was still as fierce as ever. In fact, it was getting fiercer: a whirlpool sucking more and more bodies into it. The Scourers' ranks were swelling as reinforcements still flocked in from the town's outskirts. Jayne and Temperance were increasingly beleaguered, struggling to hold position behind the oil drum. Mal and Wash, in the shuttle, were offering air support but only of a limited kind. As for Zoë and Jane, the bar they were in was completely surrounded. They could probably maintain a defense if they stayed inside it but Mal doubted they would be able to shoot their way out. They were cornered, in other words. Trapped.

Trapped.

Mal flashbacked to another time, another planet. He remembered a small squad of Independents facing an onslaught of Alliance troops. He remembered a young Browncoat called Bendis succumbing to a hail of gunfire. He remembered dozens of Alliance ships descending in the dawn sky like a host of unholy angels.

Here, now, in Coogan's Bluff, it was Serenity Valley all over again. Except…

The people converging on the town square weren't just Scourers. There were others among them, and these others were *attacking* the Scourers.

Townsfolk.

Mal recognized the fella with the beard that looked like a beaver, the guy he'd picked a fight with at the bar. And he recognized the mismatched couple, the young man—Horace—and the older woman who was either his mother or his wife. The bar owner, Billy. A few other half-familiar faces. They had guns and they were shooting at the Scourers.

"There it is," he muttered to himself. "There's that fighting spirit at last. I knew you people had it in you. All it takes is the right provocation."

And the right mixture of desperation and hope. The townspeople must have heard the fracas in the square, looked out their windows, seen Vandal and the Scourers taking hits, and sensed now was the time to rise up. Now or never. They might not win but they had nothing to lose. What was the alternative? A slow, horrible death by starvation and thirst.

This rebellion was as much the Scourers' fault as anyone's. They had sowed oppression and were reaping the whirlwind.

The residents of Coogan's Bluff harried the Scourers, fighting with a passion. The Scourers fought back, and they dished out casualties but they took casualties too. Mal saw the bandits falling back. He saw them falling down. And all at once he realized that they were ceding ground. The townspeople were winnowing their ranks.

Serenity Valley all over again—but this time the forces of rebellion had gained the upper hand.

He looked for Elias Vandal, keen to know how the Scourers' leader was handling this reversal of fortune.

The answer was, not well.

"What're you doing there, Elias old buddy?" Mal said with a little chuckle. "If I didn't know better, I'd swear you were sneaking away."

That was certainly what Vandal appeared to be up to. Unbeknownst to any of his gang, he was sloping off down an alley that led away from the town square, casting brief, furtive glances over his shoulder as he went.

"Things not going how you'd like, huh?" Mal said. "Situation gettin' too hot to handle. Thought you'd cut and run, leave your boys and girls as cannon fodder. Well, too bad, my friend. Today is not your day. Wash?"

"Yeah?"

"There's a big fella yonder in a black duster coat, thinks he don't belong here anymore. See him?"

"I do."

"Shall we go after him?"

"I do not think that is a bad idea."

As Wash turned the shuttle towards Vandal, Mal hauled in the rope down which Zoë had slid. Then he began tying a slipknot at the free end. In very short order he had fashioned a lasso.

The shuttle swooped low towards Vandal. Mal paid out the lasso, twirling it below him so that it formed a kind of vertical cone.

"Hold her steady, Wash."

"You do your job, Mal, I'll do mine."

Mal reckoned he'd have only one shot at this, and the timing had to be perfect. If he missed, Vandal would surely duck inside a building to prevent him getting a second chance.

Vandal looked up as the shuttle's shadow fell over him. He fired off a wild, frantic shot at Mal and missed. Then he was out of bullets, his gun's hammer clicking uselessly. He tossed the weapon aside and reached for his boomerblade. He came up empty-handed. Mal had no idea how or when Vandal had lost the knife, but it wasn't in its sheath any longer.

In that moment, Elias Vandal looked as bereft and helpless as Mal had ever seen him.

Then the shuttle drew level with him, and Mal, with neat, practiced precision, hooked the loop of the lasso over his head and shoulders and yanked it tight. The rope now encircled Vandal's chest, pinning his arms to his side. Mal let go of it as the shuttle sped on. Vandal stood for a second or two, trying to wriggle out of the lasso. Then the semi-slack rope snapped taut and he was plucked off his feet, up into the air.

"Yee-hah! We got him, Wash! He's dangling like a fish on the line."

"Did you just 'yee-hah'?"

"Seemed appropriate."

"Okay. So, what do you want to do with him?"

"Take him for a ride, obviously. Show him the sights. Show him them real close-up."

Human Pendant

The shuttle veered all over Coogan's Bluff, trailing the helpless Elias Vandal behind it. Wash swung him between buildings. He treated him to a very near brush with the steeple of the town's church; swept him across a corrugated-iron roof so that his toes skated over the ridges and his body quivered like a dancing marionette's. Such was the deftness of Wash's piloting that Vandal did not come to serious harm, but he did suffer more than a few bumps, scrapes, and bashes.

All the while Vandal twisted and writhed and yelled.

Mal, leaning out of the shuttle doorway, cupped a hand behind an ear and shouted, "What's that? Can't hear you?"

Vandal roared incoherently at him in panic and rage.

"You want to go faster?" Mal said. "Is that it? Wash, he's having a great time. He wants to go faster."

"No problem."

Wash eased the throttle lever forward, pouring on speed. Vandal clipped a corner of a house and went spinning round and round. His leg slammed against the gable end of a pitched roof, and he let out an agonized shriek. Mal was pretty sure his shin had just been shattered.

"Okay, Wash. Let's dial it down a notch. We don't want to kill the guy."

"We don't? Aww."

"No, this is an exercise in humiliation. Another turn or two around town, and I figure he'll be good and ready."

"For what?"

"Surrendering."

The shuttle circuited Coogan's Bluff a couple more times with its human pendant, then darted back towards the town square. As he made his approach, Wash decelerated to absolute minimum airspeed so that the combatants in the square would see the craft and its attachment coming.

The sight of Elias Vandal suspended on a rope from the shuttle was weird enough and eye-catching enough to bring about a ceasefire. Everyone craned their necks and stared. Vandal hung limp and dazed, his head drooping. If he had ever been a fearsome, imposing figure, he certainly wasn't one now. He looked pathetic, bedraggled, and beaten.

Wash lowered him to the ground. He then maneuvered the shuttle sideways, dropped the undercarriage and performed a textbook light touchdown, right next to Vandal.

Mal stepped out.

There were dozens of dead bodies all over the square, with firearms in their hands and looks of dull astonishment on their faces. There were also dozens of people still alive, with firearms in their hands and looks of astonishment—of a different kind—on their faces. The air reeked of blood and gunpowder.

Mal strode over to Vandal, who lay moaning and gibbering, still secured by the lasso. The lower part of his left leg was bent at an unnatural angle. His clothes were tattered and torn. He looked like something even a cat wouldn't have dragged in.

"Hey, Vandal," he said. "You got anything to say to everyone here?"

Vandal's lips moved but nothing intelligible came out.

Mal rested a foot on Vandal's ruined shin and applied pressure.

Vandal screamed and thrashed about. "Okay. Okay! Stop that! Please stop!"

"You want to tell us how sorry you are for starting this whole mess? Maybe you'd like to talk about your Reaver days. I'm sure you've got a lot of interesting tales from those times."

"I weren't..." Vandal mumbled.

"What's that? Speak up."

"I weren't never a Reaver."

"Oh hey now, there's a surprise," said Mal. "Did you all catch that? Turns out Vandal weren't no Reaver. He made it up. Didn't you make it up, Vandal?"

"Yeah," said Vandal miserably. "Yeah, I did."

"Louder, please. Not sure everyone heard."

Mal put his weight on Vandal's leg again. Vandal sobbed out, "Yes! Yes! I made it all up! I never was a Reaver. I've never even met a Reaver."

"Guess you thought it'd make you seem tougher and meaner."

"Yeah."

"Lend you some sorta mystique, maybe."

"Yeah."

"So what we have here, people," Mal said, "is a bogus ex-Reaver. A bandit who pretended to have a dark past. Nothing special, just a common-or-garden outlaw."

"He's even less than that," said Temperance, coming out from behind the oil drum. "He used to be a debt collector for crooks. That's what he did when I knew him, way back. Someone you'd send to get money back you were owed. A thug who'd shake people down until they coughed up. Elias *Randall*. That was his name, before he changed it."

"Randall. Vandal," said Mal. "I see what you did there, pal. Clever."

Temperance stood over Vandal. "I suppose you could say you

made something of yourself, Elias, after Bellerophon," she said contemptuously. "But it weren't much."

"This is the guy you've all been so scared of," Mal said, addressing the townspeople and the Scourers once more. "This is the guy you've bowed to and kowtowed to. Don't seem hardly so menacing anymore, does he?"

"Hang him!" someone yelled. Whether it was Scourer or resident of Coogan's Bluff, Mal couldn't tell.

"I don't know," he said. "Seems we have a truce going on right now in this square, and that's a wonderful thing, but it feels like everyone's on eggshells. Mightn't take much for the fighting to kick off again, and I don't think stringing Vandal up from a tree's the answer. I think we need something more *conclusive* than that. Something that'll bring you all some closure."

"Allow me."

The speaker was the Scourer called Shem Bancroft. Beneath its stippling of sticking plasters, his broad, round face registered a range of emotions. To Mal, above all else, he seemed disillusioned and downcast.

And disillusioned and downcast was exactly how Shem was feeling.

Shem's long-harbored suspicion that Elias Vandal was a fraud had at last been vindicated. That stuff Vandal spouted about being a former Reaver had impressed him at first, but the more time he had spent in the man's company, the more he began to think that it must only be a boast. You didn't come back from being a Reaver. Once you were a Reaver, you stayed a Reaver until you died. Vandal was a miscreant, yes, and vicious, but there was always a level of calculation in anything he did. His savagery was never without purpose, and Reavers, by all accounts, were purposeless, driven only by instinct and appetite, pure chaos made flesh.

By the time these doubts set in, however, Shem had got in too deep. He had invested heavily in Vandal's legend. He had come to derive much of his self-esteem, his identity, from being Vandal's second-in-command, the one who had been with Vandal from the outset, the first Scourer. The respect other Scourers accorded him was respect earned from his closeness to their leader, not for anything Shem himself was or did, but he took it nonetheless. He knew he didn't deserve it but it was better than none.

The offworlders had reduced Vandal to a broken, blubbering wreck. By rights, Shem should hate them for it.

But he had watched these same offworlders give four Scourers a Christian burial when they had nothing to gain from doing so. The offworlders—not only their Shepherd but this man Malcolm Reynolds too—had a kind of decency about them.

Perhaps, Shem was thinking, they had done him a service by bringing Elias Vandal low. Perhaps here, at last, he had a chance to assert himself, be his own man. Be free.

"Shem," Vandal croaked. "Shem…"

"It's over," Shem said to him sorrowfully. "I can't go on. You've been like a father to me, Vandal."

"Yes. Yes. A father."

"And I hated my father. Hated him like hell."

Jayne Cobb stepped forward, holding out Vandal's boomerblade. "Maybe you'd like to use this," he said. "It'd be appropriate."

Shem looked round at his fellow Scourers. "Any of you want to grab this knife off me, stop me doing what I'm about to do, go ahead. But think about this. You've been followin' this man for months, some of you for years. Ask yourselves, did you do it 'cause you admired him or 'cause you were terrified of him? Did you do it 'cause you wanted to be part of something or you just didn't know what else you wanted out of life? Me, I got swept up in Vandal's slipstream. But I look at him now, the way he is, and I wonder why. Maybe there's some of you feeling the same."

Nobody said anything in reply, but Mal saw a few Scourers nod their heads.

"I'm tired," Shem said. "Sick and tired. I imagine there's a fair number of you itchin' to start shooting again. The folk of this town ain't going to forgive us in a hurry, and us Scourers are probably afraid that if we don't take care, don't stand up for ourselves, they're not gonna show us any mercy. You may or may not have seen that there are as many of them around here now as there are of us. They've got their act together like no town before, and that's mostly down to these offworlders. Comes a time when you just have to accept that what you've been doing all along—even though you enjoyed it, maybe thought it made you a big shot—is wrong."

He straddled Vandal, boomerblade held high.

"And here's where I put it right," he said.

"I shoulda known you'd turn on me, Shem," Vandal rasped. He looked too exhausted and in too much pain to do anything but speak. "That day we met and you almost shot me in the back—I shoulda killed you then. And now the time's come. Now you've got your chance again and I can't do anything about it. Well, go on then. Do it. Do it, you useless piece of horsecrap. Just remember, you'd have been nothing without me. Nothing! And when I'm gone you'll be nothing again."

Shem brought the boomerblade down on Vandal like an executioner's ax.

A spasm passed through Vandal's entire body from head to toe. Then he lay still.

"Nothing?" said Shem, lifting the bloodied knife. "Yeah. Maybe I am. But now so are you."

Dragonwing Protection Services Inc.

Mistrust simmered in the air. Townsperson stared at Scourer; Scourer stared at townsperson. Mal had a nasty feeling violence was about to break out once more. Even with Elias Vandal dead, there was still plenty of animosity to go round. The residents of Coogan's Bluff scented victory. The Scourers feared defeat. It was a highly combustible mix, as unstable as nitroglycerine, and any second now it might just explode.

He glimpsed Zoë and Jane peering out through the bullet-riddled window of Billy's Bar. He was minded to tell them to take cover. Same went for Wash, who was looking on from the doorway of the shuttle. This was far from all over.

Then came a high-pitched roar, the sound of jet engines.

Lots of jet engines.

A flotilla of aircraft loomed into sight above the rooftops. Leading them was a shuttle, the twin of the one already parked in the town square.

Inara's.

The other half-dozen aircraft were high-spec personnel transportation skiffs. Each bore a corporate logo on its fuselage: the words "Dragonwing Protection Services Inc." below a roundel containing a simplified image of a dragon offering a human figure its wing to shelter under.

Dragonwing. Mal recognized the name. It was a private security company. Presumably the one Inara's friend hired from time to time. He guessed Inara had got word from her friend that the security specialists were en route and had gone out to meet them in her shuttle and accompany them on the last leg of their journey to Coogan's Bluff.

The skiffs were narrow-bodied enough that, with a little bit of skilled aviation, they could set down in the middle of Main Street, while there was room in the square—just—for Inara's shuttle to alight alongside the other shuttle.

Hatches opened in the skiffs, and scores of security specialists filed out onto the road. They mustered, and proceeded to enter the square, marching in lockstep. They were well-armed and neatly uniformed with black tactical vests, iron-gray fatigues and peaked caps with the Dragonwing logo emblazoned above the brim.

Their commanding officer made straight for Mal. The look on his face—not to mention the snub-nose 50-cal submachine gun he was carrying at waist height—said he meant business.

"You," he barked. "Unholster that pistol and drop it on the ground."

"Whoa, whoa, whoa," said Mal.

"You have to the count of three to comply, Mr. Vandal."

"Mr. . . ? Now hold on a second. This is a case of mistaken identity."

"One," the commander said.

Several of the security specialists had joined him. Mal was looking down the barrels of more submachine guns than he cared to count. At the same time, the bulk of the Dragonwing employees were fanning out throughout the square, taking up positions whereby they had everyone covered and all the exits controlled.

"Two."

"Okay." Mal moved his hand slowly towards his holster. "I'm complying." He drew the Liberty Hammer with forefinger and thumb around the base of the butt and held the gun up so that everyone could see his hand was nowhere near the trigger. Though he would have liked to shoot the hell out of these goosestepping ex-soldiers and soldier-wannabes, he knew he was hopelessly outgunned. However much lead he put into them, they would return the favor tenfold.

"Put it on the ground," the commander said.

As Mal bent to do so, Inara came hurrying across the square from her shuttle. She placed herself between him and the security specialists.

"Commander Rodriguez, this isn't Elias Vandal," she said. "*That's* Elias Vandal." She pointed to the corpse. "This is Mal Reynolds. You know, one of the people you've come here to help?"

Commander Rodriguez squinted at Mal. "Sure looks like a lawless bandit leader to me."

"I'll take that as a compliment," Mal said, "seeing as how it comes from such a fine, upstanding figure as yourself, who is in no way a glorified gun-for-hire. That's a very pretty uniform, by the way. Hangs off you nicely. Tell me, was it tailored? And those buttons—so well polished."

"Ah," said Rodriguez. "Yes. It must be you. Miz Serra said that Mal Reynolds was a wiseass."

"I like to think of myself as endearingly witty."

Rodriguez motioned to his subordinates to lower their guns. "Then who *are* the bandits here?"

"The raggedy fellas," Mal said. "The ones who look in need of a bath. Only, while in a sense you and your people have come in the nick of time, Commander Rodriguez, in another sense you're too late. There's kind of a détente going on right now, and I'm worried you may have upset the balance of it."

"No," said Shem Bancroft. "No, Reynolds, we know when the jig's up. We are not taking on a private security army as well as the rest of you. No way. That'd be insanity." He let the boomerblade fall to the ground and raised his hands. "We yield."

One after another, across the square, his fellow Scourers likewise discarded their weapons and raised their hands. Some did it willingly, some reluctantly, but all did it.

Mal felt the last of the tension ebb out of him.

As the Dragonwing specialists began singling out and rounding up the Scourers, Zoë and Jane emerged from Billy's Bar. Jane sprinted over to Temperance and flung her arms around her.

"Oh my God, Mom! Are you okay?"

"Better now, my love. So much better. You?"

They hugged hard, Jane burying her face in Temperance's chest, too overcome with joy and relief to answer.

Now a man sashayed over from one of the Dragonwing skiffs towards Inara and Mal. He was tall, well dressed, and exceedingly handsome, and moved with a grace a ballet dancer might envy. Mal didn't know whether he admired him or resented him.

"Who's this?" he asked Inara.

"My friend Stanislaw."

"Ah. Him. He came good on his promise, then."

"Did you ever doubt it?"

"Being as I've never met the guy and have no idea what he's like, I maybe did."

"Stanislaw?" Inara said as the new arrival drew level with them. "This is Malcolm Reynolds. Malcolm Reynolds, Stanislaw L'Amour."

The two men shook hands. L'Amour's grip was firm and dry, and he smelled terrific, like sandalwood and cloves.

"Mr. Reynolds," he said. "Inara's told me… well, nothing about you."

"Oh."

"I jest. She mentions you all the time in her waves."

"She does?"

"Fondly, for the most part. Sometimes with exasperation."

"I have that effect on people."

316

"What she never mentioned was quite how good-looking you are."

"Uh, thanks," said Mal. "And you, er, are wearing a nice cologne."

Inara grinned at his discomfiture.

"So, not to quickly change the subject or anything," Mal said, "but you came through for us. Earlier than scheduled, what's more."

"It's not always ideal to arrive prematurely," said L'Amour. "At parties it's downright impolite. And in bed. But in these circumstances it's no bad thing."

"Just sayin' it's appreciated. The Scourers have a camp in a ravine north of here. Your Dragonwing guys may want to check that out. And there's a bunch of towns and villages up-county where there's a Scourer presence. I imagine the people there'd welcome some security specialists coming in and kicking bandit butt."

"Consider it done. Now, Inara dear, I'm parched. Where can a fellow get a drink around here?"

"That looks like a watering hole," Inara said. "Let's see if they're serving."

Inara linked her arm with L'Amour's and together the two of them strolled off in the direction of Billy's Bar, heads together, chatting conspiratorially.

Zoë ambled over to Mal's side. "Why are you looking at him like that?"

"At who?"

"The beautiful man."

"He so great? I mean, what does he with his perfect haircut, chiseled chin, and hefty bank balance have that I don't have?"

"Nothing, sir. Nothing at all."

Mal scowled. "Him and Inara look like just friends to you? They don't to me."

"If Kaylee is to be believed, you needn't feel threatened by him. Not where Inara is concerned."

"Who's threatened?"

"Not you, plainly," Zoë said with a wry smile. "Now, sir, with your permission, may I go and kiss that blond fella over there in the palm-tree shirt who's hopping up and down to get my attention? I think he thinks he's done something brilliant that deserves a reward."

"Permission granted, Corporal."

Time For a Party

That night the residents of Coogan's Bluff put on a shindig because, well, why not? A terrible burden had just been lifted from them. They had been reprieved from a communal death sentence. There were loved ones to be buried, of course, and mourned; and there was damage to be repaired. But those were concerns for another day. Now it was time for a party.

In the town square, a five-piece band—fiddler, accordionist, guitarist, banjo player, jug-blower—led a rollicking hoedown. Everyone danced, their faces flushed in the firelight. A hog roast sizzled on a spit. Billy Kurosawa did a roaring trade in booze. Plenty of water was drunk, too. The town's wellheads had yet to be repaired but the discovery of a hoard of water stored in jerry cans at the Scourers' camp meant there was a decent quantity of the stuff to go round in the meantime. To the thirsty townsfolk, the liquid was almost as intoxicating as alcohol.

Partying as hard as anyone were the crew of *Serenity*. Simon tried to teach Kaylee some of the formal dance steps he had learned in school; Kaylee tried to teach Simon how dancing could also be about just letting your hair down and having fun. Zoë and Wash swayed slowly together in a clinch, in spite of the up-tempo music, their eyes closed. Shepherd Book showed himself to be rather nimble-footed, to the great amusement of River and Jane. Inara and Stanislaw L'Amour were definitely the most elegant couple there, each gliding around the other with consummate poise.

Mal sat contentedly on the sidelines with a beer in hand, until a local lady insisted he be her dance partner. She was the mature woman who was perennially escorted by a much younger man, and as she and Mal capered together, Mal took the opportunity to ask her if the fellow, Horace, was her husband or son. The answer was son. The woman, it turned out, was a widow and clearly in the market for remarrying. Mal had a clear impression he was being sized up as potential bridegroom material. He'd been here before with a certain YoSaffBridge and for that reason alone the situation made him more than a tad uncomfortable. He was relieved, therefore, when Commander Rodriguez beckoned him over and requested a moment of his time.

Away from the celebrations, Rodriguez told Mal that his team had found three young women at the camp at Brimstone Gulch.

"They're in pretty poor shape—bedraggled, malnourished, abused," he said. "You could call them 'camp followers,' except there was nothing voluntary about the role. We're going to return them to their families in their respective hometowns."

"And the Scourers? What are you going to do with them?"

"It's a tough one. We're not law enforcement. We have no formal powers of arrest. Technically we're *breaking* the law by detaining these people. If I had my druthers, I'd cull the lot of them like vermin. They don't deserve to live after all they've done."

"How about handing 'em over to the Feds?"

"Can be done, but it's tricky getting the Feds interested in what happens on a remote planet like Thetis."

"Talk to Mr. L'Amour. I imagine he can fix it. With his resources he can fix most anything."

"Not a bad idea," said Rodriguez. "He's already making

arrangements for civil engineers to come and rebuild the town's wells. He's a useful person to know."

"But if you do take the Scourers to the Feds, Commander, I'd consider it a personal favor if my name was never mentioned in connection with any of this."

"Understood. And, Mr. Reynolds? I'd like to apologize for nearly shooting you earlier. I've heard what you and your crew did for this town. You have my respect."

He tipped his cap to Mal.

Mal saluted him back.

Elsewhere in the square, Jayne sat on a bench, nursing a bottle of whisky. Simon had advised him against drinking on top of all the analgesics he had taken. Mixing booze with pain medication was, he had said, a bad idea. But the way Jayne was feeling, anything that numbed him—whether it came from a pharmacy or a liquor store— was worth putting inside him.

Several women asked him to dance but he turned them down. He wasn't in the mood.

When another woman came up to him, he was all ready to make his excuses. Then he saw that it was Temperance.

"Hi, Jayne."

"Hi, Temp."

"Not joining in the fun?"

"Dancin' ain't for me. Anyways, my side hurts. Dancing'll only make it worse. I like listening to the music, though."

"Mind if I…?"

Jayne patted the bench beside him.

Temperance took the whisky bottle from him and had a swig. Wiping her mouth, she said, "There's something I need to tell you."

"Okay."

"About Jane."

"You going to say sorry for not telling me about her before? It's fine. I'm all right with that. You had your reasons, I guess. The main thing is I know about it now, and I'm here, and I want to do what's right by both of you."

"If I can stop you right there…"

"No. Let me have my say. I'm thinking I'm going to stay on Thetis. I'm not saying you and me, Temp, we have to get back together necessarily. Don't even have to live together. But I've got a daughter and I need to be around for her."

"Oh, Jayne." Temperance's tone was rueful, wistful.

"I've made up my mind. I've not told Mal or the others about it yet. Maybe tomorrow. I was thinking, with Gillis dead, Coogan's Bluff could probably do with a new mayor. Mayor Cobb. Has a certain ring to it."

"Jayne, listen. There's a whole lot you don't know. A whole lot you should know. Remember Vandal this morning, when he talked about how he and I slept together?"

"Kinda hard to forget," Jayne said. "Not a pretty image to have in my head. But you thought seducing him was a way to get him off our backs, and I suppose it might've worked, if you only hadn't gone and burned half his face off straight afterwards."

"What Vandal said, his whole version of events—it's a lie. A complete distortion of the facts. I mean, yeah, I went to his apartment with him. But it weren't to sleep with him. That wasn't my intention at all. My intention was to flat-out kill the motherhumper."

"Oh. I see."

"Yeah, kill him, then go collect you, and we'd both leave Bellerophon on the first available commercial flight, to avoid any repercussions. That was the idea. Only it didn't go according to plan. Vandal—Randall as he was then—jumped me the moment we got through the door. Started tearing at my clothes. He was only after one thing. I fought back. I… I tried to get him off of me, but he was so much bigger than me, so much stronger…"

The hand holding the bottle trembled. Temperance was battling hard to keep her emotions in check.

"He…" she said. "He hit me again and again. Hit me until I was barely conscious. You can guess what happened next."

She took another slug of whisky.

"I don't have much memory of it, to be honest. I thank God for that. What I do recall is afterwards, when he climbed off, he said to me, 'Don't think you've just got out of paying Cain Stephenson what he's due. He wants all his money back, every last credit. You don't cough up, and I'll find that colleague of yours and I'll do worse to him'n what I just done to you.' The moment he said that, I just saw red. Randall went to the kitchen to make coffee. I got up off the floor and I staggered over to him. I grabbed the first heavy object I could find. I don't even remember what it was. I clubbed him with it, then I shoved his face into the gas flame. I shoved it into that flame and I held it there until I heard his flesh crackle and smelled burning meat."

Jayne looked at her, both appalled and impressed. "Damn. Damn, damn, damn. Then what?"

"I meant to kill him," Temperance said. "Really I did. But even after I'd burned him, he was like a raging bull. He kept coming at me. His face was all charred and blistered, half his hair was gone. The pain alone would've stopped an ordinary man in his tracks, but Randall, he was just mad. Madder'n hell. I had to get out of there, and I just ran. I ran and kept on running, running like the Devil himself was on my tail. I knew Randall wouldn't stop until he'd caught up with me and killed me. I knew, too, that after I was dead he'd search for you and he'd kill you as well. So I did the one thing I now most regret in my life. The one thing for which you have no right to forgive me, and yet I wish you would. I abandoned you."

Jayne said nothing.

"I abandoned you," Temperance continued, "and I did it because I wanted to protect you. I wasn't thinking quite straight, but in my head it made sense. If I quit Bellerophon and never had any contact with you again, it meant Randall would have a much harder time finding you. He would have no idea where to start looking. More importantly, it'd stop *you* looking for *him*. Because I knew you, Jayne. I knew what you were like. If I'd come to you, all beaten up and bruised and…"

"Raped."

"Raped. Yeah. If you'd seen me like that, what would you immediately have tried to do?"

"Find the man who hurt you and kill him."

"Exactly. And, by going up against someone like Elias Randall, you'd likely have wound up getting yourself killed instead. You were a mean proposition back then, but Randall, he was a whole order of magnitude meaner. I was saving you, Jayne, or so I hoped."

"Okay," said Jayne uncertainly. "Okay. Well, I guess that explains everything. Mostly. But then, why couldn't you just have got in touch with me later? You could have sent me a wave from wherever you fetched up, told me to come join you. You know I'd have come."

"Yes, that crossed my mind," said Temperance. "Trouble was, by the time I'd recovered and gotten myself back on an even keel, I realized I was pregnant."

"Don't see why that'd be such a problem."

"Oh, it'd have been a problem."

"Maybe I'd have thought it was a good thing. Maybe I'd have risen to the occasion."

"Think back, Jayne. You and me, we always took precautions, didn't we?"

"Sure, but no birth control method's foolproof."

"No, but still we were super careful. And Elias Randall was not careful at all, if you catch my drift."

Jayne stared at her. Then stared harder at her. Then his frown of puzzlement morphed into horrified understanding.

"*Gū yáng zhōng de gū yáng.* You mean…?"

"Jane ain't yours. She's his."

The song the band were currently playing was crescendoing towards a climax. The fiddler sawed frantically away at his violin, while the accordionist's fingers flew up and down the keys. Dancers whooped and stomped, all flailing arms and twirling skirts. The music and their cheering merged in glorious harmony, skirling up to the starry heavens.

"She's his," Temperance went on, "but only biologically. In every other respect she is nothing to do with him. That's why I named her after you. Because, even though you weren't her father, I wanted you to be. It was my way of reclaiming her from Randall, by associating her with a man I loved."

Jayne was quiet. Then, eventually, he said, "All this while, you've had me believing *I* was her father."

"No," said Temperance. "If you look back, you'll realize I never said as much. You all made that assumption. You took the idea and ran with it. Not once did I come out and say in so many words, 'Jane is your daughter.'"

"But you didn't deny it either. You let us think it."

"Because, I'm afraid, it suited my purposes. It got you—and by extension your crew—invested in Coogan's Bluff's plight. It made it personal."

A half-dozen vicious insults lined up in Jayne's head, but he stopped himself spitting them out. "You used us, Temperance. You used *me*."

"And you have every right to be angry at me, Jayne. I just want you to know I did it for Jane's sake."

"I nearly got myself killed fighting Vandal, and all because I thought I was fighting for Jane. For my daughter. I'd never have done it if I'd known the truth."

"No, and I'm sorry. That's all I can say. I'm sorry. I tried to atone for it. That's why I surrendered to Vandal. I felt so bad about it, I hoped that sacrificing myself would make amends. I knew that you'd have looked after Jane if Vandal killed me. You'd have been a great father to her."

"And I'd have been none the wiser about not being her real daddy."

"Would that have been so terrible?"

"Guess not. At least now I don't have to have that illusion anymore."

He grabbed the whisky off Temperance and downed several gulps. Then he gestured towards Jane with the neck of the bottle. She, River, and Kaylee were now dancing together, having the time of their lives.

"So, what are you gonna do?" he said. "You gonna tell her? About Vandal?"

"What do you think?"

"I think it'd be a difficult conversation. 'Hey, Jane. You know that man who nearly destroyed this town and threatened to make you his sex slave? Funny thing. He's your old man.' Can't imagine her taking *that* well."

"Me either," said Temperance.

"But you can't carry on letting her believe I'm her father when I'm not. Ain't fair on either of us."

"No, I agree. I'll explain to her that it was a misunderstanding. I'll tell her that I should have made things clearer and I didn't. I'll give her the same reason I've just given you: it was expedient. She'll probably hate me for a while, but she'll get over it. She's a pragmatic girl."

"And who'll you say is her real father? Because now she'll want to know more than ever."

"Some guy. Like I've been telling her all this time. Just some guy I once met. It doesn't matter who he is."

The song ended. There was a brief pause, then the band struck up a lolloping waltz.

For a time Jayne watched the crew and the townspeople mingling merrily together, grins on every face. Mal had cut in on Inara and Stanislaw L'Amour, the latter relinquishing his dance partner graciously. Mal and Inara made a fine couple. They moved in perfect synch, their gazes locked. The glow on his face was reflected in the glow on hers. Only thing was, neither of them was smiling. If anything, they looked sad, as if they knew this might be the last time they danced together like this.

The scene grew hazy. Jayne rubbed his eyes.

"Jayne?" said Temperance. "You okay?"

"This planet," Jayne said. "So little water. So dusty. So gorramn dusty."

"That Which is Most Precious..."

Serenity took off.

There had been farewells, but for most concerned they had been brief and strained. During the few days it had taken Kaylee and Wash to get *Serenity* spaceworthy again, it had become common knowledge that Temperance had misled everyone about Jane's paternity. Nobody was best pleased at how they'd been manipulated.

As the ship left atmo, Jayne retired to his bunk, slamming the door shut behind him.

"Go away!" he barked when there came a knock a minute later.

"It's me." River.

"Don't care. I said go away."

"I've got something for you."

"What?"

"Open up and I'll show you."

The last person Jayne felt like dealing with now was moon-brained River Tam. Still, he let her in.

"Sorry to interrupt your moping."

"I'm not moping."

"Jane wanted you to have these." River was clutching an

envelope and his woolen hat. "She slipped them to me while we were saying goodbye."

"I thought she might want to keep the hat," Jayne said, taking both items off her. "That's why I didn't ask for it back. Kind of a souvenir." However, he wasn't sad that she had returned it.

"Read the letter."

Jayne ran a thumb under the flap of the envelope and took out a scrap of paper covered in untidy handwriting.

"You just going to stand there?" he said to River.

River nodded.

Jayne shrugged and began reading.

Dear Jayne,

Here's your hat back. I guess you maybe might have wanted me to keep it, but it's yours and I don't really need it, being as it's a hat for keeping your head warm and Thetis is a hot planet and keeping your head warm ain't exactly a priority here. Besides, it's your lucky charm hat. Don't seem right I should have it.

I'm writing this letter because I just wanted you to know that even though you aren't my dad after all I kind of liked it when you were. It may only have been for a short time but I liked knowing you and I liked shooting your gun Vera and I liked how you looked out for me.

I'll probably never know who my real dad is but, whoever he is, I kind of hope he's just like you. That's how I'll always think of him. Gruff and snarly but underneath it nice, like you.

Mom has this old Earth-That-Was proverb kind of thing she likes to trot out from time to time. "That is most precious which lasts least long." Having you as my father didn't last long but it sure was precious to me.

That's all I have to say.
Yours, Jane

"Jane wasn't ever yours," River said. "I told you. She never belonged to you, but you should treat her like she did. That's what I said. And you did treat her like she was yours, Jayne. Because you're good that way."

Jayne read through the letter three more times in a row. When he next looked up from it, River was gone and *Serenity* was soaring into the boundless emptiness of the Black.

ACKNOWLEDGMENTS

I am indebted to Yen Ooi for authenticating and enhancing my Mandarin curse words so that I didn't end up looking like a *liú kǒu shuǐ de biǎo zi hé hóu zi de bèn ér zi.* Creative swearing is the best fun.

— J.M.H.L

ABOUT THE AUTHOR

James Lovegrove is the *New York Times* bestselling author of *The Age of Odin*. He was shortlisted for the Arthur C. Clarke Award in 1998 and for the John W. Campbell Memorial Award in 2004, and also reviews fiction for the *Financial Times*. He is the author of *Firefly: Big Damn Hero* with Nancy Holder and several Sherlock Holmes novels for Titan Books.